WHAT SHE LEFT BEHIND

WHAT SHE LEFT BEHIND

An Audrey Wilson Mystery

C.M. Miller

iUniverse, Inc.

New York Lincoln Shanghai

What She Left Behind

An Audrey Wilson Mystery

iUniverse, Inc.

For information address:
iUniverse, Inc.
2021 Pine Lake Road, Suite 100
Lincoln, NE 68512
www.iuniverse.com

ISBN: 0-595-27821-3

Printed in the United States of America

Acknowledgement

My deepest appreciation to the following:

In Ohio and St. Thomas——my family and friends, *City Beat* and *Horizons* Magazines and the *Cincinnati Enquirer*. 1480 WCIN and 1230 The Buzz.
In Georgia——-my family and friends. 1380 WAOK radio
Worldwide——-my readers, especially all of the book clubs who were kind enough to select my books.
A special thank you to all teachers, pediatric therapists and social workers. You are the sunshine and rain that nourishes our children and make them grow.

ATLANTA

─────────────── ▼ ───────────────

"Come on Remmi!" Lonnie pulled his wife through the maze of cars. "Hurry up or we won't get a good spot."

He tightened his grip on his wife's hand and jerked her across the street.

"Look like they havin' some kind of party up in there." Remmi hung back, hesitant in approaching all these people dressed to the nines while the homeless couple sported dusty rags. Lonnie touched her face and kissed her lips softly and smiled. To him, Remmi could hold her own with any of them phonies. He wished he could get her to see that.

Lonnie liked nights like this when folks were all dressed up pretending to be more than they were. He could spot a wannabe bourgeoisie Negro in a minute. They were the ones who'd dig into the pockets of their rented or borrowed clothes to give him change while looking down their nose so hard their eyes crossed. He would lay odds that some of these people out here fakin' and shakin' were as broke as he was.

The couple set up in a space near the entranceway. Lonnie started warming up on his sax while Remmi sang. People passed them by like they were a part of the urban scenery.

An occasional car rolled up and slowed to a stop in front of the entrance to the Hotel Renaissance on West Peachtree Street in downtown Atlanta. Groups of people in varying hues milled about the entrance, talking, smoking, ignoring the occasional brother requesting spare change. The smell of unwashed vagrant's skin blended in with the partier's perfume, automobile exhaust, cigarettes, cooking food and some unidentifiable city smells. A salad of conversation, laughter, engines revving and car horns blaring, whetted the appetite for the main course—

-the excitement that big cities routinely dish up to salivating crowds. Aiming to please, the Renaissance opened its arms and welcomed them inside in droves.

The spindly man and woman, dirty and disheveled from the grime of the street, performed just left of the doorway. Skinny, dusty brown Remmi Watson crafted a popular tune with her frail voice. Her husband Lonnie accompanied her on the alto sax. A few passersby clapped politely or tossed coins into an upturned hat. Some wrinkled their noses, regarding the musicians as one would ants at a picnic. People were too busy squinting into the tinted glass windows of expensive cars star-gazing to mind the street performers. Two or three well-known musicians had already been hustled into the front door of the hotel. A local movie director and an actress were spotted after that. Cars more expensive than some people's homes moved along the avenue all evening long——a veritable cavalcade of stars. No one was listening to Lonnie and Remmi's weak performance anymore. They were too busy gawking at the white limousine that had pulled up to the curb and stopped.

The driver exited, moving quickly to help the passenger from the back of the car. The woman was slender, stylish, in her mid to late thirties. She handed the man a folded bill before walking toward the hotel door on thin, cinnamon colored legs. She was tall, nearly six feet, maybe more taking into account the height of her slim heeled shoes. She wore her confidence as evenly as she wore her expensive attire, moving toward the entrance with deliberation and purpose.

A sudden tepid gust interrupted the humid night air, kicking a bright yellow square of paper along the ground. Stopping suddenly, the woman adjusted the gold lace wrap around her shoulders before continuing. The body fell so close to her feet that she nearly stumbled over it when it hit the pavement. Her screams pierced the night air, curdling the blood that pooled from the body out into the street.

CHAPTER I

▼

"Girl, you look like you could use a drink."

"I already had two." Audrey squirmed in her seat.

"Well maybe you need something stronger." Renita said, snapping her fingers at a passing waiter. Renita was good at snapping her fingers at people. It was surprising that somebody hadn't dashed a drink into her face.

"It's these damned shoes." Audrey reached down and adjusted the skinny straps of the shoes. "These bad boys pinching my feet so bad I feel like taking them off and throwing them in the trash."

"You paid almost four hundred dollars for them shoes. I know damn well your cheap ass ain't about to throw away nothing." Renita took two glasses of champagne from the waiter's tray and dismissed him with a flick of her manicured hand. She sipped. "I can see you cutting off part of your foot first."

Audrey shot Renita a smirk.

"Very funny. I'll have you know that there is no way in hell I'd pay four hundred dollars for a pair of shoes." Audrey took a deep sip from her glass. "But they cost too much too hurt this bad."

"Suck it up, Sister. At least you look good." Renita tilted her glass and Audrey picked up the other one and they clicked a salute before drinking.

"See you could be like Melodious Jones." Renita nodded toward the buffet. "Look at her."

Audrey followed Renita's gaze to the short, hippy woman stooped over the display of food. She hobbled down the receiving line collecting a heaping scoop of everything she saw. She was in obvious pain, but not enough to keep away from the buffet.

"This that fat heffa's third time up at the food table. The bitch look like she ready to take a shit."

Audrey laughed. "Girl, you crazy."

It was nine thirty on Friday night and the CRUTCH benefit was well underway. The Lenox Room was filled beyond capacity with CRUTCH members from Ohio and its neighboring states who had made the trip to Atlanta for the annual gala.

Due to the overwhelming turnout the reception ran thirty minutes over while people played catch-up with members they hadn't seen in years. Attendees languished over dinner, murmuring bits of gossip or marveling at baby pictures. Feeling that they were losing control of the event, the organizers scrambled to get the presentations done in the time remaining.

The announcement was made for this year's winner of the *Patron Crutch Award*. Applause rang out as Ed Dixon approached the stage. He accepted the handshake and hearty slap on the back from the moderator. The hostess slithered up to him in a white form fitting dress, kissed his face and handed him the golden trophy.

Audrey checked her program and frowned.

"What are they doing?" She said to the people at her table. "Ed's award is not supposed to be presented until the end of the evening."

"I guess they had to make some changes since the dinner ran over." Syd Lawson replied, squinting at the crème colored program. "You're right Audrey, the *Patron Crutch Award* was to be given near the end of the presentations."

"Maybe this *is* the end." Bobby said with a snicker as he worked at the food on his plate. They were serving dessert and Bobby had one of each of the five offerings in front of him.

"What...?" Audrey said in a panic. "But what about *our* category? They were supposed to announce the *Champion* before the *Patron*."

"Girl why don't you shut up about that damn thing." Bobby cast an impatient gaze at his sister. "Don't worry, you gon' get your little award. They probably moved Ed up because he told them he's got to get back to Rosemont tonight and collect some rent." Bobby snickered.

Audrey ignored her brother and tried to relax. She shifted in the straight-backed chair and checked her watch. It was almost nine thirty. They had been there since a little before eight, missing most of the opening reception. Which was good...for her feet.

The delicate silver Manolo Blahnik sandals she had splurged on for the event cost way too much to be so uncomfortable. The strappy shoes bound her feet and held her swelling toes tighter than slaves coming from the Mother Land causing rays of pain to shoot from foot to head. She could have sworn she heard her throbbing toes' tiny muffled screams from beneath the table. The thought of spending several more hours in the vise grip of the shoes, and the torture device that slimmed her hips so that she could wear her favorite slinky dress, was almost more than she could bear.

She would have ordered another Vodka, but she didn't want to be so sloshed she couldn't make it to the stage when her name was called. They'd be there at least another two hours so she'd better suck it up. That would be a challenge since she was so uncomfortable she could hardly concentrate on what was being said.

Audrey distracted herself by playing with the antique garnet bracelet her mother had given her as a graduation present. Following tradition, Audrey's mother had presented her eldest daughter with the bracelet making her promise to pass it on to her firstborn. Audrey remembered welling up with pride as her mother snapped the clasp shut. The moment was particularly poignant as it came at a time when Audrey was dealing with a personal tragedy. It amazed her how her mother could always apply the proper poultice at the right time for anything that ailed her. How did her mother know that she was in such pain at that time? Perhaps it was mother's intuition. Whatever the reason, the exchange had deepened their already close bond. Her mother had been on her mind so much in recent weeks. She'd taken the piece of jewelry from the safety of the armoire in her closet and packed it for the Atlanta trip. Wearing the delicate marcasite bracelet with its deep red-brown stones made her feel as though her mother were sitting there with her. Tracing the intricate design of the heirloom Audrey felt her parent's presence stronger than ever.

This was the first time the CRUTCH banquet was held outside the Greater Cincinnati area and Audrey had looked forward to coming to Atlanta all year. The organization refused to break the economic boycott of downtown Cincinnati by having the event there. When someone suggested they have the banquet in Atlanta, everyone on the committee agreed. To ensure they didn't run into the same kind of cold, unwelcome wagon they had in some of their local hotels, CRUTCH sent an envoy to check out the southern city the previous year to see if everything met their standards.

When they began arriving the last week in July, everyone was beyond pleased with the city and its accommodations. Southern hospitality was alive and well and resided in a huge plantation-style mansion in the *"city too busy to hate"*.

Now Audrey turned her full attention to the man on the stage. Ed Dixon was one of her oldest clients. Soon after she opened her own financial services firm, Ed, who'd worked for years as a school janitor, signed on with her firm trusting her to grow his savings. Now he was one of the leading real estate barons in the Midwest. He stood behind the dais, accepting the award for revitalizing some of the most deteriorated residential property in the region. He looked nothing like when she first met him years ago. A modest man, Ed Dixon mumbled a few words of thanks before returning to his seat.

Audrey knew almost everyone at Ed's table. He sat next to his wife Elise and their son Ed Jr. Seated next to Ed Jr. was real-estate consultant Hap Leroy and his wife Minerva. Rounding out the party was Ed's attorney, business partner, and Audrey's former lover, Jules Dreyfus. The woman sitting next to Jules looked like super model Elle MacPherson. Everyone in the room noticed her as she glided to the table with Jules. Audrey's sister Renita made a point of nudging her whenever Jules and the super model touched hands or put their heads together and whispered intimately as new lovers do.

Audrey hadn't seen Jules in a while. His life post-Audrey seemed to agree with him. He was still tall and lean and firm. The texture of his skin, cut of his hair, and the clothing that he wore exuded his new wealth. Together, he and his date looked like a million dollars. When the woman rose, presumably to go to the ladies room, Audrey felt a rush of envy. She wouldn't acknowledge any romantic feelings for Jules so the only explanation she could think of that would cause her jealousy would be the woman's absolutely flawless appearance.

Like Audrey, Elle wore a slinky silver dress; only hers was about ten sizes smaller than Audrey's. With her golden hair, shimmering dress and glowing skin, "Elle" seemed iridescent. Audrey swallowed the emotion that stuck in her throat like a thick green glob of phlegm. She took another gulp from the flute and smiled at nothing in particular, pretending not to look at the shimmering goddess that had everyone's attention. The woman turned heads as she passed through the crowd. Delicate stilettos enhanced her slender legs that looked nothing like Audrey's more substantial ones that were encased in the tight, shiny dress like sausages. If the super model's feet were hurting her you sure couldn't tell by the way she glided through the crowd.

Audrey knew she was being silly. Her legs, though far from thin were curvaceous and firm from working out. She enjoyed a good meal and wasn't about to trade off fried chicken for skinny legs, so she worked out everyday to keep her muscles toned. She'd been blessed with the womanly curves that many would die for. But Audrey had always envied women with slender legs and tiny feet.

Cranky and irritable, Audrey displaced her annoyance onto anyone or anything it would adhere to. Her real problem was that she was missing Marsh and was tired of seeing everyone coupled off. She hadn't spoken with her boyfriend since the Sunday before she left for Atlanta. She'd left him a couple of messages before leaving Rosemont on Wednesday. Though it had been a busy few days, thoughts of him wove in and out of her daily activities, sticking and pinching at her mind, prickling her insecurities.

The waiter passed again and this time Audrey chose a soft drink. She sighed and took a sip of her ginger ale, waiting for the announcement of the next winner.

"Where are you going?"

Her brother Bobby rose suddenly, bumping into her chair as he moved away from the table.

"To take a leak. Who are you, the potty police?" He looked around the room distractedly. He was in a hurry, not looking at her as he talked. He must have had to pee really badly, Audrey thought.

"What if they announce our category while you're gone? I don't want to go up there without you."

"You just want somebody to lean on cuz yo' coins achin'." Bobby said in a poor imitation of a southern accent, bending over like he was hobbling on a cane. Then he straightened and addressed Renita. "Renita, why don't you go down to Grady Hospital and get your sister a walker."

"Oooh, that's, cold!" Someone at the next table said. Several people within earshot snickered. Audrey glanced over at the table next to them. Jill Witherspoon cast a look of feigned pity in her direction.

As children, Audrey and Jill had attended Rosemont Academy but they hadn't moved in the same circles. Jill was a financial consultant as well, but unlike Audrey, her business had flourished over the years. She catered to all of Southwest Ohio's most wealthy professionals. She never missed an opportunity to flaunt her success.

With gleaming black hair flowing down her back like a dark rolling river against glistening nutmeg colored skin, Jill Witherspoon was a showstopper. She was decked out in a soft white fabric that looked like linen. The affect would have been too casual for this affair on anyone else, but Jill was working it like an overseer works his whip. She looked fantastic. Seated next to her was her current boy-toy, a twenty-something Marc Anthony clone. The other seats at the table were filled with her usual stuck-up entourage. Bobby knew Audrey hated Jill and here he was putting on a show for her. Audrey was *too* embarrassed. She glowered at Jill and rolled her eyes before shooting hot daggers in her brother's direction. He just laughed and kept on walking.

"Come in here trying to be cute with your old bad feet ass." He was walking away from the table, still speaking loudly enough to give his audience at the next table something to laugh about.

"Go to hell, Bobby." Audrey fanned him away with her hand before grabbing her drink. Now she wished she had chosen something stronger. She was miserable sitting there all stuffed into her clothes. The last thing she needed was Bobby's immature comments making her feel worse.

"Shhh!" Renita shot them an ugly glance. "Why don't the two of you behave? Some of us want to hear the program."

Audrey rolled her eyes. Bobby continued walking toward the rest rooms.

Their table was all the way live. Renita and her band had scored a gig at the Renaissance and would be playing there the entire weekend. Syd Lawson and her girlfriend Carmen Bausa were there cuddled up like they were alone. Bobby had decided to come stag so he and Paul Radford could hang out in the street, as dogs are wont to do.

Paul had played professional basketball with Bobby. Cleveland drafted them both the same year. Bobby was the team's shooting guard; Paul, the Cavs power forward. Each had been a consistent player until a plague of injuries and bad luck had sidelined them. When Larry Nance joined the team Paul's basketball career was pretty much over. Soon after his final year in the sport he had become more famous for his public speaking than for his skill as a basketball player. He sat at the table, his rangy frame draped over his chair looking over the rims of his stylish glasses. His tawny skin glistened in the soft, ballroom lighting. He watched his former teammate move away from the table his eyes still and unreadable. He caught Audrey looking at him, smiled and winked. Audrey returned the smile. Paul was probably her brother's closest friend and certainly the most admired athlete in Bobby's circle of pro ball players. Bobby would be staying at Paul's East Cobb mansion during the visit.

Paul excused himself and headed toward the restroom. Audrey looked after him wistfully. Why couldn't she be in the company of an attractive, successful man like Paul?

Audrey was in Atlanta without a date. Her boyfriend, Marshall Fixx, had an emergency with his son Toots and was spending the weekend with him in Boston. Audrey did a bad job at playing the supportive girlfriend. She knew that it was important for Marsh to be with his son, but this award was important too. Audrey was getting national recognition for her work with the people in the

Rosemont community and she wanted Marsh to be there. It really hurt when he chose this weekend to go to Boston. He'd said that Toots had been giving his mother all kinds of trouble and he had to go up there and straighten him out.

"Couldn't you at least come with me until the ceremony is over and fly to Nantucket from Atlanta?" She had asked him.

"This is my son I'm talking about Audrey." She remembered him looking at her like she had spinach stuck on her tooth. "I won't compromise when it comes to him. I'm surprised that you would expect me to."

"I'm not asking you to compromise anything!" She'd spat back at him angrily. He made her feel like a clinging vine and she knew better than that.

"I just wanted you to share this award with me." She tried not to sound like she was begging. "The feeling, I mean."

It wasn't until she said the words that she realized just how letdown she really was. But it wasn't the first time he'd disappointed her. Marsh was so detached lately. She could tell by his body language that he wanted to put an end to the Atlanta discussion. He patted her head and kissed her forehead in a condescending, dismissive way. That's when Audrey got pissed.

"Don't you patronize me Marshall Fixx!"

"I wasn't. I was just trying to be supportive."

"Well if you want to support me you'd bring your ass to Atlanta." She snapped.

He shrugged and shook his head impatiently. His mind seemed to be somewhere else. It was like he just wanted Audrey to go home so he wouldn't have to deal with her and what ever it was she was feeling. Marsh inhaled to keep from saying anything else upsetting. He grabbed her face in his hands and kissed her softly on the lips then pulled away slightly.

"It's your award, Audrey. You worked hard for it." He held her at arms length as he spoke. To Audrey the distance felt more like a mile.

"You go have fun in Atlanta. I'll see you when you get back…"

That's not the way it's supposed to go, she had thought. He was supposed to beg her not to leave without him. But he didn't. Instead, he started kissing her; moving his hands to the places on her body that would get him maximum results with minimal effort. She guessed he assumed a good strong sex session would cancel everything else out.

Unfortunately, Marsh wasn't up to the task. He lay next to her snoring less than twenty minutes after he'd started what Audrey had come to think of as fore*lorn* play. Audrey remembered staring at the clock and feeling lonely, angry, and unsatisfied when the encounter was over. Maybe they needed some time apart.

Perhaps a brief separation would stoke the embers that had been cooling gray over the past few months of their relationship. Not to mention the fact that she and Renita could hang out and be hot in Hotlanta.

Audrey and Renita decided to take the trip south a few days before the banquet. Renita had lived in Atlanta in the late 1980s and knew her way around the city. Audrey left instructions about her change in plans and anything upcoming with their office manager Dorothy, and left her cat in the care of Mrs. Mashburn who lived in the house next door. She called Renita back to let her know she was ready to leave Rosemont. The sooner the better.

Their plane touched down early Wednesday afternoon. The sky was clear and pale blue and the air was sticky hot. Each time Audrey flew in to Atlanta, she was struck by the number of yellow, brown and deep ebony faces in and around the busy airport. We certainly seemed to be running things in this southern city, she thought, at least on the surface. They picked up the boxy economy car Renita had reserved, loaded their bags and drove toward the downtown Marriott Marquis. During the first few minutes of the ride the scenery sped past them so quickly it was hard to take it all in. But when they were just outside the city traffic suddenly ground to a halt. They spent what seemed like a ridiculous amount of time trapped behind a rusted out white Chevy truck that was plastered with miniature red and white replicas of the old state flag and various stickers proclaiming the driver's opposition to the new Georgia symbol. Audrey and Renita looked at each other and shook their heads. A few vehicles sported American flags that had flapped proudly when cars sped up the freeway. But like everything else the flight of red, white, and blue was stilled as the traffic slowed into a jam. It took them nearly an hour to go the last eight miles of the trip.

Renita pulled into the hotel driveway and stopped on the other side of the huge lighted fountain in the courtyard of the hotel. They stood near the car as grinning bellmen uniformed in maroon jackets with gold trim, grabbed their bags and slid them into a brass rolling cart and waited while they checked in. Ten minutes later the sisters were in their room on the 20th floor. The bellman pulled back the drapes and the women viewed the sprawling city, its blue sky topped by a gray smog haze. Audrey handed the man some rolled up bills. He tipped his hat and was gone.

They spent the first day seeing the city...Little Five Points, touring the historical Sweet Auburn District, and visiting The King Center. Their visit coincided with The National Black Arts Festival and the streets were filled with every kind of people there to sample food and soak up culture. The next day Renita took her to a salon and Audrey got her hair braided. Afterwards they went to Lenox Mall and Phipps Plaza to do some shopping.

They ended the evening Upstairs at the Renaissance for Renita and the band's opening. Audrey was so exhausted from their busy day that she couldn't stay for the entire evening. She got a cab and took the short ride to their hotel.

It wasn't just the activity that had drained her. She was starting to have a strange feeling about Marsh. She missed him. Throughout the day, she had called him three times. There was never an answer and he hadn't returned the calls. He was to have left for Massachusetts Thursday. It was now Friday night and she hadn't heard from him in nearly a week. Though their relationship had become strained of late he'd always returned her calls…even when they didn't have much to say to each other. She hadn't heard a word from him since the discussion they'd had about him going to Boston. It wasn't like him not to at least call. Something was wrong.

*   *   *   *

The announcement was finally made for Community Push, Audrey and Bobby's category. Though they had already been given the nod to receive the *Champion Award*, the wait was still nerve-racking. Audrey craned her neck, panning the room, cutting her gaze around the clusters of people in search of her brother. Bobby was nowhere in sight. She checked her watch. How long had he been gone? It seemed an eternity but it had only been about thirty minutes.

The announcer began calling out the names of the nominees. Polite applause swept through the crowd. In the distance, she caught the quick easy glide that caused her rapid breathing to steady. Slightly winded and glistening with perspiration, Bobby moved to help Audrey out of her chair just as their names were announced.

He and Audrey looked at each other and smiled. They had worked so hard to build their business. To be recognized this way was gratifying to both of them. Bobby looked down at his sister and kissed her cheek. They linked arms and headed for the dais, riding the wave of thunderous applause that almost made Audrey forget the sharp, pinkie-toe pain determined to upstage them.

CHAPTER 2

Around eleven o'clock the awards had been given. The attendees hung back, reluctant to see the evening end. Everyone at Audrey's table seemed torn between going home for the evening and finding the next best party. Renita and the fellows had to get upstairs to prepare for the evening show. The rest of the group decided to take the party over to *Ambiance*, a jazz club next door to the Fox Theater. They would round out the night by returning to the Renaissance to see Renita, Lloyd, and the guys.

"Why don't you go clubbin' with your family." Lloyd suggested to Renita. He lit a cigarette, took a quick pull on it and exhaled. "Ya'll are coming upstairs anyway. Me and the fellas can handle the first two sets."

Renita beamed, relieved that Lloyd had made the offer. She didn't want to impose on the band, but she also didn't want to spend the entire night working.

"Oh, my gosh!" Renita gazed at Lloyd in bug-eyed amazement. "Lloyd is giving me a pass! The world must be coming to an end. Let's get outta here before he changes his mind."

She kissed Lloyd's cheek.

"You all go ahead." Audrey said. "I need to go back to the room and change these friggin' shoes." Audrey didn't even want to think about doing anything else. The sore, puffy appendages that used to be her feet, told her to call it a night. But she didn't have the heart to follow her mind. Especially since Renita didn't have to go right to work. But she wasn't doing anything else until she got rid of these shoes. The mere thought of changing into her comfy eel skin slides and putting an end to the crippling pain, bathed her in relief.

The slam-patter of shuffling feet and the roar of boisterous conversation filled the lobby as hundreds of people pushed toward the front doors. Occasionally someone would approach Paul for an autograph or congratulate Audrey on winning her CRUTCH Award. She smiled and clutched the gleaming trophy closer to her breast.

Audrey looked around and realized that she and Paul had gotten separated from the rest of their group.

"Where's Renita? I was hoping she would go with me to the hotel so I could change my shoes."

"I think she got so carried away with being given a pass that she started running and hasn't stopped yet." Paul kidded as he munched on candy. He was chewing on oval pastel almonds that he rattled in his hand as he talked. He popped another one into his mouth and then extended his hand toward Audrey. She frowned at the candy-coated nuts and shook her head. Paul shrugged and popped another and then said between crunches.

"Maybe they went on ahead to get a table. I'll go with you to change your shoes." He offered her a warm smile.

Paul Radford was the brother Bobby never had. When Bobby needed a model of how to build on ones celebrity, Paul was the example that he used. And what an example he was.

Paul had played professional basketball several years before parlaying his talents into motivational speaking, which led to his hosting his own talk show. The irony in this was that Paul had overcome a crippling speech impairment that plagued him the first twenty years of his life.

Through extensive therapy and incredible determination, today he was one of the most sought after orators in the nation. With his trademark designer glasses, fair complexion and reddish-brown hair, made more distinctive by the jagged shock of silver on one side, Paul Radford was a familiar face locally and nationally. He had done exactly what Audrey and Bobby had been teaching their clients to do. Paul used his role as a professional athlete to facilitate his becoming a model for what young people could do when they could no longer play the game. He had done what he could to overcome the speech impairment and he would do whatever it took to reach any goal he set for himself. The Wilson family was proud to know him.

Audrey studied his face for a moment.

"Paul, where are your glasses?"

His hand shot to his face and his small eyes darted around as he tried to think. "I must have left them in the men's room."

He darted into the bathroom and Audrey perched gingerly on a nearby love seat and waited. She searched the crowd for her party, hoping the stampeding crowd would not stomp her foot. In a few minutes Paul was back with a hopeless look in his eyes.

"You'd be amazed at how many pairs of glasses I lose."

"I'm sorry."

He waved his hand. "It's no big deal. I've got another pair in the car."

As the two of them neared the outer door, it became apparent from a change in energy in the air that something was wrong. Audrey heard bits of conversation from people around her.

"They say somebody jumped…" One of them said.

"It's a woman. She was pushed out the hotel window…" Somebody added.

"Did she get hit by a car?" Another voice queried.

"No man, she jumped off the roof." Someone else replied.

Audrey wrinkled her forehead in concern. She grabbed Paul's hand. He was pulling her forward. She planted her sore feet and resisted.

"What's going on up there Paul?"

"It's sounds like someone took a nose dive onto the pavement." Being six foot eleven, he could see the activity ahead of them and discern that the police had already cleared the body away and were letting people through a narrow opening cordoned off by yellow crime tape. He pulled at her arm, trying to get her to move forward. But Audrey wouldn't budge.

"My God, you're kidding." Audrey gasped, turning her head away. "I don't want to see it. Is there another way out?"

"I'm sure there is." He too now looked away from where they had been headed. Paul took her arm and they pivoted in the direction from which they had just come. "We'll probably run into Bobby on the way." He said.

"Where'd he go anyway?"

"He went to the men's room."

"Again? Did you see him the last time you were there?"

"No. But I imagine they have more than one bathroom in here. Knowing Bobby he's probably somewhere getting some phone numbers." Paul smiled down at her, but Audrey wasn't in the mood to be humored. The festive crowd had morphed into a gawking mob of rubber-neckers, pushing and shoving to get a closer look at the grisly scene. The thrill of the strange city was dulling, she felt herself longing for the slow pace of home.

"What about Renita, Syd and Carmen? Where are they?" Audrey struggled to find a familiar face among the growing swell of people in the hotel lobby. Paul placed his hand on her back supportively, trying to calm her anxiety.

"Don't worry," he touched her nose with his finger playfully. "They might already be at *Ambiance* now. We'll change your shoes and meet them there."

They took baby steps through the thick crowd until they reached a bank of escalators that led them to the west wing of the building. The din faded and the crowd thinned as they moved to the back of the hotel. Audrey hobbled to keep pace with Paul's long strides, wincing with each step. The thin straps sliced into her baby toes, creating burning, watery blisters that would likely incapacitate her before this was all said and done.

"Paul. Paul! Slow down." She thought she'd lose consciousness from the pain. When she suddenly felt herself being lifted and carried toward the doorway, Audrey was surprised and impressed. Paul had lifted her into his arms and carried her like the hundred fifty pounds that she struggled with on a daily basis was nothing. When was the last time a man had literally swept her off her feet? She searched her mind for a memory that wasn't there.

They stopped in front of the bell captain's post. A young man with a ruddy complexion and a sharp goatee, tipped his black cap and hurried over to them asking if they needed assistance.

"I've got the ticket for the car in my breast pocket." Paul told Audrey. The candy-sweet smell of the almonds mingled with his warm breath when he spoke. "Fish it out so we can give it to this guy and get outta here."

Audrey put her silver purse in the hand that held the award and did as Paul said. She breathed in the heavy musk of his cologne, feeling the heat rise from his firm chest as she snaked her hand into his jacket pocket. Grabbing hold of the small pink paper square, she handed it to the bellman, who tipped his hat again before trotting off to get the car.

She had expected Paul to deposit his load in one of the long intricately carved wooden benches that flanked either side of the sliding glass door. But he showed no signs of tiring, or the need to put her down. It was a relief to her swollen feet and she was going to milk the moment for all it was worth. The milk soured when she noticed him looking curiously at her puffy red feet. Audrey flushed hot with embarrassment.

"I guess it's kind of a lucky break for me that you wore these horrible shoes." He brushed her face with his in a way that was sweet and unexpected.

"What do you mean?" It felt so good being wrapped in the big man's arms. Though she appreciated the attention, she felt no physical attraction to Paul. This somehow made it easy to relax and accept his kindness.

"Bad shoe choice not withstanding, you look exceptionally beautiful tonight, Audrey. It's not often a woman gets me to show my chivalrous side." He leaned down and whispered into her ear. "I'm at your service. Anything I can do to help ease the pain, just say the word."

Oh, Jesus! Don't start no mess, Paul, she said to herself. Audrey didn't respond to whatever it was he called himself doing. She looked in the direction the bellman had gone, wishing he would hurry up. Paul probably meant nothing by it, but his attempt to make this anything but her using him as a rickshaw was a presumption she wasn't in the mood to deal with. Her feet hurt! She just wanted him to hold her—-period. He could keep all the cutesie stuff to himself.

She felt suddenly sad and lonely for Marsh. He was supposed to be holding her, telling her how pretty she was and how proud of her he was. She had envisioned him sweeping her up, taking her to their hotel room and making love to her like he did when they first met. But Marsh wasn't here tonight. He was in Boston. With his ex-wife.

The car finally rolled into view and stopped in front of them. The young man opened the passenger door wide and Paul placed Audrey gingerly onto the seat. He handed the bellman a couple of bills and took his place behind the wheel of the car. They were at the Marriott in no time.

Paul waited the five minutes it took Audrey to change her shoes and do a quick make-up check and they were off to meet the rest of their party at the club on Peachtree Street.

*   *   *   *

When Audrey and Paul arrived at *Ambiance* nearly thirty minutes later, the rest of their party was already there and seated. Except Bobby. The couple pushed their way through the thick, noisy crowd, past the bandstand to their table.

Everyone in the room was kicked back, bobbing their heads as the bassist took his solo. Applause flooded the room when a young man with a horn approached the microphone. The house band was raising the roof with a lively rendition of the standard, *Blue Skies*. Audrey turned all the way around to admire Marvin Jones, the young trumpeter who played with the throw back style of a classic jazz legend. The crowd cheered, giving the baby-faced man a rousing ovation as he moved the horn from his mouth, stepping to the mic he motioned toward their table.

"I'm going to impose on a good friend that we have in the house tonight." Marvin said. "She gave me my first big break when she chose me to accompany her on her album, *Soaring To New Heights*. She's a wonderful friend, teacher, and singer, Miss Renita Wilson. Give it up for her, Club Ambiance." The audience applauded politely, craning their necks to see who he was talking about. Marvin bent over the mic and in the soupy strains of someone who spent countless hours in smoky jazz venues, said, "Come on Renita. I need some help up here, girl."

It didn't take too much coaxing to get Renita to the stage. The kid with the horn went into the intro and Renita belted out the jazzy song the band had been playing, driving the crowd wild. She refused the request for more when the song was through, thanking the audience nearly a dozen times before kissing Marvin's cheek. She whispered a few words into his ear. He laughed. Renita rejoined them at the crowded table near the stage.

"Miss Wilson will be performing at midnight all this week Upstairs At The Renaissance. Ya'll be sure to check her out." Everyone clapped and nodded their heads as if saying they'd be there. Marvin blew Renita a kiss that she caught and shook like dice before releasing it to the crowd. He laughed. "We gon' take ten right about now. Everybody drink up and be nice to the wait staff. Thank you."

Renita was still slightly winded from the performance as she turned up a highball glass and emptied it. Audrey looked over at her and beamed proudly. The waitress brought over another round along with bowls of pretzels and chips that they munched on as they laughed and enjoyed one another.

"Where my drink at?"

Everyone looked in the direction of the questioner. Bobby Wilson stood before them wearing a silky soft, tan long-sleeved shirt that opened at the neck to display a thick serpentine chain that glistened in the dim light. Sleek tawny leather pants accentuated his athletic thighs and butt. The slacks were inappropriate for the smoldering July heat, but Bobby was as cool as an ocean breeze. If he sweated it didn't show. Audrey smiled at her baby brother, who looked like a party in a bottle. He knew how to enjoy life like no one else she knew.

"Where the hell you been?" Paul asked him.

"Had to take care of a little business." He grinned at his friend Paul, who winked knowingly. They slapped five and made barking dog sounds.

"Well I hope ya'll took a shower when you got through." Renita shot sarcastically.

"Mind your business, girl." Bobby replied, motioning to a passing waitress. He ordered a Heineken before grabbing a handful of pretzels and popping them one by one into his mouth.

"You missed Renita showing out with the band." Audrey said with pride.

"Seen it before, heard it before." Bobby said nonchalantly.

Renita cast a scowl in his direction. Audrey watched her sister. Something was bothering her. She'd noticed an almost indiscernible edge to her demeanor earlier that evening. Audrey knew it would be fruitless to try to talk to her now. She'd get the scoop from her later.

Audrey's attention was pulled away from Renita and drawn to the three policemen who had just entered the club. A hush swept through the room as everyone watched to see where the officers were headed.

Audrey was surprised when the club owner pointed toward their table. A minute later they stood before her brother who looked up at them as surprised as everyone else.

"Bobby Wilson?" The policeman who stood nearest him said. His blonde hair was trimmed into a neat crew cut, accentuating his angular frame. The wide shoulders most likely offered good support when he needed to apply a strangle hold.

"What's up?" Bobby jerked around to face them, agitated.

"You want to step outside, or you want to do this in here?" The cop was just as belligerent.

"What's this about?" Audrey asked. She didn't like the man's tone. The deputy ignored her, motioning to one of his colleagues who pulled Bobby from his seat, knocking the chair onto the floor. He spun Bobby around and handcuffed him like his substantial frame weighed no more than a feather. The other cop read him his rights.

"I said, what's up, man!" Bobby was loud. Angry.

"You're wanted for questioning in the death of Simone Denton."

CHAPTER 3

▼

The police led Bobby toward the door. He would be transported to the Forsyth Street Detention Center for questioning. Still numb from the initial shock, the group scrambled to get their things, pushing through the crowd to the front of the club while more than a few club patrons gave their assessments of what had just occurred.

"That was FUCKED UP!"

"DAAAAM! You see how they treat us? A brother can't even get his party on without being harassed."

"That's how APD is, dawg, always fuckin' wit us!"

The speculation continued as they neared the door. The owner rushed over and Paul shoved a fistful of bills at him before he could speak. Judging by the appreciative look on the man's face, it must have been more than enough to cover their check. A flurry of comments swirled around them as they moved toward the exit. Now it seemed everyone in the crowd recognized Paul or Bobby. And everyone had an opinion.

"Hey, that's that dude that's on that show…what's it called?"

"Naw, man. He used to play ball.

"That one in the leather pants play for the NBA."

"Uh hum, and I think that other one does too, girl. They sure are fine…"

"I know ALL the Hawks. I never seent that dude before."

"I know that cat! I played ball with him at Run-N-Shoot."

"You a Mutha fuckin' lie!"

They continued to push through the crowd that seems to have gotten much thicker since the police came in. They continued to deflect comments.

"I think he play on one of them teams up North."

"Might a known…"

"Yeah, girl. They always comin' down here starting some shit."

"Uhm Huh. And you know he gon' get off, just like Ray Lewis…"

Audrey marveled at how quickly the crowd had turned on them. The negative sentiment for professional athletes and entertainers with the money and connections to wrangle through the legal system was apparent. The group finally made it to the street, dodging commentary all the way.

They got into Paul's black Hummer and he chugged through the heavy nighttime traffic to the detention center on Forsyth Street. He stopped the truck across from the large gray structure and turned completely around to face them.

"Maybe we should talk about this before we go in there." Paul said.

"Talk about what?" Audrey cast him a quizzical gaze. "Bobby needs us. We're wasting time."

"Bobby has been accused of murder. He wasn't with us for parts of the evening." Paul reasoned, looking from one of them to the other. "What are we going to say about his absence?"

"We're going to tell the truth is what we're going to do!" Audrey looked at him like he'd lost his mind. "You don't think he's guilty, do you?"

"Of course not!" Paul returned the crazy look she was giving him. "But these are the cops. All they need is the tiniest shred of evidence that his time is unaccounted for and he's done." He looked at them again for reassurance. "I think it's better we go in united when we talk about Bobby. Now I ask you again, what are we going to say about Bobby's absence?"

No one responded. Still shaken by what happened, it was too soon to give rational thought, much less voice it.

"Why don't we go over to that McDonald's?" He pointed across the street. They all shrugged as if being pulled by the same string and started piling out of the boxy vehicle.

They looked on in silence as Paul fed coins into the meter. The steel contraption whirred in acceptance, giving them two hours until it required more. The anxious party moved in the direction of the restaurant. A morose pall hovered over the table as they sat in stunned silence while Paul ordered coffee for them all. He returned to the table with a tray full of steaming paper cups. Everyone grabbed one, but nobody drank. Paul broke the silence.

"Did any of you know Simone?"

They shook their heads. Audrey had heard Bobby mention the mother of his son sparingly over the years. She had never met the woman. She and Renita first learned that Bobby had a son when a picture of the boy fell out of his wallet. He said little about him and the more they asked, the more withdrawn he became.

They knew that the woman and the boy lived in Atlanta and that his name was Simon. To Audrey's knowledge, the woman and child had never visited Bobby in Ohio. When she and Renita asked, Bobby wouldn't entertain their questions about the boy or his mother. After a while, they stopped asking.

She'd surmised that Bobby didn't care much for the mother of his son. The few times he said anything at all about her it wasn't flattering. He'd call her out of her name, even admitting on several occasions that he hated her. But did he hate her enough to kill her?

According to the police, former pro basketball player Bobby Wilson had made one last free throw by propelling his ex-girlfriend from a tenth floor window. That was ridiculous! Her brother wasn't a killer.

But Paul was right. He had been away from the group several times during the evening. Where had he been? Why was Simone at the Renaissance that night? If Bobby knew she was there, why hadn't he said anything about it?

Audrey looked over at Paul. His face creased with worry as he looked into space for a long time before turning his attention to his coffee cup. Audrey wondered again if he thought her brother was guilty.

"Are you sure you didn't see Bobby when you went to the men's room?" Audrey touched Paul's hand, searching his face for answers.

"I didn't see him." He raised his shoulders in an exaggerated shrug. "Maybe he went to a different one than the one I used." He paused and they all knew that there was only one restroom on the floor where the banquet was held. Could Bobby have gone to another floor to use the bathroom? He could have, but why would he?

"This is bad ya'll." Paul said. "It's Friday night. They won't even hear the case until Monday morning at the earliest." Paul cracked his big knuckles so loud Audrey jumped.

"I'm afraid that if we tell the police he was away for an extended period of time, he may never get out of there." Paul continued. "Maybe we should tell them that we were together all night——that none of us were away from the table for more than a few minutes."

He searched all of their faces for a third time, this time noting the reluctant, affirmative nods.

*   *   *   *

It was nearly two a.m. when the police started interviewing them individually. The detective who questioned Audrey, Detective Cameron Grissom, asked her a string of questions and she dredged up the staged responses they'd all agreed upon.

The Detective was average height and weight. The dull light ricocheted off his baldhead but did little to illuminate the dreary room. He wrote on a frayed pad with a black ballpoint that he held in stubby, pink fingers. His face showed no emotion, but Audrey felt pressure nevertheless. Apparently, the rest of her party had experienced a similar level of stress from their meetings. Each of them re-entered the lobby after the ordeal, ashen and on edge, glad to be welcomed into the bosom of their loved ones.

They all gave the same story about coming to the banquet together. No one mentioned Bobby being gone but a couple of minutes to go to the restroom. They each recognized that there could be consequences for not being forthright with the authorities, but they couldn't talk to the cops until they knew what was going on. So they told the police Bobby had been with them all night. They'd decided that until they'd spoken with Bobby that would be the story they were sticking to. Their agreement was to say as little as possible and pray that the ordeal would be over soon.

They were told not to leave the city until they were authorized by the police to do so. Once they were back in the lobby, Paul suggested they go to his home north of the city and try to sort the whole thing out. The five of them piled into his SUV and rode in silence north on I-75 to the Roswell Road exit and through the streets of East Cobb County.

Streetlights disappeared and soft gaslights replaced them as they wove through the exclusive residential area with sprawling lawns, rolling driveways, or hidden entrances leading to unknown splendor behind dense foliage. Paul made a right turn and steered the car up a slight incline and into a long driveway with stone pillars on either side. He touched a button on the dash and one of the four garage doors opened and suddenly everything was bathed in light. When the car came to a stop, they exited like zombies and followed Paul into the house.

He led them into a massive, minimally furnished living room. The huge fireplace, its most distinctive feature, was embedded in a striking wall of jagged stone that must look magnificent filled with yellow-orange flames. The tawny oak floors glistened with a buffed finish that doesn't come from drug store cleaning products. Original paintings and limited edition prints decorated the walls. Beautiful soapstone statues sat on the floor or on glass tables. An African patterned rug supported a heavy stone coffee table. A sectional leather sofa enclosed the set, giving it the feel of an African tribal summit. Paul offered them seats by waving his hand in the direction of the soft brown couch. They sat down in the spacious room, the air thick with a deafening silence.

"I'm going to put on a pot for tea. The bar is in the corner if anyone wants anything stronger." He pointed a long, stiff finger toward an oak cabinet on one side of the room before departing for the kitchen.

No one moved to fix a drink. Audrey scanned the room while everyone else busied themselves with their own thoughts. The clattering sound of approaching wheels on hard wood jolted them back to the present. Paul wheeled a gilded gold caddy into the living room. He removed a lovely patchwork cozy, displaying a beautiful floral teapot. Matching cups, saucers, creamer, and sugar bowl completed a set that any housewife would be proud to own. Gleaming silver flatware fanned attractively atop white linen napkins. The second tier contained everything anyone could possibly need for the perfect cup of tea. Audrey looked at the big man quizzically. She would never have guessed a man like Paul Radford would be so particular about something like tea.

He placed lace doilies on the saucers before gingerly adding delicate teacups. With extended pinkie, he poured the steamy brew and passed a cup to each of them. It wasn't until Audrey sipped and the heat scalded her mouth that she felt wakened enough for her tongue to be functional once more.

"Paul, did you know Simone?" She asked after setting the cup onto the saucer. The slightest tinkle of glass meeting glass interrupted the silence as Paul landed the cup on the saucer. His eyes clouded pensively before he spoke.

"I met her." He looked at Audrey, then at his cup. The tremble of his hand was almost imperceptible.

"What about the little boy?" Renita asked. She sipped from her cup and then looked at Paul with steady eyes. "Do you know Bobby's son?"

"I may have seen him before, I can't really say for sure. It would have had to have been a while ago if I had." Paul said, and then looked away. "Bobby probably would have spent more time with him, but he hated that bi...he hated Simone."

It seemed to embarrass him that he'd almost let the expletive slip. He walked over to the caddie and poured himself a fresh cup of hot water from a stainless steel kettle on a second tier that Audrey noticed only when he'd touched it. It had been hidden underneath a cozy that matched the one that had covered the floral container on top. He dressed the liquid to his tastes and sat next to Audrey on the sofa.

"Where is the boy now?" Carmen asked. She sat next to Syd with a concerned look on her face. She had been orphaned at an early age and the thought of the young boy being motherless must have affected her in a much different way than it did the rest of them, Audrey imagined. Syd put her arm around her girlfriend before looking over at Paul for an answer that would ease Carmen's worried heart.

"I'm not sure." He replied. "I think Simone has family here—an aunt and some cousins in Midtown. I'm sure they will take care of the boy."

"How can we know for sure?" Audrey asked, looking from Paul to everyone else in the room. "Do you know her name?"

"No. I don't know her name." He replied a little too sharply, and then added. "I would think Bobby would be able to help you with that information." His voice trailed off when he saw the hurt and confusion return to their faces. "Don't worry, I'm sure they'll let us talk to him tomorrow." He spoke the words to reassure himself as much as them.

"Do you think Bobby will step in and take responsibility for the boy?" Carmen was still not convinced that the poor motherless child was free from harm's way.

Paul snorted in response to her question.

"I'm sorry. But I can't see any way in hell Bobby Wilson would raise a ten year old boy." He looked at Renita and Audrey and shrugged apologetically. They averted his gaze. It was true, the thought of their brother taking a step that came anywhere close to concern for another human being, let alone a child, was laughable. He'd never played a role in the boy's life and from what Paul was saying he blamed the neglect on problems with Simone. But they all knew that was an excuse. They all knew Bobby.

"No need to apologize." Audrey touched Paul's shoulder with her hand. "I don't think Bobby would ever be a candidate for Father of The Year either."

"What's the kid's name?" Syd asked.

"Simon." Paul almost whispered it. "She named him after herself."

"Simone and Simon." Carmen smiled. "That's nice. I'll bet she really loved him." She looked off dreamily. Syd patted her leg comfortingly.

"The poor boy will surely be traumatized by this." Renita said. "To lose his mother and father at the same time."

"But he hasn't lost his father." Audrey said. "Not yet. We've got to get Bobby out of that place." She set her cup in its saucer with too much force, spilling a few drops over the side.

"We will." Paul assured her. "We'll find out about the boy, too."

"I sure hope that he's going to be all right." Carmen's sympathetic words were nearly inaudible.

"Stop worrying so much. We'll find out tomorrow what will become of him." Syd yawned and looked at her watch. "It's almost four o'clock. Where can we crash for the night, Paul?"

"I'll show you." The three of them rose and left the room.

He returned soon and took Audrey and Renita to a spacious room with two double beds.

"I hope the two of you don't mind sharing a room." Said Paul as he showed them a small full bath on one side of the room. "The rest of the house has been shut off."

"This is fine." Audrey said. "Thanks, Paul…for everything."

"No problem." He looked at them both and winked. "We'll get to the bottom of this tomorrow." He closed the door; the plush carpeting muffled his footfalls.

Sleep hit her like a ton of bricks. The last thing she remembered was his words. We'll get to the bottom of this tomorrow. She closed her eyes with the prayer that she'd wake in the morning and find it had all been a bad dream.

CHAPTER 4

▼

Early Saturday morning Paul's home was alive with the bustle of his overnight guests. Everyone was anxious to get up and get downtown to find out the latest development in the situation with Bobby. Paul called the Detention Center but wasn't able to get anything but the run-around. Frustrated by the futility of trying to get information by phone, their hope was that it wouldn't be as easy to dismiss the small group if they confronted Bobby's accusers face-to-face.

The plan was to stay there until one of them was able to speak with Bobby. If they were denied, what could they do? Stage a sit-in? Vivid flashes of film footage with civil rights workers being demoralized and beaten flashed in Audrey's head. But she had enough sense to recognize that those things were not relegated to the South. There was probably less chance of such an incident happening here than there was outside her hometown in Cincinnati.

She tried to divert her fears by calling Marsh. She could use his moral and professional support. There was no answer. Her calls to him had remained unanswered and unreturned. She'd have to put that out of her mind for now. Her bother's life was on the line. He needed her, even if Marshall Fixx did not.

When they entered the police station, Audrey was surprised when the mention of her name to the clerk garnered looks from the surrounding desks. The familiar face of Detective Cameron Grissom surfaced from the rear of the room. He still had the same deadpan expression he'd worn last night.

"Miss Wilson. Your brother would like to speak with you." His eyes were as still as a mannequin's. "But I need to ask you a few questions first."

Grissom nodded to a female detective with her butt propped on the edge of the desk of the only other woman officer in the room. Both wore their hair in tight, chemically relaxed auburn tinted buns held in place by bobby pins and cosmetology cement. Weighted down by her police gear, the butt leaner fell in behind Detective Grissom who took Audrey's arm and led her to a small, stuffy room to the right of where they'd been standing. Grissom waved his hand to a gray metal chair that was pulled slightly away from a matching gray table. The lady cop took a position against the wall. Grissom closed the door and then took the only other chair in the room.

"So you're visiting Atlanta from Rosemont, Ohio?"

"Yes." Audrey leveled her voice. "We're here attending an awards ceremony. Bobby and I were nominated for a CRUTCH this year." Stop rambling! She admonished herself. Her nerves were on edge. The whole scene reminded her of the time she was held for the murder of her friend Norma Jean Strange. Her friend had entangled her in an embezzlement scheme and Audrey was later arrested for Norma Jean's murder. Audrey chased the painful thoughts away, trying to focus instead on the moment.

"Where was the banquet held?" Grissom asked.

"The Renaissance Hotel." Audrey decided she'd better stick to direct responses to his questions. He'd already asked the same things before. She figured he must be trying to trip her up.

"Did your brother leave the room during the ceremony?"

"No. You asked me that last night." Maybe if he knew she was on to him he'd stop this waste of time. She was wrong.

"You know, that's exactly what your sister said."

"Because that's exactly what happened." She held his gaze, feeling his eyes burn into hers like acid. It was hard for her not to blink.

"We have witness testimony that the suspect was away from the table a good portion of the evening."

"Well your witnesses are wrong." Audrey said with more conviction than she actually felt. She immediately thought about that heifer Jill Witherspoon. She probably couldn't wait to run to the police and trash Bobby.

"Well we also have witness accounts that Bobby Wilson arrived at Club Ambiance much later than the rest of you."

"I thought you were only concerned with where he was during the banquet."

"Miss Wilson, I'm only concerned with the truth."

Grissom's mouth was pulled so far into a frown that there was no mistaking the fact that he thought she was hiding something. At what point had this interview become an interrogation, she asked herself.

"How long was the banquet?" He pressed on.

"Three or four hours."

"Which one was it? Three, or four?"

"Four, I think."

"And you claim your brother never left the table?"

"No. Well…he may have gone to the bathroom. I wasn't watching him all night." Audrey felt herself caving in.

"So you really don't know if the suspect was away from the table long enough to go upstairs, kill Simone Denton and return to the banquet."

"That's ridiculous!" Audrey creased her forehead, turning her lips into an evil frown. "He wasn't gone that long."

"Did you partake of any alcohol during the ceremony?" Grissom asked.

"I had a couple of drinks."

"How many."

"A couple would be two." Audrey ripped sarcastically. The detective ignored her snide remark and took the questioning down a different path.

"You're older than your siblings, aren't you?"

"Yes."

"I'll bet you've had to pull your brother's bacon out of the fire on more than one occasion throughout your lives."

"No more than any other big sister would."

"Have you ever lied for him?" Grissom slid the question at her like he was skimming stones on a pond. Her brow wrinkled into a frown and she didn't respond. Grissom didn't pursue it.

"Where did you go when the ceremony concluded?" Grissom sucked his teeth, looking at her sternly, trying to read her verbal and physical language.

"You said it yourself, Detective. We went to a club on Peachtree Street called *Ambiance.*"

"Your entire party?"

Audrey squirmed in the stiff, straight-backed chair. She'd already been told that they had testimony to the time Bobby made it to the club. There was no way to wiggle out of the question without telling a bold-faced lie.

"It was so hectic at the Renaissance that some of us got separated. Bobby came in a little after I got there."

"Did you ask your brother why he'd gotten there so much later than the rest of you?"

"Did *you* ask him?" Audrey was sick of talking to this guy. "Maybe he was chipping golf balls behind the hotel, and then took a flight to Chicago, disposed of the bloody knife and clothes and then made a bee-line back to *Ambiance* to relax and party after a hard night of murder and mayhem."

Grissom curled his lips into a snarl and shot his partner a quick glance. The policewoman hadn't moved or spoken since the interrogation began. Grissom shifted his sights, cutting his cold eyes into Audrey's defiant ones.

"I'll take you to see your brother now." Audrey stood and followed Grissom out of the room and down a narrow hall. The woman officer followed her.

Bobby sat at a table in a tiny room that was an identical twin to the one she and Grissom had shared. As soon as the door closed, she rushed to him and they hugged. Then she pulled away from him angrily.

"What the hell is going on Bobby?"

"Sit down Audrey." They both took one of the metal seats on either side of the small table. Audrey reached over and grabbed his hand.

"What's going on, Bobby?" She asked again.

"They're telling me that Simone had defensive wounds that could have been made when she was warding off her attacker. They think that attacker was me."

"Why would they think that? Did you see her last night?"

"I called her. I was kind of mad because when she read about the awards in the paper she started hassling me." He waved an irritated hand in the air. "I ain't come here to see her. I came here to party."

"But you did see her."

"Yeah, I saw her."

"Why didn't you tell anybody? And why was she staying at the hotel?"

Bobby rose abruptly, jabbing his elbows back in angry frustration. He wanted to hit something...or somebody.

"Dammit Audrey, you sound like the fuckin' cops." He paced the floor like a caged tiger. He stopped, faced the wall and tried to relax. "She kept buggin' me and I went to see what the hell she wanted."

The knot in Bobby's wide shoulders softened.

"What did she want?" Audrey asked gently.

"She wouldn't tell me. When I got there, she said she couldn't talk right then. That she was expecting somebody. She asked me to leave."

"Did you?"

"Yeah, after I cussed that bitch out."

"Why'd you cuss her out?"

"Cause she begged me to come up there and then acted like she didn't have time for me when I came. Plus I knew that she was really just going to ask me for more money." Bobby huffed.

"Did she?"

"No." He answered, returning to the table and taking the seat he'd abandoned. "She wanted me to start spending time with Simon. That's when I really went off. How the hell she expect me to spend time with him when I live almost five hundred fuckin' miles away?"

Bobby's nostrils flared. His deep brown skin glowed red beneath the surface.

"Did you hit her?" Audrey's eyes narrowed in concern. She looked down at his hands. She didn't see any marks, but if he slapped her with his open hand…

"We had a fight." His gaze was unwavering. "But I ain't kill her!"

"I know you didn't, Bobby." Audrey grabbed his hand and gave it a supportive squeeze. He jerked it away.

"She caught me off guard." Then he mumbled, "I shouldn't have gone off on her like I did." Bobby swallowed back emotion, sliding his gaze away from his sister's piercing glare.

"Simone wanted the boy to have a man in his life but she approached me the wrong way. I cain't blame her for wanting her, uh…our son to have a male influence in his life. Why wouldn't she come to me? After all, I *am* his father."

Bobby was quiet for a moment. Audrey knew that it was hard for him to talk about this so she waited patiently for him to continue. He scratched his head, looked at the ceiling and then continued.

"I called you in here because I need to ask you a favor." His eyes pleaded with hers, searching her face in desperation.

"I want you to take care of my son for me."

"What? Why are you saying this to me?" Audrey drew back in her seat. "They are going to let you out of here soon aren't they?"

"To tell you the truth, I don't know." He licked his lips, hesitated, and then continued. "I need a lawyer. Depending on what you told the cops, the rest of ya'll might need a lawyer one too."

CHAPTER 5

▼

Marshall Fixx sat in front of the wide screen TV Saturday afternoon at his friend Ike's house watching the basketball game.

"What's takin' so long with the food, man?" he hollered in the direction of the kitchen.

"I'm not your fuckin' short order cook, Fixx."

"How 'bout getting me a tonic?" Marsh's hunger attack was sudden and vicious. He needed something to quell the growling monster in his belly.

"All I got is beer and Maalox." Ike replied.

Marsh frowned. He looked around the messy space with its collection of fast food containers, empty beer cans, dirty cocktail glasses and various articles of clothing Ike had stepped out of when they became too filthy to be worn any more. Ike had given the air a few sprays from a can of room freshener, but the space still reeked of unwashed armpits, stinky feet and flatulence. Marsh's skin started to itch and he scooted to the edge of the worn recliner. He swiped the back of his neck with this hand to make sure there was nothing crawling there.

"Don't you have a woman who could come over here and help you with this?" He looked from Ike to the pitiful looking sandwiches he'd set before him on the tray. Marsh picked one up and looked at it suspiciously.

"If you don't want to eat it, don't. Be that much more for me." Ike grabbed one of the fat, sloppy sandwiches and tore into it. He chewed a few times before swallowing, and then turned a can of beer up sucked its last few drops and tossed it in the direction of an overflowing can. It hit the wall and then clanged upon the dusty wood floor.

Marsh shrugged and took a bite of his sandwich. It was so good it almost made him forget about his filthy surroundings.

"This is pretty good." He said around chews.

"I don't need you to tell me I make a good sandwich, Fixx." Ike looked over at his friend as he took another bite and chewed.

"You ought to be over your wife's house anyway." Ike picked his teeth with his finger. After examining his find, he put the digit back into his mouth. Marsh drew back in disgust.

"She's not my wife, and I'm here because you begged me to stay with your stankin' ass."

After eight years of taking more shit than any woman should have to bear, Ike's wife Freda had recently walked out on him. He tried to make light of it but as the days turned into weeks and weeks turned into months and she still hadn't returned, Ike Pace's loneliness was apparent. He truly had begged Marsh to stay at his place. Marsh was tempted to stay with his parents as he usually did when he visited Massachusetts, but he knew his buddy Isaac was in trouble. So, he ignored his friend's sloppy house and messy ways and descended upon the Pace household on Friday afternoon, his shoulder ready for his friend to lean upon.

"You know, you'd feel a lot better if you'd get someone to come in and clean a couple times a week, man." Marsh changed the subject, dodging his friend's comment about his ex-wife. He didn't want to start a conversation about Marlena. But it was too late. Like an old hen, Ike was pecking around for every detail of Marsh's meeting with Marlena. Marsh surmised it was easier for him than dealing with his own emptiness.

"If Marlena is acting the way you said she was last night, it's just a matter of time before ya'll get back together." He passed Marsh a beer. "What are you afraid of anyway?"

"I'm not afraid of anything." Marsh felt edgy all of a sudden. He cracked open the top on the beer and took several long swallows. He didn't understand himself what had happened last night.

He and Toots had returned from a day of shopping before catching a ball game at the boy's school. It was late when they'd returned and he knew that Marlena would be mad. He hated the thought because things had gone pretty well until then.

When he'd arrived Thursday night, Marlena had been slightly distant, but affable. She opened the door and her fragrance rushed out, pulling him in like the hands of a seductive sorceress.

She was absolutely lovely. He had nearly forgotten how much she appealed to his senses. Her brown hair, lightened with blond highlights, gave her honey gold skin an added glow. She wore a billowy white shirt over slim black slacks. Her smooth feet were bare. When she padded toward the stairs to call Toots, Marsh felt his muscles flex. He made himself stop watching her, turning instead to examine the walls.

"I see you've been working." The walls were decorated with varying sizes and shapes and textures of her artwork. The look was bold and striking, just like the artist herself. She walked toward him, pointing to different pieces and explaining how she'd come up with the idea for each one.

Marsh scarcely heard what she was saying. Her nearness and her smell—all rosemary and lavender and natural things that soothed and electrified simultaneously, made him dizzy. When Toots finally came down the stairs, Marsh was so relieved he could have kissed him. They hugged instead.

"Aren't you forgetting something?" Marsh said to the boy.

"Your horn." Marsh looked down at him and smiled. "I haven't heard you play in a while."

It was because of Marshall Fixx, Jr.'s early interest in the instrument that had led to his nickname. Toots ran back upstairs to get it.

Before they pulled out of the driveway he'd given Toots a stern warning about his behavior at school and about being more respectful to his mother.

"She's never at home Dad." Toots had looked at his father, then out the car window.

He knew the boy was lonely for him.

"That's funny, your Mother says the same thing about you." Marsh's jaw tensed. His ex-wife called him more than once after Toots had stayed out all night or skipped school. He had been giving his Mother a lot of lip and was being a regular little knucklehead. Marsh hated to enter the territory where he was headed, but he had to find the root of the problem.

"You doing drugs, boy?"

"No!"

"Then what are you doing?" Marsh could no longer keep the anger out of his words.

"Minding my own business."

Before Marsh knew it, he was reaching to slap Toots hard across the mouth. But Toots ducked and shot up his elbow to catch the blow.

"God dammit, boy!" Marsh's hand burned from the impact of running into the bony angular appendage that sufficiently defended Toots against his father's assault.

"Get out of the car!" Marsh's command thundered fire red anger. Toots scooted over as far as he could on the passenger side, but he didn't open the door. Marsh flipped a switch and unlocked all the doors. He exited the car, jerked the door open and snatched Toots out of the car. The hot words that bubbled like water on a stovetop, got no farther than his throat when he saw that the boy was crying. Marsh melted like butter. He pulled his son into his arms and held him until his trembling tears quieted.

"When are you coming back?" Toots asked him.

"I don't know." He stroked the boy's head. Embarrassed, Toots pulled away. He opened the car door and pulled it shut behind him. Marsh stepped to the driver's side and slid behind the wheel. He adjusted the mirrors and fastened his seat belt.

"What am I supposed to do?" Toots asked sullenly. "Mom's never home…"

"Son, you're not a baby. If your Mother has to work late you should be okay on your own for a few hours. She leaves a number, doesn't she?"

"Yes." Toots looked down, unable to look his father in the eye after giving such a flimsy excuse for his behavior.

"You know I'm here every weekend that I can be." Marsh ran his hand through the boy's tightly curled hair. "You need a haircut." Toots jerked his head away. He wrinkled his face in adolescent defiance.

"Dad—when are you coming back?" Toots refused to be dismissed. He wasn't going to stop until his father answered the question.

Marsh knew what his son wanted to hear. He didn't want to lie to him, but he hated watching his pain.

"I need to get some things squared in Ohio, T. Then we'll see."

Toots gave him that you're full of shit look that kids give their parents when they know they're just that.

"Don't look at me like that. What do you want me to do—lie to you?" He grabbed the boy's shoulder and squeezed it hard until he had his attention.

"Toots, things aren't as easy as they sometimes seem."

Toots averted his gaze. Marsh released him and started up the car. Looking over his shoulder, he guided the rented Lincoln away from the house. They sat in silence as the car took them down the quiet street. It was as if they were both waiting until there was distance between Marlena and the conversation before they continued.

"You got a girlfriend out there, Dad? Is that why you left Mom?" His big eyes were moist with pain and concern for his mother. Marsh felt like a dog knowing his son knew the reason he and his mother were no longer together. "You do, don't you?"

"I have a lady friend in Ohio." Marsh confessed.

"What's so good about her that you don't want to be with me and Mom?" Toots looked at him like he really needed an answer.

"Is she prettier than Mom? Do you have more fun with her than you do with me?" Toots looked away, his jaws puffy with hot, angry air. He turned to face his father once more.

"Is it the sex? Is it so good you'd rather stay with her than Mom?"

Marsh screeched on the breaks, jolting the car to a stop and slamming the gearshift into neutral. He turned to face his son, shocked.

"Don't you ever talk to me like that again!" He pulled the boy toward him holding both shoulders firm; he shook him until Toots opened his smoldering eyes to face the man who was nearly his mirror image.

"I'm your Father, Toots, and I'm human. I've made mistakes in the past and I'll make more in the future. But you listen to me, and you hear me good." He jerked his son's shoulders making the boy look him square in the eye.

"I love nobody or nothing on this earth the way that I love you. Do you hear me?" He looked into the boy's eyes. A slow tear rolled down his face and Marsh pulled the Toots to him.

The tension he had felt between them since he'd first seen Toots that evening melted away. He was once again the funny little kid who liked nothing more than laughing. To Marsh, the boy's laughter was the sweetest sound he could ever hear.

They relaxed into the rest of the evening, cramming as many activities as they could into the allotted window of time. When they were each completely spent, they decided they'd better head for home. The problem was it was two o'clock in the morning.

He hadn't called Marlena and he'd kept his cell phone off because he didn't want anyone to interrupt his time with Toots. He was expecting a good cussing out when he brought Toots home. In spite of this, Marsh was disappointed when she went into the verbal assault. She could barely wait for the sound of Toot's bedroom door closing before the tirade began.

"What the hell is wrong with you keeping my son out till all hours and not calling?"

"I'm sorry, Marlena. We…"

"You don't have to tell me you're sorry. I was married to your sorry ass, remember?"

"Look. I know you're upset, but…"

"You don't know shit!" She was pacing now. Her hands flew wildly as she ripped him up and down about his behavior.

"You swoop up here when you're in a parenting mood and tear apart everything that I've worked so hard to put together for Toots and me. Then as soon as he gets used to you, you're on a plane going out of his life until the next moment of guilt forces you to come out here again."

He stormed over to her and grabbed her shoulders, making her face him.

"You know that's not true! I love Toots and you know it. I'd do anything for him. Besides, if I remember correctly, *you* called *me*."

Now Marlena was shaking, rumbling like a volcano. He mistook the origins of her agitation for rage. It shocked him when she suddenly collapsed into tears. Had he *ever* seen her cry? She was the toughest woman he'd ever known.

"My God." He pulled her to him. "Honey, I'm so sorry." He wiped at her tears. She was sobbing without abandon now. He pulled her over to the sofa and held her, letting her release the pain that she had held all this time; from the initial betrayal until this very moment. She hadn't allowed him near her, turning a deaf ear to any apology or explanation. She had walked away from him like he was a bad movie, like all she had lost was the price of admission.

Marsh lifted her face and looked into the big brown red-rimmed eyes. All the guilt he had hidden came flooding back, and with it a tidal wave of regret. Before he could rise from the sea of shame, he was kissing her, and she was kissing him. She pulled at his clothes until his clean, bare brown skin was shaded in silhouette by the dim light. Through tears and heartache, their lips moved to every part of each other, anointing the open wounds his betrayal and her hate of him had opened and left exposed for so long.

He unbuttoned the big shirt, pulling the lace bra from her small firm breasts, sliding the tights over her high rump and down her slender thighs. He listened to her gentle moans as he massaged her thighs, and then pulled at the lacy panties, kissing at the soft, furry warmth that he had once cast aside as cold, lifeless tundra.

They moved together on the overstuffed sofa, the room's bright colors accenting the music of their lovemaking. Marsh touched her with his fingers, with his tongue, gulping in her familiar sweet heaven like a man who'd been without food. He'd missed her. He wouldn't let himself really consider how much, until that moment.

Marlena opened her legs leading him inside her. Marsh lost all control, shuddering, throbbing, releasing. He closed his eyes and cried out, hating that he'd come so far to come so fast.

Marlena kissed his forehead and smiled. They held each other, silently. He was afraid to break the silence with words. Words—-those pesky things that complicated what had a moment before seemed so simple.

"What do you want to do?" Marsh asked. He watched her in the dim light, glad to be able to cover his weakness for her behind the shield of darkness. He feared what his eyes would reveal.

"What do you mean?" She mumbled. Her tone was not what he'd hoped for. Cold? No—-but not that warm either.

"I mean—-you want to get back together?" He inched the words out like a timid groundhog, peeping out of the safety of its burrow, hoping.

"You think giving in to an urge during a weak moment is a good foundation for a reconciliation?"

Now he was irritated.

"I wasn't giving in to some urge, Marlena." He sat upright causing her to nearly hit the floor. "I love you. I've never stopped loving you."

"I'm sorry Marsh, but I just don't trust you."

"It was one mistake, Marlena. One! It happened almost five years ago. Can't you forgive me?"

"I've tried Marsh. I really have. But…" She looked away. He pulled her chin back toward him.

"But what?"

"But nothing, Marsh." She rose and he followed her. She pulled the big white shirt on, quickly buttoning the tiny buttons. Her hands trembled, making her angry. She gave up on the buttons, pulling the thin cloth around her small frame and closing it in a tight fist. She looked up at him. Instead of afterglow, wild rage filled her eyes and lighted her skin.

"It's time for you to leave."

"What? Why?" Marsh was hurt. Didn't she feel anything for him?

"I need to think about this. All of it, not just what happened tonight." She softened, touching his hand in a way that asked for his understanding.

"For years I haven't been able to think about you without thinking about a whole bunch of negative thoughts at the same time. I'd like to see if I could give the thought of a reconciliation serious consideration, without all of the other stuff getting in the way." She gave his hand a squeeze. "I think you should do the same."

She led him to the door and closed it softly behind him. He stood at the door like a dog that was used to curling up with master, suddenly banished to the dog-house. He didn't want to talk to Ike about what had happened that night. His friend studied his face, waiting for the juicy details.

The sandwich that tasted like a chunk of heaven a moment ago, now stuck in his throat. His appetite gone, he slid the plate onto the messy cocktail table. Ike was right. He should be at Marlena's instead of sitting in this musty house with his musty friend. He thanked Ike for the sandwich and left.

CHAPTER 6

▼

Except for an occasional hello in passing, Audrey hadn't spoken to Jules Dreyfus for more than two years. They'd met while she was looking for legal help for her client, Ed Dixon who was the prime suspect in the murder of a Rosemont socialite. Now here she was again seeking legal aid. This time for her brother Bobby. Jules had attended the banquet last night. She hoped that he was still in town. A quick call to his office in Rosemont let her know that he was also staying at the Marriott Marquis and would be in the Atlanta area for another few days.

She, Renita, Syd and Carmen had Paul drop them off at the hotel around ten that morning. As soon as she'd showered and changed, she had the front desk ring Jules's room. She hadn't expected a woman to answer the phone.

"Oh! Jules Dreyfus, please." Audrey didn't know why, but she was annoyed having to deal with a "go between" before she could speak with Jules. She assumed the person on the other end was the Elle-looking chick from last night.

"Hold on a sec, he's in the shower." Audrey frowned into the phone as she heard muffled laughter before Jules picked up the receiver.

"Hello." He sounded so damned happy she was even more annoyed. Why did everyone seem to have someone right now but her?

"Jules, it's Audrey."

"Audrey? My goodness, what a surprise!" Jules paused a moment. His voice dropped a few octaves before he continued. "How are you?"

"I'm okay. I…"

He cut her off, rattling on with the giddiness of a child.

"I saw you at the banquet last night. I'm sorry that I didn't stop by your table. I kept meaning to do that but before I knew it, the dinner was over. Then afterwards, all that chaos outside. That poor woman——ah boy! Big cities. They're all full of violence and crime."

"Jules, that's sort of why I'm calling." Audrey twisted the cord around her index finger. "I don't know if you've heard the news, but Bobby was picked up last night and is being held in connection with the death of that woman."

"What? You're shittin' me."

"No." She hesitated a minute. "I need your help."

There was a sigh, then an extended pause. Audrey was beginning to feel like she'd made a mistake calling her ex-lover. He was probably still mad at her for dumping him. Now to have the gall to ask for a favor——he must be lovin' this.

"I'm down here on vacation, Audrey. I've got a flight chartered for Savannah tomorrow." Then he whispered. "I'm not alone."

"I know you're not alone Jules, your friend answered the phone." Audrey shook her head and looked up at the ceiling. She didn't have time for this foolishness.

"Look, I'm sorry I bothered you on your vacation. I'll let you get back to whatever you were doing."

"Wait, Audrey. I didn't say I wouldn't help your brother." There was a pause. She felt nervous waiting for his response.

"I'm just a bit surprised that you would call me. I thought you and Marshall Fixx were…where is Marsh, anyway? I didn't see him at the banquet."

"He couldn't make it." There, she'd said it, now her ex could sit and gloat knowing that she had dumped him and now her current significant other was treating her as though she weren't that significant.

"Oh." He paused. "I understand."

"No, you don't. It's very complicated and…look, he's not here and my brother needs help. Can you meet me at the Detention Center on Forsythe Street? That's where Bobby is being held."

"Yeah, I'll do it. Where are you staying?"

"Right here at the Marriott."

"Yeah? Well, why don't we meet downstairs at the cafe? You can fill me in on what's happened so far."

*   *   *   *

A variety of breakfast smells met her at the foot of the escalator. She made a right turn toward the source of the aroma, the hotel restaurant. Jules was already there. He smiled and they embraced awkwardly before the hostess approached and led them to a rear table with a lovely view of the massive gold fountain and pedestrians pounding the hot Georgia pavement. Jules ordered two coffees from a skinny, long-faced waitress and he and Audrey made small talk while they waited.

Jules looked rich. The disheveled, fidgety, slightly shy guy she'd met years ago in her old office building was gone. The man seated across from her was a matured version of the Jules Dreyfus she'd known. His graying, dark blonde hair was brushed away from a face that was tanned and attractive. The only lines on his face were the sexy crinkles around his blue-green eyes. His neat white teeth glistened like he was in a toothpaste ad. Audrey didn't know if he was really that much better looking or if she was so attention starved that she wasn't seeing clearly. Whatever the reason, a part of her wished this was a social meeting. But it wasn't. Bobby was being held for murder and she needed Jules to free him.

The coffee cups and two glasses of ice water were set before them. Jules rummaged through the condiments looking for his favorite sweetener while Audrey put her cup to her lips and sipped.

"So how have you been?" he looked up from his cup, sprinkling sugar on the table instead of in the coffee. Audrey pointed down at the mess and smiled. He was still the same Jules.

"Oops!" He started brushing and blowing the granules away from him. Audrey shook her head and wiggled out of range of the sugar assault. There was laughter in her voice when she spoke.

"I'm doing fine. It's really good to see you."

"You shouldn't have broken up with me Audrey." He was blowing harder now, trying to clean away more grit.

"Let's not go there, okay." She was already kicking herself. She damned sure wasn't going to let him kick her too.

"If that's what you want." He finally got a couple of packs of sugar into the cup and started to stir. "Just wanted you to know the door's still open." He laid the spoon on the table, looked at her and smiled.

"Doesn't look like it's open to me." Audrey thought about the woman's voice she'd heard over the phone when she called him.

"What...? Oh, you mean Heather." He fanned the air dismissively. "Trust me—-the door's still open."

Audrey looked into her cup. Her heart let out a tiny whoop that he wasn't serious about the super model. Not that it mattered; she was quick to tell herself.

"Tell me everything you can about what led to Bobby being picked up." He said before taking a sip of coffee.

Audrey told him about coming to the banquet with her party from Rosemont. Before the ceremony began they met and mingled with other attendees but for the most part, they were at the table all night. She told him that Bobby had been away from the table for a while before their category was announced.

"How long was he gone?"

"I don't know." Audrey shook her head, looking up at the ceiling trying to estimate how long Bobby had been away from the rest of the party. "I can't say for sure. It could have been ten minutes, maybe twenty. I don't think it was more than thirty."

"And this woman had a room upstairs in the same hotel. Twenty or thirty minutes is plenty of time to hop the elevator and pitch someone out of a window."

Jules' casual tone made Audrey shudder. Bobby couldn't have done this. He couldn't be that cold——to kill someone and then return to the table like he'd just stepped out to smoke a cigarette. Maybe she was wrong about the time. She didn't think he was gone long enough to commit the murder. It probably wasn't anywhere near the amount of time she'd led Jules to believe. The only reason she'd noticed Bobby's absence was because she was afraid he wouldn't return in time to accept the award with her.

"CRUTCH keeps written and video records of these events. It would be easy enough to check the time of the announcement of the Community Push Awards segment." Jules reasoned.

"That's true. And Bobby left a little after Ed Dixon accepted his award." She looked up from her cup.

"That was a long time, Audrey." Jules said in a troubled tone. Audrey frowned.

"Even if Bobby was gone thirty minutes or more before our category was announced, if it doesn't fit into the official time of death, they would have to release him." She pounded the table for effect.

"Not necessarily." Jules wanted to stop her from boarding a train that was going nowhere. He grasped her fist and held her in his warm azure gaze. "There's no way that they can pinpoint the exact time of death. The police could very easily include that thirty minutes in the window of time that they are investigating."

Audrey's expression fell. Jules squeezed her hand and comforted her with soothing eyes.

"But people saw her hit the ground. The time of death should be evident." Her eyes searched his desperately.

"At this point, they're probably still trying to determine if she was killed in her room and then pushed. It may even be a suicide." Jules added. "We shouldn't have any problem getting Bobby released on bond. What happened when you talked to the police?"

"Well…we didn't exactly tell the police everything."

"What do you mean?" His eyes pulled together sharply, puckering the space between them.

"I mean, we all agreed that we would say Bobby was never out of our presence except for a few minutes to go to the bathroom before the beginning of the presentation portion of the ceremony.

"What? Audrey, that wasn't smart. If Bobby is guilty, you could all be in a lot of trouble for deceiving the police.

"I know it was stupid, but none of us had spoken to Bobby and we didn't want to tell the cops anything that would help them build a case against him."

"Audrey! If the man is innocent the police will figure that out during the investigation and he'll be freed. You all didn't do anything but make things worse for him." Jules was raising his voice and irking the shit of her.

"What do you mean, *if?*" Of course he's innocent. And what planet are you living on where only guilty people get convicted of crimes?" Audrey's nostrils flared. She pulled her hand away from him, leaning inwards, daring him to challenge her further. Jules opened his palms in surrender.

"Calm down, honey." He looked up as a man and woman approached then sat at the table behind them. Jules leaned closer. "I didn't mean to make you mad." He said softly, waiting until the blazing fire across the table quieted to a slow burn before continuing.

"You're absolutely right. Innocent people get picked up and imprisoned everyday. I wasn't trying to dismiss your reasoning. I just want you to know that your actions may not have helped Bobby and will most likely hurt him."

Audrey's eyes were suddenly full of tears. She had been up all night and was exhausted. She was afraid for her brother and wanted to get him out of this mess. Audrey told Jules what Bobby had said about not saying anything else until he gets an attorney. That he had advised them all to do the same.

"Sounds like good advice." Jules nodded his head at the waitress who had returned to top off their coffees. "So you guys want the family discount?"

Audrey frowned.

"Is that supposed to be funny?"

"Lighten up, girl." Jules moved to touch her hand but she pulled away. "Look, it doesn't sound like they have much of a case." He took a sip of coffee. "What else did Bobby say?"

"At first he wouldn't tell me anything about what he'd done that night. Then his story changed. That troubled me."

"Do you think he's guilty, Audrey?"

Audrey welled up this time letting the tears flow without restraint. She shrugged and let out a ragged sigh.

"I…I don't know."

Jules moved over to her side of the booth and held her while she cried. He enfolded her in a warm familiarity that she missed and needed. But he was the wrong one to give it. Where the hell was Marsh?

She accepted a forehead kiss and the consoling words, wishing the kindness were coming from her man. Jules pushed the tiny braids away from her face, tilted her chin up and looked into her eyes.

"When did you get these little braids done?"

"A few of days ago." Her voice was heavy with the weight of her tears. She put a napkin to her face. When she pulled it away it was smeared with tears, Cargo olive mascara and sheer mahogany foundation. "Renita took me to a salon the other day."

"They look real pretty. I'll have to thank Renita next time I see her." Audrey gave him a weak smile. He took one of the skinny plaits and ran his fingers along its length. "Marsh is a fool for not coming down here with you."

Audrey looked away. On the other side of the windowpane the fountain flowed. People came and went, dodging too fast cars in the downtown Atlanta traffic. She hated that he'd dredged up the subject because she still hated Marsh for not being there to help her through this. Jules turned up his glass and drained the water from it before setting it back on the table. He spoke around the chips of ice that he crunched.

"Don't worry, Audrey. I'll go see Bobby today." He patted her hand reassuringly. "Everything is going to be fine."

CHAPTER 7

▼

When Audrey returned to the room Renita wasn't there. Feeling lonely, she gave Paul a call. He answered the phone on the second ring and seemed excited to hear her voice.

"Have you heard anything new about Bobby?" He asked.

"No." She said.

"I have an idea. Get a hold of Renita and you guys come stay out here."

"No, I think it would be best if we were downtown near Bobby."

"Why? You can't do anything but wait for them to untangle this mess. Until then, you're running up a huge hotel bill and paying for expensive downtown dinners. If you come out here you've got full run of the place—-tennis court, pool, running track, weight room, sauna. My housekeeper cooks everyday and you could have one of the cars to get around town in."

How could she pass all that up? She and Renita had upgraded their room from the standard Renita initially had as part of her package to perform. So they where paying a pretty penny for the suite they were staying in. It was nice, but Paul was offering them a stay at his mansion—free! She accepted his invitation and was hanging up just as the click of the lock told her Renita had returned.

She looked haggard and slightly disoriented. Audrey ran over to her, concerned.

"What happened to you?"

"Nothing" She wiped her nose with the back of her hand. "I'm just tired, I think I may be coming down with a cold."

Audrey gave her a curious look as she pulled off her jeans and plopped down on the bed. Bobby's involvement with Simone's murder was getting to all of them, but Renita seemed to be taking it particularly hard. Or was it something else?

"Where've you been, Renita?"

"I went for a walk. Have you heard anything more from Bobby?"

"No. But I did meet with Jules Dreyfus. He's considering representing him."

"Oh. That's good…" Renita mumbled, drifting off. Audrey walked over to her bed and saw that Renita had fallen asleep. She shook her shoulder.

"Renita? Renita?"

"Huh…what." Renita startled. Her eyes popped opened. She wiped at the drool that had streamed onto her cheek. "Oh, shit. I fell asleep?"

"Yeah. Are you sure you're all right?"

"I'm okay, I said." Renita looked at her sister like she was getting on her nerves.

"I was just worried about you, that's all." Audrey remembered the conversation with Paul and told Renita about his offer.

"Sounds good to me. I don't give a shit where we stay. Since he's giving us transportation I can get rid of that expensive ass rental car."

Renita sounded cranky and preoccupied. Audrey knew that eventually she'd tell her what was wrong. She shrugged and started packing.

"Well get your stuff together. He'll be here in about an hour."

*   *   *   *

The original party from Rosemont was dwindling. Syd Lawson and Carmen Bausa stopped by Audrey and Renita's room to say goodbye. Still concerned about Bobby and his son, they promised to call Audrey at Paul's to get daily updates on the situation.

No sooner had they said their good-byes than Paul was at the door. Renita called a bellman to wheel their bags downstairs. They checked out and got into Paul's roomy SUV.

The afternoon sun shown bright and heat radiated from every surface. Audrey found the thick southern humidity stifling. She was glad to be in the air-conditioned coolness of the vehicle.

They sped north on I-75 to the Roswell exit, turning onto Paper Mill Road. In the light of day Audrey could fully appreciate the beauty of the sprawling mansions on the way to Paul's. It never ceased to amaze her the waste and excess of the American way of life. They passed countless rolling green lawns decorated with colorful floral banks welcoming visitors down endless driveways made of stone or brick. Well-groomed, sun tanned people ran or walked with equally pampered children or dogs. With the exception of the occasional black and Asian faces the scene was Norman Rockwell to the nth degree.

Renita was quiet during the trip, dozing off for most of the ride. Her dark shades had come loose from one ear, causing the glasses to hang askew on her small brown face. Audrey made a promise to herself to have a good talk with Renita as soon as they got situated at Paul's. This was a difficult thing for all of them. It surprised her that Renita, who was usually the stabilizing force of the siblings, seemed to be falling apart. Audrey didn't know if she had the strength to support both her brother *and* her sister right now.

The sigh Audrey released was one brought on by a long, painful exhaustion. She didn't know if she'd have the energy to deal with everything she had to do. Audrey hadn't even begun the process of seeing about Simon. Paul looked over at her and smiled. He grabbed her hand and gave it a comforting squeeze.

"Try not to worry. You can only do so much." Paul snuck glances at her between focusing on the road. He spied Renita in the rear view mirror. "Renita is a strong sister. She'll make it through this."

"What are you, a mind reader or something?"

"No. Just a concerned friend." He nodded toward the sleeping Renita and then glanced at Audrey. "No matter how old they get, they're still your little brother and little sister. You can't help but worry." He patted her hand with his before placing it back on the wheel.

Audrey was constantly reminded of all the loving, caring people that were in her life. She appreciated Paul's friendship and told him so. He smiled, guiding the truck into the curve of the driveway.

A huge, mottled coated mastiff bolted across the lawn and into the garage with a healthy gait. The animal faced the door of the car, his long pink tongue extended, waiting for attention from his master. Paul touched the garage door opener to close it and turned off the ignition. A tiny beep alerted them that the doors were unlocked. Renita woke and stretched before reaching for her bags.

"Don't worry about those, I'll bring 'em in." Paul said to her. The dog issued a low, threatening growl to the visitors, making them feel unwelcome. Renita growled back before reluctantly releasing her grip on the bags and letting Paul bring them into the house. He led them inside, through the large living room where they had spent a good part of the night, to the bedroom they had shared.

"This is Danger." Paul said, referring to the beast panting beside him. "I hope no one has dog phobias." The dog barked. "Behave, Danger." Paul ordered and then addressed his guests. "One of you can stay here and the other down the hall, unless you want to bunk together again."

"We'll use this room, Paul." Audrey had a feeling that if she didn't stick close to Renita she'd never find out what was wrong with her.

"You sure?"

"There's plenty of room in here." She told him. "There's no need in dirtying up the whole house."

"Suit yourself. The cleaning lady has to clean it whether someone's there or not."

For the first time Audrey thought Paul sounded a bit arrogant. He made it a point to refer to his "help" whenever the opportunity presented itself. Then she thought maybe she was just playa hatin'. The man was a self-made success, the very definition of The American Dream. Why shouldn't he gloat? Audrey had read so many articles on Paul Radford's rise to fame and fortune that she practically knew his entire biography by heart. Bobby had filled her in on the few sensitive details that Paul had kept from the media.

He was born in a small West Virginia town whose chief industries were coal, kaolin, and the Klan. The family was close knit but extremely poor. Bad became worse when Paul's father was killed in a mining accident, leaving his mother to raise Paul and his four sisters alone. His earliest memories were of doing every thing that he could to make money to help his mother support the family. In spite of his assistance, Paul's mother still had to work morning and night to provide for her children. Since his mother was hardly ever home, Paul was forced into an adult role when he was very young.

Family life rapidly deteriorated. The youngest sister died of pneumonia. The oldest washed up on the bank of the river after being missing nearly a week. The two middle girls were taken by the state when it became increasingly apparent that their mother couldn't care for them.

At some time during his adolescence, Paul developed a severe stuttering problem. As a result, he endured torturous teasing from his peers. In spite of his speech impairment, he put his whole heart into everything that he did. Paul was an average student but he was an exceptional basketball player. A talent scout spotted him when he was sixteen years old and his mother signed a release that made him the property of the West Virginia Eagles, a now defunct expansion team of the NBA. The Cleveland Cavaliers eagerly drafted Paul Radford when his old team disbanded. But since he wasn't as flashy and articulate as some of his teammates, Paul's role on the team was marginalized. He knew that if he didn't become a better speaker, he'd be doomed to mediocrity. He took control of his speech problem by spending years in intensive therapy. After more than two years in therapy his first post game interview left everyone amazed. He was a natural in front of the camera. Commercial endorsements and business opportunities came pouring in. Today he is one of the most sought-after personalities in the country. He had disassociated himself from his impoverished roots, assimilating into the new rich class in which he now circulated. Poor stuttering, back hills bred Paul Radford was now a star. And the Wilson's were guests in his sprawling Georgia mansion.

Once he'd left them alone, Audrey and Renita started putting up their things. Audrey walked into the spacious closet and lined up her shoes. Static erupted from the small radio near the window. She turned to find Renita flipping the dial looking for a station.

The heavy beat of the extended club version of an Incognito tune brought them both to the center of the room. The sisters twisted and shook, gyrating to the thick melodious congas. Renita bent her head and shook her long dreds. Not to be outdone, Audrey wiggled her hips from side to side, shaking her braided extensions to the beat. They were so engrossed in the rhythm that they didn't know Paul had returned.

"Aaaah shucks now!" Paul bopped into the room like it was a house party. "I know ya'll can move better than that."

He squeezed in between them; shaking before one and then the other, limber, moving like a boneless chicken. He put his hands on Renita's hips. She wiggled them toward him. The two of them meshed their bodies together seductively. The height contrast didn't stop them from moving in sync to the beat. Paul grabbed Audrey's hand, turning her body and gliding toward her. She could feel herself stiffen, not willing to join in the dirty dance. He leaned in and whispered. "Relax, Audrey. It's just a dance."

Exhausted and stressed from carrying the weight of all that had happened during the last twenty-four hours, Audrey opened somewhat to his suggestion. The music chipped away the tension. She didn't know why, but she felt the need to keep her distance. She'd known Paul for years. What was she afraid of? She told herself to relax and let the music and the man take her. After all, it *was* just a dance, she told herself—relax.

Audrey jutted her behind in Paul's direction. Renita clapped her hands and laughed. It seemed to be what they all needed. Paul put his hands on each wide hip.

"That's it. That's it!" He instructed.

Her hips moved like they and the drums were one.

"Whooowee!" Paul looked down at her. Audrey felt wanted and sexy and good.

"Work it now. Shake it but don't break it!"

No sooner had he said the words than Audrey felt a crook in her middle-aged side. She grabbed at the ache and they all laughed. By this time the music had changed and they fell winded onto one of the big soft beds. The trio laughed like kids. Paul gave each of them good-natured hugs, before lifting himself from the bed.

"I gotta make a run, ladies. I can see I don't have to tell you to make yourselves at home." He dusted the wrinkles out of his wide-legged tan slacks.

"If there's anything you need and you can't find, ask Martha. Her room is at the end of the hall."

Not only does he have "help" Audrey thought, but he has "live-in help". She had to give the brother his props. If you're going to be part of the nouveau riche, don't half step. Paul was gone in a flash, leaving Audrey alone with Renita and the contemporary jazz of WCLK. She left the bed and walked over to the stereo and turned down the music. She plopped back down next to Renita who was pre-occupied with a goldenrod square of Hotel Renaissance stationery.

"So what's up?"

"What do you mean, what's up?" Renita scratched her forearm absentmind-edly.

"You've been acting kind of strange, Ren." Audrey leaned closer and nudged her.

"I'm okay, Sissy. Just tired." Renita yawned and sat up. "With all that's been going on we still have to do the Renaissance gig." She let out a sigh pregnant with exhaustion.

"I'm sorry, Renita. I've been so caught up that I forgot. This isn't just a vacation for you."

"That's okay. I just hope the manager doesn't cancel our contract." Renita poked out her bottom lip and looked at the doorway before cutting her eyes at Audrey sheepishly. "I hate to say it, but I was kind of pissed at Bobby for fuckin' up my groove. He put us in a bad situation with the Renaissance." She waved the yellow sheet of paper toward Audrey, but didn't give it to her to read. "This is a note from Lloyd saying that the hotel wants to renegotiate our deal."

"Can they do that?"

"Shit...*can* they?" Renita snorted. "We'll be lucky if they even call us back. And we're concerned about them putting the bad mouth on us. The last thing we need is to get the reputation of being one of those groups that brings trouble to every event."

"You think they'd do that to you?"

"Who knows? We've got to do what we can to ward off anything of the sort." Renita sighed. Tiny puffs hung beneath her eyes and her shoulders slumped. "Lloyd had to really do some hustling this morning just so the manager would let us work tonight. It's not just Lloyd and me. We'd be fine, but the boys need this gig. They really worked their asses off last night."

"I can't believe that the manager of the Renaissance is blaming you because your brother got arrested in connection with Simone's death."

"It's had a sharp impact on business. The crowd was real thin last night and there's no guarantee it will get any better." Renita shook her head reflectively and then said, "I can't say I blame the manager. A woman gets thrown from a window in his hotel and the prime suspect is the brother of someone who's performing at his establishment. I can see where he'd be a little put off."

"Point taken." Audrey said, and then tried to cheer her sister.

"You guys are so good. They'll call you back." She locked gazes with Renita. "Honey, don't feel bad about your misgivings about Bobby." Audrey rubbed her aching back before giving her sister's hand a supportive squeeze. "I'm not even sure if I believe he's completely innocent."

"Really? Why do you say that?"

"He wouldn't open up to me the first time I saw him at the Detention Center. The next time his story had changed. And then there was that comment about us all needing attorneys." Audrey rolled her eyes and shook her head in dismay.

"That doesn't sound good." Renita drummed her fingers on her knee. "Why would he advise us to get lawyers unless he was guilty and…"

"And unless he knew we could be guilty of obstructing justice for covering for his ass." Audrey cast her sister an annoyed gaze. "I just wish Bobby would get his life together."

"I know. He's had every opportunity in the world and he continues to act a fool." Renita closed her eyes and let the music take her to a better time and place.

The stereo emitted the soft, clear tinkle of a piano in an otherwise quiet room. Renita grabbed her stomach suddenly, but not before the growl of hunger interrupted the gentle music.

"Damn girl!" Audrey looked at her like she had cracked a loud fart. "When was the last time you ate?"

"Shit if I know. I guess at the dinner last night."

"Well, let's go to the kitchen and rustle up some grub." Audrey said, happy to be in motion.

They left the bedroom peeking into rooms as they traveled the long hallway to the front of the house. The cookware extending from a wood beam rack, the huge stove and refrigerator were stainless steel. A chunky butcher block was an island in the center of the room. The counters were deep mahogany colored tile and the back splashes looked like teak.

"This isn't a kitchen." Renita said. "It's a food preparation center."

They laughed.

"The boy must do a lot of entertaining." Audrey said after giving an approving whistle. She ran her hand along the glistening refrigerator that covered nearly half of one side of the room.

"It is a requirement for a man of Mr. Radford's stature."

The voice sounded like it was manufactured for an old horror flick—sinister accent of some unknown European origin and all. Audrey and Renita whirled around to see a tiny, dark brown woman with a dowager's hump that rounded her back enough to take several inches off her height. She looked from one of them to the other like she'd just found roach droppings in her spotless kitchen.

Audrey smiled and extended a hand. She wasn't sure of the correct way to acknowledge "the help" but she knew that being polite was in the first few pages of any etiquette manual.

"You must be Miss Martha."

Apparently, Martha had skipped the first chapter of the civility handbook. She didn't reach for Audrey's hand nor did she return the amiable words. Her gaze was dull, unfriendly. Embarrassed, Audrey drew her hand away.

The woman was spooky, like a black and white ghoul living in a world of vivid color. Renita ignored the shriveled Film Noir queen and started looking around the kitchen like the housekeeper wasn't even there. Martha didn't like that.

"Can I help you with something?" She shadowed Renita, hoping her tight words and close presence would cause the usurper to back down. Renita continued looking in the refrigerator like a health department inspector.

"We'd like dinner please. Do you have anything prepared?" Renita had no problem relegating the servant to her position. The little prune of a woman responded as though Renita were a hypnotist who'd uttered the properly programmed suggestive phrase. Martha cupped her hands together like they held a secret.

"Dinner isn't until seven. Would you like something from the noon meal?"

"What you got?" Renita looked down her nose at the little woman impatiently like she was used to dealing with "the help". Audrey pitied anyone who had the misfortune of having to deal with her little sister in that capacity 24/7.

"Lunch today was roast chicken, buttered new potatoes and asparagus spears." Martha recited the menu robotically. "I can serve you that."

"Sounds okay with me; how bout you, Audrey?" Renita closed the refrigerator door and rested her hands on her hips.

"Fine." Audrey murmured, blown away by her sister's gall.

"What about dessert?" Renita was no longer looking at the little woman, but continued the visual inventory of the room.

"Chocolate layer cake, Ma'am."

"Great. Can you bring in a bottle of Riesling with dinner?"

"I'll have to check the wine cellar, Ma'am."

"Run along and check it, dear." Renita said dismissively making a flicking motion with her hand that Audrey had only seen in the movies. "We'll have our lunch in the dining room, Martha." Renita turned and left the kitchen. Audrey picked her jaw up from the floor and followed her.

"Why, I must say I'm impressed." She told Renita when they entered the dining room.

Renita waved at the air.

"I've seen her type a million times. She only feels good when she's being dogged out so I say dog her ass down."

"Damn little sis, don't be so mean." Audrey chided. She pulled out a chair and was about to sit, but changed her mind. "You can have that ole sissy wine. I'm going to fix me a drink. Want one?"

"What the hell?" Renita said.

Audrey went over to the bar and fixed them both gin with tonic and lots of ice and lime. They sat and sipped their drinks for a few minutes before Martha entered with two steaming plates of aromatic food. She arranged two silver place settings and then set the dishes before each of them. Martha filled crystal goblets with water and positioned them to the side of their plates. She placed the pitcher in between them before stepping away from the table.

"We seem to be out of Riesling, Madame." Martha reported. Renita nodded slightly.

"That'll be all." She said.

"Enjoy your dinner." The servant said dryly before making her exit.

Audrey snickered and dove into the plate. Renita had started eating even before Martha left. They ate like there was no tomorrow. The meat and vegetables were sumptuous. The bread was melt in your mouth fresh. Just as they were finishing up the last few bites, Martha was back with a dessert tray and a coffee pot.

She set two steamy cups before them with the cream and sugar caddies and gave each of them a huge chunk of moist, deep brown cake nested on dessert plates.

"Would you like ice cream with your cake?"

"That sounds good Martha, give us each a scoop." Renita pushed her plate in the woman's direction. She scooped a fat dollop of vanilla onto their plates, refilled their water glasses and disappeared to the kitchen. Audrey could have sworn she levitated.

"That's one scary bitch." Audrey issued an exaggerated shiver.

Renita just sucked her teeth lazily and turned her water glass up. Before long, they each leaned back in their chairs rubbing fat, gluttonous tummies.

"That was good." Renita groaned.

"Uh huhn." Audrey looked over at the bar, too lazy to move. "It's your turn to fix drinks."

"Shi…I ain't fixin' nothin'. Tell that ole hag to get in here and freshen our drinks."

They felt her cold glare before they saw her. They slanted their gaze in the direction of the door. Sure enough, there was Martha.

"I'm…sor…we…" Audrey knew they were cold busted. Renita didn't give a damn.

"Martha, we'd like two gin and tonics with plenty of crushed ice and lots of lime."

Martha did as she was told. She removed their plates and sat thick white cocktail napkins on the table before them. She fixed the drinks, served them and was gone. The liquor was good but nearly too strong for Audrey who favored a higher tonic proportion than gin in her drinks.

"You don't think the ole' girl is trying to get us drunk do you?" Audrey suppressed a burp.

"Shit, I don't care what she trying to do," Renita pounded her fist against her chest and belched loud and unashamed. "Whew!" She burped again. "Long as she keep up this kind of service, she ah ite with me." She raised her glass and took another sip.

"Now, maybe we should talk about what's going on with Bobby and how we can get his butt out of jail." Renita picked her teeth with her baby finger before taking another sip of her drink. "Do you really think he could be guilty?"

"I don't know what to think. What I do know is that he hated Simone. He was always a hot head and once he signed with the NBA it was like it fed his over-sized ego. Who knows what he's capable of?" Audrey left her chair and started to pace, her clogs slapping at the backs of her heels.

"I can't tell you the relief I felt when Jules said he'd talk to Bobby."

"So what did he ask for in exchange? A sniff from a pair of your old panties?"

"That's disgusting." Audrey wrinkled her nose at the thought. "He seemed a bit reluctant to help Bobby."

"No kidding?" Renita snorted. "Bobby has never been one of his favorite people because he always upset you so. We both know what a butt hole Bobby can be. What did you say to Jules to get him to go see him?"

"I just asked him, is all." Audrey stopped pacing and inspected her glass. "You want another drink?"

"Sure." Renita said. Her eyes were already so heavy-lidded they were barely open. "What the hell? Pour away."

Audrey refreshed their drinks and brought them to the table. She raised the glass to her lips but suddenly felt she'd had enough and put the glass down. Her stomach was full and if she had much more to drink she wouldn't remember her own name, let alone be lucid enough to help Bobby.

"Why do you think Bobby never let us meet Simone and her son?" Renita sipped the drink and savored the potent taste of the gin before continuing. "Every time I tried to get the address or phone number from him he'd weasel out of it some way. I thought of looking it up on my own, but I didn't know the lady and I didn't want to get cussed out by some angry baby daddy mama."

"Probably a wise decision on your part." Audrey responded.

"Don't you know? The last thing I need is some baby mama drama." Renita was drunk. She plucked a pale yellow Jordan almond from the candy dish in the center of the table and popped it into her mouth.

"Uhm, these are pretty good." She said crunching. She pushed the dish toward Audrey who declined with a disgusted wave of her hand.

"I hate them things. Getting back to the subject, Bobby is being held down-town and unless we get some answers they may send him over to the Federal Pen. We need to go see him." Audrey reminded her.

"They can't send him to the Federal Penitentiary unless he's tried and convicted. We're not about to let that happen." Renita said. Audrey was glad to see her snapping out of her funk. The food and liquor had bolstered her spirit." Let's go see him and then we need to contact Simone's aunt."

"We should be able to get her full name and phone number from Bobby."

"It's a good idea to find out all we can about Simone and whether the old lady is going to provide for the kid." Renita added. "Maybe we can entice her if she's not too keen by offering to set up a fund for his care."

"That's a good idea. Waving a little money in front of her may make her more apt to tell us about Simone." Audrey concluded. "Let's go."

CHAPTER 8

▼

Alcohol basting didn't seem to affect Renita's driving. She handled Paul's Volvo like she owned it, blasting a classic rock station and floating in and out of traffic like the rest of the speeders. Maybe they were all drunk too. Audrey had poured a travel cup of Martha's strong coffee for herself and sipped herself to sobriety while mashing her foot on an imaginary brake. Renita pulled into a lot across the street from the jail. It wasn't until they got out of the car and walked toward the Detention Center that Renita seemed a bit wobbly.

They entered the drab sand colored building blinking to adjust to the bright lighting, roar of telephones, office machines and shuffling feet. The thought of being surrounded by law enforcement completely sobered them both. They sat in the sterile waiting area in virtual silence checking out the activity around them.

It was almost six o'clock before they were finally admitted to the room where they would see Bobby. The gruff, brown skinned guard with the baldhead and bad attitude was the same one who had been there when Audrey had visited before. Having to work a double shift most likely added to his already irritable mood.

"Wilson!" he barked into the microphone. The two of them startled alert, sprang from the hard plastic chairs they had been sitting in and walked over to the desk.

"Follow the white line to room A19 and wait." The guard's attention was already turned toward the man who was standing behind them. As directed, Audrey and Renita followed the white line painted on the floor, entered a tiny room and waited.

Before long the door clicked open and Bobby stood before them. His face was haggard and covered with a day's growth of scratchy looking stubble. He shook his head at his sisters and turned as though he were about to leave.

"Bobby? Bobby!" they flailed questions in unison.

"Where are you going?"

His back was toward them so his sisters couldn't read his face. The guard looked at him curiously.

"Bobby, get back here." Renita said.

"Are you all right?" Audrey asked sympathetically.

Bobby turned back toward them. He shook his head before folding his long body into the chair. The muscular, uniformed guard stood by the door watching their activity.

"I talked to Jules Dreyfus today…"

"Yeah, he was here." Bobby cut Audrey off. "He said he'd take the case."

"So does that mean that there is a case?" Renita asked.

"It's bullshit." Bobby said, and then explained, "They want to try to railroad me just because somebody said that a tall black man was seen leaving Simone's room shortly before she died." He waved his hands animatedly as he spoke. "As many people that were at that hotel, why the hell they have to pick me?"

"How many people in the hotel that night had an argument with the mother of their son who ended up taking a dive from the tenth floor?" Renita had run out of patience with Bobby. Bobby shot his sister an angry glare. Audrey moved to defuse the impending eruption.

"You did go to her room." She said gently, remembering their last conversation.

"Yeah, but I was only there a few minutes."

Audrey cut the guard a sideways glance and lowered her voice further. "So where were you all that time you were gone from our table?"

"I met this honey at the banquet and we went away for some quiet time. Well, we weren't *that* quiet. Heh, heh…ooo wee! That girl could holler." Bobby laughed. He reared back in his seat. "We were holed up in the stairwell downstairs. We kicked it for a minute, then I came back to the table."

"You're disgusting!" Renita turned around in her chair like she couldn't stomach the sight of Bobby. Audrey impaled her sister with an impatient glare. Bobby's recklessness irritated her too, but they had to stay focused on the reason for their visit.

"What was her name?"

Bobby looked at Audrey like that was the most stupid question she'd ever asked in her whole life.

"Hell, I don't know her name. I'm not even sure if I could accurately describe her. She was tall and blonde; the kind that hang around pricey hotels picking the pockets of rich business men."

"Did she tell you if she had a room number?" Renita asked.

Now he was looking at Renita like she'd asked an even stupider question than Audrey's. He just shook his head without responding. Bobby rubbed his hands through his low cut hair and eased back into the chair. He looked down at the floor like he wished they'd just go away.

"Room number? Ya'll don't get it, do you?" He searched the face of one of his sisters and then the other. "I meet women all the time. They take one look at me and see dollar signs and they wanna get with a celebrity. I take a look at them and see tits and ass and I wanna hit it. We on the same page now?"

Audrey blushed. Renita threw her hands up like she wanted to strangle him, but a stern look from Audrey settled her down. Audrey had heard all the stories of basketball groupies who stood around waiting for a chance to be Miss Right Now. It was business, each side looking to fulfill a need. Bobby hadn't played ball in years, but any black man over six feet tall wearing expensive clothes got the same kind of attention in public as if he'd stepped on the street wearing a jersey, high-tops and dribbling a basketball.

"We didn't go to a room." Bobby continued. "I already told you, we did it on the stairs. I did what I had to do and came back into the banquet area."

"When did you find out that Simone was staying at the Renaissance?" Audrey was getting tired of pulling information from him. She wished he'd just spill it so they could all go home.

"Not until the night of the dinner. She was standing near the concierge area when I was talking to a partner of mine. Apparently she'd heard about the banquet and our nomination and thought she'd use the opportunity to try to squeeze me."

"Did you fight?"

"We had words. I figured it was just a matter of time before she'd hit me up for some cash. She kept pressuring me to come up to her room. I told her to get her dumb ass out my face; that I would deal with her some other time. She got loud, made a scene." He flicked his hand. "I ignored that bitch and walked away."

The sisters cringed at Bobby's off-color terminology of his son's mother. But neither of them called him on it. They didn't want to do anything that would make him stop telling them what happened.

"So you went to see her later?" Renita queried.

"Simone had this sadness about her. It seemed like her eyes were crying even when she was happy. I felt bad for talking to her the way I did so I went to the room number she gave me. First there wasn't any answer. When she finally opened the door she told me to come back later." Bobby released a disgusted sigh. "Ain't that some shit? That's why I hate that scheming bitch." He licked his lips. "I grabbed her round the throat. I was going to punch her but I just pushed her up against the door and came back downstairs. That's the last time I saw her."

"Was there somebody in her room?" Audrey asked him.

"Well, why do you think she wouldn't let me in? Maybe she wanted me to come up there to make the muthafucka jealous."

"Why would she have a room at the hotel when she lives here in town, anyway?" Renita wondered.

"Simone was a ho. She goes where the money is. All the conventions and shit that's going on downtown, she probably wanted to be closer to the action. She's got a condo out in Sandy Springs that I'm paying' for." He pounded his chest with his fist for emphasis. "I guess being downtown was more convenient for her."

"That would make sense except for one thing." Audrey injected.

"What's that?"

"Simone had Simon with her."

"She did?"

"Yeah. Why would she have the kid with her if she was downtown hookin'?" Renita wanted to know.

"Who the hell knows? Maybe she didn't have a sitter for him and she wasn't planning on bringing her tricks to the room…I don't know. I never did understand that chicken-head heifer."

"Maybe she wasn't there for that kind of meeting." Audrey offered. "If she opened her door, but wouldn't let you in, maybe she was busy with somebody who was not a john."

They were quiet for a moment as they considered what that could mean. Audrey looked around the dreary room breathing in the faint odor of disinfectant and cigarettes. Then she remembered her last conversation with him and the questions they'd come to ask him.

"Bobby, the last time I was here you asked me to take care of your son. He was in the room with Simone the night of the…Friday night. According to the police he's in the custody of Fulton County Child Services."

"Did you talk with them?"

"Not yet. Every number I called led to a dead end. I've got the address. I'll have to go there first thing Monday morning."

Bobby seemed genuinely disappointed.

"We need to know anything you can tell us about Simone's family. We need names, phone numbers, addresses, the whole nine." Audrey took a pad and pen from her leather tote, prepared to write.

"You can get Dorothy to access my address book at the office. If I start trying to give you that stuff off the top of my head you'll never get anywhere."

Audrey wrote their office manager's name on the top of the pad. Dorothy Lofton was handling everything with both businesses and much of her and Bobby's personal affairs as well. Luckily, Audrey had had the foresight to push the important things on their calendar to a later date. Things were slow at the office so it was a good time to be away. It was unfortunate that their absence was extended because of a tragedy like this.

She was still scribbling when the guard alerted them that their time was up. Audrey and Renita hugged Bobby so tight that he pulled away before he became emotional.

They left the facility in silence, each in too much pain to speak. In Audrey's mind, the best way to overcome a bleak situation is to take action. They headed back to the East Cobb mansion. Audrey would call Dorothy's line and leave her a message to get the information as soon as she came in Monday morning. They wouldn't be able to get in touch with anyone at Child Services before Monday either. Until then, they would just have to wait.

CHAPTER 9

▼

"So what are you going to do?"

Ike asked the question for the second time, and for the second time, Marsh didn't have an answer. Ike sat on the overstuffed recliner with his leg hanging over one arm of the chair. At ten fifteen on Saturday morning, Marsh left his bedroom in search of his host. He found Ike in the living room sucking on a can of beer. He'd swallowed four of a six-pack as they talked over the next few hours. Trying to save himself an extra trip, Ike brought back both the remaining cans the last time he went to the kitchen. Marsh couldn't help it. He had to let Ike know that he was going down a bad path.

"Don't you ever drink water or tonic or anything that doesn't contain alcohol?"

"This is *my* house. I do what the hell I want." Ike burped and took another swig.

"I'm not trying to get in your business, Ike. Just don't let Freda's departure ruin you."

"What?" His heavily hooded eyes opened like he had been slapped sober. "Man, I'm celebrating. Don't worry about me, Fixx. When I'm through partying, I'll clean up and put the whole thing behind me. Right now it's just a relief to be able to be a stankin' ass man and not have some bitch on my back about every little thing."

Ike shook can number four before chucking the empty cylinder toward the pile of trash near the waste can. Just to irritate his guest, Ike ripped the top off a new can dramatically, it's air escaped in a loud rush for freedom. He looked at Marsh with a silly grin on his face.

"So what you gon' do?" He asked again.

"I don't know what to do." Marsh left the chair he had been sitting in and started to pace. Driving home from Marlena's last night, he'd felt a tremendous high. For years he'd thought about and dreamed about what he'd experienced last night. He and his ex in the throws of passion, making up for the time they'd lost due to his mistake. When it actually happened it was surreal, like an out of body experience. A force was pushing him near her, making him take her without thinking or caring about the consequences. He'd nearly cried when she was receptive; the flame within him igniting a place in her he thought was cold and dead. She'd always been so standoffish whenever he visited Toots. Marsh thought she no longer had feelings for him.

But that hadn't been the case last night. Making love with Marlena had been like New Year's fire works, volcanic eruptions, and nuclear explosions all going off at once. At least it had been for him. Afterwards, she'd had no trouble asking him to leave. She was so hard to read. He knew she enjoyed the sex, but like before, she put him out afterwards.

"I can't tell you what I'm gonna do until we talk things through." He finally said. "We can't just rush into something. And we have to consider Toots."

Ike took a swig of the beer and burped.

"Shit, Toots will be all for it. You know the only reason he's been acting up is to get attention. He playin' botha ya'll. He knows as soon as he shows his little ass you'll be on a plane and all up in his face."

"I know." Marsh stopped wearing out the carpet and sat back down. "There's something else I need to think about too. Someone rather, and that's Audrey."

"That chick in Ohio?" Ike waved both hands at Marsh like he was the biggest sucker in the candy store. "Why? You ain't proposed to her or no shit like that, did you?"

"No, Ike." He looked at his friend like he'd lost his mind. "I didn't propose to her. But we do have a tight thing happening. I'm not sure how attached she's become, but I can't just walk away from her like the past year never happened."

"Man, please! The only reason you been with her is because you couldn't be with Marlena. Now that Marlena gave you the green light you gon' try to do the right thing by somebody you don't even want?" A lazy belch slid from beer-wet lips. His heavy lids were nearly shut. Ike hiccupped and then expelled a goofy giggle. Marsh just looked at him and shook his head. "I'm taking advice from this guy?" He said to himself and shot Ike a disgusted glare.

Marsh left the chair and started pacing again. He stopped in front of Ike and looked down at his lazy friend who spoke more than a little truth. He had used Audrey to fill a void. Marsh hated to admit it, but it was true.

"It's not that I don't want Audrey. We got a good thing together. But I might have a chance to get my family back. I have to at least try——if that's what Marlena wants. Even if it doesn't work out." Marsh looked down at the floor and added. "But I don't want to hurt Audrey."

"Man, kick that bitch to the curb. She probably down there in Atlanta with her heels behind her head anyway."

*   *   *   *

Dawn was just beginning to break when Audrey woke and showered. Renita hadn't come in from her gig last night at the Renaissance. She didn't know if Paul was in. If he wasn't, that meant she had the house to herself. Unless Martha was there.

Audrey pulled on a pair of jeans and a tee shirt and opened the bedroom door. The aroma of fresh coffee pulled her in the direction of the kitchen. She moved over to the long, heavy oak sideboard. Martha was laying out a buffet of fruit, eggs, grits, hash browns, pancakes, biscuits, sausage, and smoked salmon swimming in gravy. She eyed Audrey then turned and opened the oven. The hot, warm smell of something wonderful spilled into the kitchen, flooding the grateful space with the comforting aroma of baked goods. Martha closed the oven door, giving the bread more cooking time. Audrey suppressed a whimper of disappointment. Martha faced Audrey and spoke in clipped tones.

"What would you like for breakfast, ma'm?"

"My name is Audrey. How would you like to be addressed?"

"You can call me Martha."

"Thank you Martha but I can get my own breakfast."

"Look. This is my job." She held the coffee pot toward Audrey and she nodded. Martha poured a cup of the steamy dark fluid into a white china cup. "Don't come in here dragging that Negro guilt burden. I do this kind of work because it is what I choose to do. I don't find it demeaning, degrading or any other kind of "D". Long as I get "D" paycheck I don't care what anybody thinks about what I do." A southern accent replaced the contrived old world dialect Martha had assumed before.

Audrey eyed the old woman curiously, opened her mouth to respond but thought better of it. Martha was right. It did make her uncomfortable that Paul had a black maid. She'd never known a black man to have servants. Though she assumed Marsh did at his parent's home in Nantucket, she'd never visited him there. It wasn't like she didn't have "help" herself. Audrey used a cleaning service once a week that many of the people in her association used, but these were people who worked for a corporation and you rarely saw them. The only thing you knew was that your house was always well dusted and clean when you came home from a hard day's work. If you wanted laundry, dry cleaning, or any other service performed, you filled out a card and left the dirty clothes in a specified area. It was very impersonal.

"I haven't seen anyone else this morning. Have you seen Paul today?" Audrey felt the need to fill the space with conversation. Martha didn't share her feelings.

"Yes, ma'm." She busied herself wiping, cleaning, and checking the stove.

"Will he be joining us for breakfast?"

Martha stopped what she was doing, stood stock still like she was dealing with a chatty adolescent who'd just severed her last nerve. She turned to face Audrey. The weird Transylvanian accent was back.

"Mr. Radford had his juice and went for a jog like he does every morning. He'll eat at his leisure. I didn't hear anyone come in last night (Audrey knew she meant Renita) so I assume you will be eating alone."

Martha's withering glance made Audrey cast her eyes downward. With one caustic slash of her tongue Martha had implied that Audrey was a ninny and that her sister was a slut. The housekeeper returned to her duties. Audrey fingered the lovely white embossed roses on her coffee cup, relieved when Martha had gone back to her tasks. She finished putting the food, china and silverware on top of the buffet.

"Can I get you anything else, ma'm?"

"No. Thank you, Martha." Audrey replied weakly. Renita would've made Martha fix her plate.

She left Audrey alone with enough food to feed a small army. Audrey took a moment to observe the beautifully decorated room that was warm and cold at the same time. Audrey didn't like this room. There was a strange chilliness to it. It was almost as if Martha had her own icy thermostat with its needle locked in the discomfort zone.

Audrey walked over to the long table and grabbed a heavy white embossed plate. She culled a heaping spoonful of everything there and carried the plate to the dining room. Her chair faced a set of French doors that led to a veranda. She looked out into the backyard and a beautiful view of the woods beyond. Audrey was about to put a forkful of salmon into her mouth when she looked outside again. The patio looked so inviting she left her place at the table and opened the sliding doors.

She took the waterproof cover off the iron furniture and went inside to collect her plate and coffee. The morning's warm, clean newness immediately lifted Audrey's spirits. She ate her breakfast and decided that a walk might release the guilt she had about her gluttony. Perhaps the clean air and exercise would help her organize her thoughts as well. She needed to figure out what to do next to get Bobby out of the mess he was in.

It was still too early to start making calls. Neither Paul nor Renita was there and she wanted them to go with her to the Detention Center that morning. She hadn't brought her watch outside with her, nor had she brought anything to write down her thoughts. Maybe going for a walk would kill some time if nothing else.

Audrey trapped over a wooden bridge, stopping to peer over the side at a school of fat white and orange coy. The black spotted fish gathered at her feet, begging for food. When nothing was forthcoming, they slithered beneath the murky water. Bullfrogs croaked from somewhere in the rushes. Audrey inhaled, closing her eyes to drink in the peace and freshness of the new day. After a moment, she stepped down the planks and moved toward the thicket of trees in the distance.

Two Belgian fence espaliers, lush with fruit flanked a small stone path that was nearly hidden by an overgrowth of ornamental grass. Bushy muscadines toppled a rounded trellis and just beyond the overhang of leaves and grapes was an octagonal gazebo. Audrey ascended the broad wooden stairs and took in the breathtaking pastoral scene before her. Looking to her right a view of hazy mountains, skyscraping pines and bustling city was a painter's delight. She turned, taking in the rest of the grounds.

A barely perceptible, unkempt area beyond a clay tennis court caught her eye. Letting her nosiness be her guide, Audrey stepped down from the gazebo and walked behind the court. Just beyond a thicket of brush stood a wooden shed with an aluminum roof. Audrey squinted at the structure curiously. Why would Paul have this run-down lean-to in the midst of such opulence? The sound of bustling feet snapped Audrey's head in the direction of the sound. She turned and was surprised to see Paul running up to her with a strange look on his face.

"Audrey!"

"Oh, hey Paul. I was going for a walk."

"That's not a good idea…I mean, alone. Just a couple of weeks ago a brown bear was spotted near here." Paul's chest rose and fell as his breathing stabilized from his sprint.

"You're kidding!"

"No, really. I wouldn't want anything to happen to you." His eyes darted nervously toward the shed. She laughed to herself. He seemed so uneasy Audrey forgot her curiosity. Some of the manliest men were afraid of spiders and snakes. Maybe Paul was just afraid of the forest. Or was there something in that shed he didn't want her to see?

"Why don't you come with me?" She had a feeling he'd refuse. She was right.

"Why don't we go back to the house?" He said, guiding her in the opposite direction. "I've been up for a while and I'm hungry. We could talk about what we need to do to help Bobby over breakfast."

"I've already eaten." She said.

Paul continued to move her toward the main house. Soon they were in the patio. She looked over at the table and noticed the dishes she'd left outside were gone. Martha had probably been watching her the whole time. Perhaps Paul wasn't afraid. He obviously didn't want her wandering the grounds. What was out there that he didn't want her to see? Again she longed for the slow pace of Rosemont. She missed her house, her cat and her life. But she wouldn't be able to leave here until Bobby was freed. Audrey threw her hands up in defeat and followed Paul to the house.

CHAPTER 10

▼

"My brother killed his baby momma."

"What are you talking about, *Cherie*?" Franchot ran his index finger from Renita's frowning lips down to her small round breasts. He circled a nipple before pinching it between his fingers.

"Ow!" She slapped his hand. He laughed and pulled her to him, kissing her until she went limp in his arms. She hated herself for being here with him like this. But she couldn't help it. When she saw him Thursday night, standing out in the crowd like a celestial body, she forgot for a minute the words to the song she was singing. She pushed away the swish of painful memories that kicked her hard in the gut. Franchot Arnaud. Her one and only love was standing right in front of her as she performed that night at the Renaissance in Atlanta.

Renita's first thought was to run, either into his arms or away so that she could feel or reject the sweet pain that being with him would bring. Running away would be safer. Though her heart was full of longing and her head full of curiosity, not tempting fate would definitely have been easier. But it was already too late. There was nothing to do but thrust herself into the feeling and let it run its course.

Liar. She had said never again. But it wasn't true. Why had she made the promise to herself, her sister and God? Renita was already bundling an emotional poultice to apply on the wound the self-betrayal would leave. She'd have to smooth it over the guilt she'd feel at having to lie to Audrey about spending even one minute with this man. The remaining mixture would have to be used to repair the chasm of disappointment her action would rip through her relationship with Lloyd. There was nothing she could say to make them understand how she would want to have anything to do with Franchot Arnaud.

She was able to compose herself and get through the night's performance but it seemed like the longest night of any she could remember. Toward the end of the session she searched the room from her position on the stage and no longer saw him. This gave her a feeling of relief and disappointment. Despite her ambivalence, she found herself panning the room anxiously, seeing if she could spot him.

They finished the last set. Renita thanked the crowd and headed for the lounge. She was on her way out of the restroom when she stopped cold. Franchot stood before her. His tall, perfectly sculpted frame shimmered in the dim light. His dark hair had receded and thinned a bit on top and was flecked with gray. The black tailored suit clung to him like she used to, grateful. He extended a drink and she found herself moving near him as if he had her on a string.

Franchot leaned in and kissed her, washing away the protective shell that had enclosed her for nearly ten years. Her mind tried to protest but it knew that it didn't have a vote.

"I've missed you, my love." The words rolled off his tongue and pricked her heart. Renita was afraid she'd cry at the pain of the reunion she'd thought about for so long. His accent was not as thick, but still as bewitching. The spell the words cast was as powerful as it had been when she'd met him in Brussels forever ago.

"Come with me, *Cherie*."

She took his hand and he led her toward the door. Renita's dream bubble burst when she heard Lloyd behind them.

"Renita!"

Like a little girl whose daddy had caught her misbehaving, she stopped and waited for his admonition.

"What the hell are you doing here?" Lloyd's eyed Fran contemptuously. His voice erupted from a face darkened by hatred. He glanced quickly in Renita's direction. Hurt and disappointment drew his brows inward. "You're not going anywhere with him, Renita."

People milling around the room, socializing, drinking, laughing, stopped suddenly, struck by the pending volcano that was about to erupt. Not only did Lloyd dislike this man who had caused Renita so much grief over a decade ago, but his emotion was also heightened by her refusal to commit to him. She knew Lloyd loved her yet she wouldn't entrust her heart to him. It drove him crazy.

Before they left Rosemont Renita and Lloyd had picked up the relationship that they wove in and out of for years. Lloyd was waiting for her to settle down and accept the fact that he was never going to leave her. He'd even bought her a ring but Renita had just looked at him, not touching the dazzling diamond like the act alone would indenture her to him. She refused the ring he had presented her. Undaunted, Lloyd held onto the symbol and his dream that she would soon wear it.

"Renita is a grown woman." Excitement stirred Franchot. The heat of anger intensified his French accent. "I believe she is capable of making her own decisions." He pulled Renita to him. She held up her hands silencing them both. Renita pulled out of Franchot's embrace and hugged Lloyd.

"I'm okay, Pops. Really." She looked over at Franchot, who issued an impatient gaze before pulling out a cigarette and a thin gold lighter.

"I need to talk to him."

Franchot drew on the cigarette and blew a bluish white cloud of smoke between them, masking his eyes that had grown dark with anger. Renita touched Lloyd's arm reassuringly.

"I'll be alright." She kissed his cheek. It felt cold. "I'll see you tomorrow."

A feeling of sadness surfaced as she remembered Lloyd's face; a moving portrait of anger turned into worry as he watched her link arms with Franchot and walk toward the door. She knew Lloyd was hurt but at the time she didn't care.

Talking endlessly, she and Franchot walked hand in hand to the Marriott…to his room. They made it to bed before they made it through the first year of catching up. They stayed in bed nearly all that next day. She'd been with her family during the awards ceremony and then, in it's awful aftermath and she hadn't seen Franchot since.

He'd been mad at her for not coming to his room on Friday night. When she told him about her brother and his troubles, Fran wasn't sympathetic.

Renita looked at her watch. She needed to get out to Paul's to see what was going on with Bobby. She dreaded going out there. The guilt she felt about being with Franchot made it hard for her to face Audrey. Not only that, Renita didn't want to admit it to her sister, but a part of her thought Bobby may have killed Simone. He hated the woman. Everybody knew that. He felt that Simone had tricked him into a situation that he didn't want to be in. He refused to see his son and whenever she and Audrey asked about the little boy they got cussed out. Bobby said he didn't believe the boy was really his but he didn't want to go to court; didn't think that kind of publicity would help his career. He agreed to pay what she'd asked. Venom was the glue used to seal the monthly checks that were mailed to Simone Denton. He'd be evil around that time too. She and Audrey teased him behind his back saying that it was "Bobby's time of the month" and they stayed away.

Now Simone was dead. Bobby was in jail. And Renita had to pretend she thought he was innocent. She had a real problem talking to him at the jail yesterday. She hated sitting there trying to be supportive, all the while feeling guilty as hell for thinking that *he* was guilty as hell. She burrowed deeper into Fran's embrace, pushing thoughts of Lloyd and her siblings out of her mind. Her best bet was to stay away.

*   *   *   *

Audrey spent Monday morning calling Children's Services and getting the run-around. Since she couldn't claim guardianship they wouldn't give her any information about Simon. She called their office in Rosemont and was happy to hear Dorothy's voice. It made her miss home all the more.

"I thought you all would be back here today." Dorothy was a great office manager with a no nonsense style that Audrey truly admired. The big-boned, Tuscaloosa, Alabama native was as light on patience as she was heavy of hip. She let her boss know that she wasn't all too pleased that she had to rearrange her schedule to accommodate their change in plan.

"I can't go into it all over the phone, Dorothy, but there's been a terrible tragedy down here and the fact that we've had to extend our stay couldn't be avoided."

"Jesus, be praised!" The woman's voice was full of concern. "Are ya'll alright?"

"We're going to be just fine." Audrey didn't want to worry her too much. "I'll fill you in on everything when we get back there. It should only be another few days." She hoped that were the case.

They spoke for a few more moments, Dorothy grumbling as she accessed Bobby's Outlook Express and e-mailing the addresses requested by her boss. Knowing that Dorothy was back to her usual grouchy self, Audrey ended the call. She connected her laptop and waited for the transmission from Ohio.

Audrey got everything she'd requested from Bobby's address book and felt cautiously jubilant. After calling information, Audrey was able to verify the numbers and look up the addresses. Paul went online to get directions while Audrey called Simone's aunt and her cousin. There was no answer at either place. They were more than likely at work. When every detail was taken care of or at least attempted, they were ready to visit Bobby.

It was eleven o'clock when Paul and Audrey arrived downtown. They parked the car in a lot across the street and pushed through the smells, sounds, and colors of street vendors and people heading to stores and outdoor concerts. Periodically a fan would recognize Paul and ask for an autograph. He'd turn on the charm, nodding and scribbling as devotee's fawned. Audrey was quite bored with Paul's celebrity and ready to move on. She wished she could be transported back a few days ago when she and Renita were hanging out having fun. But that was before Simone Denton had been pushed from her hotel window. Before Bobby had been picked up for murder.

Audrey was called to go inside the meeting area. Paul rose and gave her a hug telling her he'd be there when she was done. Audrey walked the painted line that was becoming all too familiar. She turned the knob this time into a much larger meeting room that contained eight different tables and matching chairs. Several of them were occupied with visitors and the men they'd come to see. Guards stood point in each corner of the room and at the door. Bobby was seated at a table directly ahead of her. They hugged for a brief, uncomfortable moment before taking their chairs.

"Are you okay?" She didn't mean for the words to waver like they were coming from the mouth of a scared six year old. But that's what happened. Bobby expression went from anger at his situation to worry for his sister.

"Are *you* okay?" She shook her head. It had been a long time since Bobby had shown concern for her feelings. Audrey hadn't had time to think about herself. She was here to do whatever she could to get him released. She questioned him point by point on the things he had told her so far. He filled in some of the sketchier details from their last meeting. She was beginning to understand why he was being held.

"Listen. I didn't tell you something the other day." He grabbed her hands and wrapped them in his massive mitts. "When I saw Simone that night I didn't just cuss her out, I hit her."

"Oh my God, no! How could you do such a thing?"

"I was feeling all bad for not going to her room at first, then when I get there she had some other sucka up in there. I hate it when a woman tries to play me." He stopped for a moment, and Audrey knew he had transported himself back to that fateful night. His gaze was chilling and distant.

"I knew she had somebody else in the room even if she wouldn't admit it. Then she asked me to set up a five hundred thousand dollar trust fund for Simon. She said she had some high-powered Atlanta lawyer and he already told her that he could attach my pension plus make sure she could draw against my future earnings. We started arguing." Bobby looked down at his hands like they had betrayed him. "I hit her. People not only heard us fighting, since she never let me in her room, somebody might have seen me hit her."

"That's bad." Audrey's head was swimming. What would Bobby tell her next?

"Did you tell Jules about this?"

"He knows. What were you able to get from Children's Services?"

"Nothing. Though I'm your sister, Simone didn't have my name anywhere in Simon's records. They won't give me any information unless you'll submit to a paternity test and we complete some kind of county paperwork. Until that happens they won't let me anywhere near him."

"I'll make the arrangements. They're trying to place him in a facility. I know I didn't do right by him all these years. I really don't even know him. But I can't let him go into one of these state places. Hell, this is Georgia."

"Bobby, I'm sure they have excellent facilities here, but I agree with you. Why should he be institutionalized when he's got family?" She looked at Bobby. She had to be careful that she didn't upset him bringing up his past attitude about his son.

"I don't mean to sound insensitive, but it seems that with Simone gone it would be the perfect chance for you to just forget about Simon." She looked deep into his chestnut irises that had softened with concern for his son. "You haven't been a father to him for ten years, why the change?"

"You're right. I've been a total idiot. I treated Simone like shit." He looked away, but not before Audrey saw the wetness gathering in his eyes. "I've been thinking since I've been in here. She didn't deserve to be treated that way. We both had sex. We were both careless. I blamed her for getting pregnant. I thought she did it to trap me. Hell, you can't be entrapped if you don't put yourself in the situation. It's time I started owning up to my responsibilities. I can't do anything else for Simone, but I can help Simon."

Audrey smiled and put the heels of both hands to her eyes to try to dam the flow of tears. All the years she had been trying to get Bobby to do the right thing. It was unfortunate that it took the death of his baby's mother and his being charged with the crime, for him to straighten up.

"Paul has a lot of pull in this town." Bobby appeared more serious than she had ever seen him. Ignoring her show of emotion, he pointed sharply as he spoke, like he was giving direction to a dull-witted child. "Tell him I want him to help you. You've heard all the horror stories about foster care. I don't want my son being abused by strangers trying to make a buck from the system."

"You know I'll do everything that I can." Audrey grabbed his hand and squeezed it.

"What about Simone's family? Do you think they'd take Simon in?"

"I doubt it. Simone's parents died when she was young. When she was about five or six she went to live with one of her father's sisters. They never got along. Simone was constantly in trouble. When she turned sixteen she left her aunt's house. I never met the woman, but if she's anything like Simone described her, I don't think I ever want to meet her."

"What did she say about her?" Audrey wondered out loud.

"I can't remember specifics. The aunt dogged her out so bad she ran away before she was legal. But apparently Simone tried to re-establish some kind of positive relationship with her when Simon was born. She used to take the kid over there at first but then they fell out about something and as far as I know they never reconciled."

"But under the circumstances, don't you think she would want to raise Simon?"

"I doubt it. I think the fallout between them had something to do with Simone's preference for those of us of the tall, dark and handsome persuasion."

"Oh, she's one of those…"

"Right. She has *conservative views* on dating." Bobby made little quotation marks with his fingers. Audrey shrugged knowingly. "She hates the fact that her great nephew is bi-racial."

Audrey looked at him and shook her head. Racism is such a waste of time and energy. A little boy's life hangs in the balance and through no fault of his own, he'll never be accepted by his blood relations. Though she'd never laid eyes on the boy, her heart was already open to him.

"Don't worry about it, Bobby. I'll make sure Simon is taken care of, even if I have to move him into my house and hire a nanny. We can pay for it out of your pension."

They both laughed for the first time since the visit began.

"What else is happening with the case?" She asked him.

"Jules came to see me again."

"Good." Audrey beamed. "If anyone can get you out of this mess, he can."

"I wish I had your faith."

Before Audrey could respond the guard moved toward their table and put a swarthy hand on Bobby's shoulder.

"Hey, Bobby man, thas 'yo time." He spoke in the gentle, friendly manner of a fan who wished he could throw a pass to the man he had admired during his years in the NBA. It comforted Audrey watching the easy way the man interacted with Bobby. Maybe he would look out for her baby brother, making his time spent there easier. Audrey stood and they hugged briefly before he was led out of the room.

∗   ∗   ∗   ∗

Paul unfolded his lanky frame from the brown plastic chair and rushed from the waiting area to meet her. He'd been wonderful through this whole thing. It helped immensely that he lived in Atlanta, making her feel less like a stranger in a strange land. Audrey didn't know what she would have done without him.

"How's he doing?"

"Okay, I guess." Audrey released an exhausted sigh. "An attorney friend of ours is meeting with the police to get this worked out."

Paul drew Audrey into his arms and rubbed her back soothingly. He held her for a moment before pulling back suddenly and motioning toward the exit. He held the door and they walked toward the parking deck across the street. Someone in a passing car shouted Paul's name. He waved to the fan without removing his arm from Audrey's shoulder.

"They don't have any real evidence on him do they?" Paul checked both ways for traffic and strode across the street.

"They've got enough." Audrey waited until they were inside the car before she continued. "When Simone learned he would be coming down here, she started calling him. Bobby felt like she was harassing him and called her the day of her death and left a nasty message on her hotel voice mail. So there are phone records that they talked."

"So he knew she was staying there all along."

"Apparently, so. He met with Simone that night and they fought. She wanted him to be more active in Simon's life and Bobby refused. There was an argument. He grabbed her by the throat and hit her. She scratched him up while trying to defend herself."

"So he lied about seeing her that night?" Paul drew back in disbelief.

"Yeah…But according to Bobby, he was only there a few minutes. He swears she was alive the last time he saw her."

"Bobby was gone more than a few minutes."

"Well so were you, Paul." Audrey shot back quickly, defending her brother. "Are you saying that anyone who went to pee that night is a suspect?"

"I didn't mean to upset you, Audrey."

"For your information," she paused, locking him in her steady gaze. "He hooked up with some woman that night. That's why he was late getting back to the table."

"Well, that's his alibi." Paul clapped his hands together like the statement brought the whole ordeal to a conclusion.

"Yeah. But unfortunately, Bobby was so busy getting deep with that woman he forgot to get her name."

"So do the police have a strong case against him?" Worry wrinkled Paul's brow. Audrey knew that he was struggling to check the emotion he was feeling for his friend.

"There were wounds on her face, neck and arms that happened before the fall. But there is nothing to prove that she was with someone other than Bobby that night.

As far as the police are concerned, he was the last person to see Simone alive."

"The police said she was in a scuffle before the fall?" Paul looked very worried for his friend. "Don't tell me...Bobby looks like he's been in a cat fight."

"I couldn't detect any scratches on him, but I'm no expert at examining that sort of thing. Besides, he admitted hitting Simone."

They were quiet for a moment. In the background, the faint sounds of traffic cluttered the air outside the car.

"The forensic people haven't completed their review." Audrey continued. "Hopefully they will find evidence that someone other than Bobby spent time with Simone that night."

"The cops must have detected something physical in order to justify holding him like this. Whatever evidence they have must be sufficient to link Bobby to Simone's death." Paul's eyes pierced hers questioningly.

"Bobby wasn't the only person to visit her room that evening." Audrey looked away. A tender lump thickened in her throat and a hot torrent of tears streamed her face. "I'm going to do whatever I can to see that the person who did this is caught and Bobby is released."

CHAPTER 11

▼

Audrey passed Bobby's instructions on to Paul about helping to move along the process at Children's Services. Paul wasn't sure if he could cut through Fulton County red tape but he promised to do what he could to see that the boy was released. He dropped Audrey off at his home.

"I'll be back in a few hours. If you need the Volvo the keys are on the hook in the kitchen." He pulled out of the garage and down the winding driveway into the bright summer day.

Audrey fingered the bracelet, tracing the smooth garnets with her finger. She was too restless to read any of the books she'd picked up while shopping with Renita the other day. She didn't want to start nibbling on whatever Martha had cooked up in the kitchen. Audrey turned on the television, clicking from one station to the next, not really paying attention to the screen. The station rested on the local news. It amazed her how much more crime there was in Atlanta than in Rosemont. The story of Simone's death and Bobby's possible involvement was only one of several violent stories being reported. Simone's story had been buried amongst all the other tales of felony and newsworthy events occurring around the same time. Audrey turned off the set. She wanted to talk to someone. Where the hell was Renita?

She picked up the white cordless phone and punched in the first four digits of Marsh's phone number before sitting it back onto the end table. For whatever reason, Marshall Fixx was avoiding her, or he was just so busy he couldn't talk. He'd said his son was having a lot of problems. Far be it from her to try to interfere with a man getting involved with his son. Maybe if Bobby had been as conscientious, they wouldn't be in Atlanta dealing with this messed up situation.

It would have been nice to have the comfort of her man right now. Audrey was annoyed with Marsh and his behavior.

"Bastard." She said aloud, curling her lips in frustration. She lied to herself that Marsh didn't matter. Beneath the surface she was more hurt than she was willing to admit. She didn't want to lose him, but she felt him slipping away.

Marsh was everything she wanted in a man. He was thoughtful, self-assured, successful and good-looking. At first their relationship was as seamless as a fairytale. With an initial rocky start behind them, they seemed destined to live happily ever after. But at some point things changed. Or maybe Audrey had been so bewitched by the relationship's promise she had refused to heed the ominous growl that knotted her stomach when she honestly assessed her relationship with Marsh. He had grown more distant with each passing day. But Audrey ignored her overactive gut and pressed on. She knew the source of her gastrointestinal discomfort resided in the city of Nantucket, Massachusetts. Its name was Marlena Procter.

Every three to six weeks Marsh flew to Boston. When their relationship was new he'd discuss his trips with her—his main office in the city, his property, his parent's cottage on the Cape, and his friends. He even talked about his son and ex-wife, artist Marlena Procter. After a while he discussed the trips less and less. Audrey didn't mind. She didn't want to keep hearing about a life that she would never be a part of. Then it got worse.

Days before his flight, Marsh would construct layers of distance until he'd formed an impenetrable cocoon. He stopped calling her a day or two before he was to leave as if Audrey's aura would depreciate Marlena's oeuvre. That wasn't the worst part. Each time he'd return, he'd be even more withdrawn than before he'd gone away. By the time he started warming to Audrey again, he'd get another call about Toots and off he'd fly, up and away from Audrey.

They hardly made love anymore. When they did it was stilted, uninspired, routine. Audrey found herself looking at the clock, counting the minutes until they were through. Neither of them enjoyed it, it had become an exercise, a thing that couples are supposed to do in a relationship and little more.

She'd left nearly a dozen messages for him since she'd come to Atlanta almost a week ago. He knew where to reach her yet he still hadn't called. "Maybe he's dead." Her worried heart cried. "Yeah," her cynical mind replied. "Dead up in Marlena's bed."

Audrey shook the angel and devil arguments out of her head. She didn't have time to try to figure out what Marsh was doing. That would take care of itself in due time. If he was sleeping with his ex-wife, wasn't a damned thing she could do about it.

She grabbed her notebook and clicked to the page with the names and numbers she had gotten from Dorothy. This time Lenora Sleighton answered after the third ring. From the mushy voice and hacking, phlegm-laden cough, Audrey gathered the smoker was just waking up.

"May I speak with Lenora Sleighton, please?"

"Depends." Lenora Sleighton couldn't have sounded less enthused.

Audrey tried to put a face to the voice on the other end of the phone. The woman sounded like Bette Davis…in *Whatever Happened To Baby Jane.*

"Miss Sleighton, my name is Audrey Wilson. I'm, well…kind of an acquaintance of Simone's. I'm terribly sorry about your loss."

"You mean Simone's death? I'd hardly call that a loss."

Ouch! Audrey didn't know how to respond to that. No matter what differences people had in life, they usually tried to act like they had a little respect for them when they died. She reckoned Lenora Sleighton didn't see the point. It wouldn't be easy to get Miss Sleighton to see her. She'd have to reach deep inside her bag to come up with something that would pique the woman's interest.

"I'd like to meet with you about your niece's son, Simon."

Lenora Sleighton didn't respond. Over the long seconds of silence, Audrey fingered through her mental Rolodex, but any ideas that surfaced quickly fell like dominos. In the end, the only thing left standing was the truth.

"Miss Sleighton, I'm Bobby Wilson's sister."

Lenora responded with a rheumy sigh that developed into a hacking cough. Audrey waited while Lenora composed herself.

"So what do you want?"

"I was wondering about Simone and Bobby's son. Are you going to formally take custody of him?"

"Are you nuts?" Now there was laughter interspersed with the ragged barking. "I was saddled with Simone for ten years. The ungrateful little cunt gave me nothing but trouble. I'm finished with her." She was quiet for a moment. "Somebody from that swanky place she's got in that ritzy neighborhood called me about collecting her stuff." She paused and expelled a half laugh half cough. "Like I need her crap in here. I don't want anything of Simone's. I'll be damned if I'm going to be responsible for that little mutt boy she got from laying around with every Tom, Dick, and Harry."

"But Miss Sleighton, if you don't take custody of him he'll be a ward of the state."

"Well that's why they have agencies like that, for little mistakes like Simon."

Audrey was so angry and disgusted that she had to hang up before she said something to this woman that neither one of them would like. She quickly made an excuse and ended the call.

Audrey sat in her bedroom at Paul's boiling mad and sick to her stomach. Bobby had been right. This woman was a piece of work. She wouldn't place a junkyard dog in Lenora Sleighton's care. Instead of wasting her time thinking about that piece of garbage, Audrey turned to the page with the numbers she had collected for The Department of Family and Children's Services. She contacted the Child Placement Division again and asked to speak to the caseworker assigned to the child of the woman who had been killed at the Renaissance Hotel over the weekend.

Cordelia St. James had a tired, yet pleasant sounding voice that got a shot of adrenaline when Audrey mentioned her interest in adoption.

"Have you adopted or considered adoption before?"

"No. Never. There are special circumstances that led to this call. If you have time, I'd like to meet with you."

Ms. St. James told her that she would be finished with her last client in a couple of hours. She gave Audrey directions to the DFCS office on Peachtree Street. The meeting was set for four o'clock that afternoon.

CHAPTER 12

▼

"Where in hell have you been?" Audrey asked frantically. She had been calling Renita all morning.

"I stayed at a friend's last night." She said cavalierly. "Where you at?"

"I'm still at Paul's. I've got a meeting at four with this woman at Children's Services. Can you come with me?"

"Where's her office?"

"Where else? Peachtree Street."

"Well I'm at the Marriott. Why don't you hop on down here?" Renita said. "We can walk through Centennial Olympic Park until it's time for the appointment."

Renita snapped the little phone shut and smiled as Fran eased behind her, nuzzling her ear.

"Every time that fawking little phone rings, you're out the door."

Renita regarded Franchot with amusement. He was less the party animal than he had been ten years ago, but he was still as possessive as ever. He wanted to monopolize all of her time. She tossed the phone into her bag and smiled. She was still mad about him, but her days of sitting at a man's feet waiting for him to tell her when to move had disappeared with her youth. Fran had been the only man to get her nose open, literally and figuratively. But that was long ago.

But it wasn't long enough as far as Lloyd was concerned. It was he who had stayed up hours on end after Renita overdosed. It was he who stuck by her through the long and painful detoxification period. Her family thought she was still touring but they didn't know that the only touring she did her last six months overseas was of the inside of a rehabilitation facility forty miles outside Paris.

Lloyd hated Franchot Arnaud because he had Renita so turned out on cocaine she didn't care about anything or anyone. Then she heard that her mother was dying. With that news, Renita made getting clean and sober her number one priority. She walked away from drugs and from Franchot, vowing never to return to either. When she came back to the United States, she moved into their family home and nursed her mother through the physical and emotional ravages of her cancer. Renita stiffened her resolve licking her addiction to drugs and love and channeling the cravings by comforting her mother.

Now she looked into his eyes, big blue pools begging her not to go, and thought about the promise she'd made long ago. She had already gone back on her promise to herself to leave him alone. Fran was clean now just like she was, so she didn't worry about betraying herself on the first part of that promise. She knew now it was the drugs that bound her to him. With the narcotics out of the picture, she could deal with Fran like she did any other man. He was just something to fill time until something else came along. She took a shower and slipped on a colorful peasant blouse and flowing skirt.

"I'll see you in a bit, love." Renita said airily. Kissing Fran on his moist lips, she grabbed her big straw slouch bag and left the suite.

*   *   *   *

On her way to find a spot along the wall where she could wait for Renita, Audrey read the names etched into the bricks by contributors to Centennial Olympic Park. She couldn't begin to guess the number of uniform rectangles engraved with individual names, many of which accompanied a company name, quote, haiku or Scripture. It made her long for the bank of the Ohio at Sawyer Point and its soothing river breeze. If she were there it would mean that everything was back to normal and that she was home.

Not that it wasn't nice here in this park. Its urban beauty was a living monument of a better time for many in the nation and the world. It had been constructed as a central meeting point during the 1996 Olympic games and gave visitors an indescribable freedom. Kids of all ages, sizes, shapes, and colors, ran into the sparkling geyser that shot upwards from five linked Olympic rings. The water roared and blended with giddy squeals as people jumped through the circles and got thoroughly soaked. Audrey eased herself onto the wall and watched the carnival of life unfold before her as she waited for her sister.

A few minutes later, Renita popped in front of her like a piece of hair on an old movie projector. She was in too bad a mood——her hip jutting to one side and a grimace twisting her face——for such a splendid day.

"I'm starving. We got time to eat something?"

"Well, hello to you too, Miss Renita." Audrey wasn't trying to let Renita ruin her state of mind. "Let's get something from that stand over there."

They purchased gyros and lemonade from one of the vendors and did more gawking than talking as they ate. The food seemed to relax the evil right out of Renita.

"I see you're still wearing the bracelet." She said eyeing Audrey's wrist.

"Yeah." She tugged the heirloom, making sure that it was secure on her wrist.

"I've been thinking a lot about Mama lately too." Renita's eyes misted.

"Remember that time we took our allowance and brought her that big bottle of *Evening In Paris*?"

Some of the lemonade went down the wrong way and Renita coughed out a laugh.

"Yeah…she wore it on Mother's Day."

"You know that was something for her to give up her Channel No. 5." Audrey remembered the light floral signature scent that lingered as her mother swished around the room. The women sat somberly for a moment as reveries of child-hood innocence took them to another place.

"Why you sitting there with that goofy smile on your face?" Renita said, breaking the silence.

"Look at those kids out there." Audrey said, squinting to protect her eyes from the sun. Two little topless girls, one black and one white, ran in and out of the water screaming like somebody was trying to kill them.

"Are you all right?" Renita's query was full of concern. Audrey knew what she was thinking. Audrey always became slightly dreamy and a little sad when she was around children.

"You know, Ren, I never thought my life would end up like this."

"What you talkin' bout?"

"See how free those little girls are? Aren't they beautiful?" Audrey sighed regretfully. "I hate aging."

"Girl, who you telling?" Renita swallowed, ridding her mouth of the last bite of sandwich. "My eyes look like roadmaps and my vision is shot to hell. In order to read anything I have to pull the paper near my face and away until I can focus. I feel like a friggin' trombone player."

"Well at least you are keeping your self slim." Audrey countered. "I have to work out like a fiend so my ass won't hit the ground. I got gray hair and aches and pains in places that are too embarrassing to mention." She frowned and then took a sip of her drink.

"Girl, you starting to scare me." Renita shook the ice in her cup and frowned.

"You should be scared. I swear, Ren, it's like you wake up one day and see a stranger in the mirror." Audrey sighed dejectedly. "An old stranger."

"What the hell are you talking about? You're only two years older than me and I know I ain't even close to being *that* fucked up."

"You're closer than you think." Audrey assured her.

"The hell you say." Renita sucked her straw extra hard, stopping when she produced nothing but the crackle of ice against the paper cup.

"I'm scared, Renita. I'm on the bad side of middle age and I ain't got nothing to show for the time I spent on this earth."

"Girl, you need to lighten up. If you ain't satisfied, get up and do something." Renita swatted away a fly and took another bite of her food.

"It's not that simple." Audrey tried to explain, "what about the continuum of life?"

"Huh?"

"Ren, don't you ever think about what your legacy will be? I mean beyond personal accomplishments."

"You know, you been acting dopier than usual since this stuff with Bobby and Simone."

"Me? What about you?"

Renita shrugged and cast Audrey a guilty gaze. Her mouth remained closed. Audrey looked away, past the band of aqua nuts into the distance. "The more I think about it, the more sure I am that I need to have Simon in my life."

"Bobby's little boy and you? Are you crazy?"

"No Renita, I am not crazy. I'm just a middle-aged woman who wants to know how it feels to have a person to depend on. Not like a man or a friend or a sibling. I think being a mother might give me a different sense of purpose in my life." Audrey picked up a pebble and dropped it over her shoulder into the fountain. "I think I need Simon just as much as he needs me."

"I can't say that I know how you feel because I don't." Renita tread lightly. "But this is a big step you're thinking of taking."

"I know." Audrey shrugged, brushing a fly away from her lemonade. "I've been thinking about it, that's all."

"But you're not married."

"Wait a minute." Audrey laughed and shook her head at her worried little sister. "Did I just hear Renita, one night stand, screw them before they screw you Wilson, imply that a woman has to be married to have a child?" Renita curled her mouth as her sister continued. "Even as a little girl you always said that you might want kids but you didn't want to get married."

"Yeah? Well I changed my mind." She pointed her empty cup to the rowdy children before them. "Kids need two parents these days more than ever. Anyone who has kids should be married. Otherwise, you're setting a bad example for your children."

Audrey looked at Renita like she had just grown a second head.

"You musta' been up all night smoking crack." Audrey sucked the last of the syrupy drink from the cup and was startled when Renita jumped up angrily, almost knocking the drink from her hand.

"Why would you say some foul shit like that knowing what I've been through?" Her hands were welded to each hip and her lip curled in an angry frown.

Audrey looked at her sister sharply. Something was bothering her and she still wasn't ready to talk about it.

"I was only kidding, Renita."

They were both treading dangerous ground with each other's past lives. Renita had been drug free going on ten years now. She had never given up alcohol though and Audrey was always afraid that her sister would relapse or trade one addiction for another. But so far, Renita showed no signs of letting anything get the best of her.

Though neither of them spoke the words out loud, Audrey knew that Renita was thinking about the incident that happened when Audrey was eighteen. She had dated Lenmore Dutton all through high school. They'd even talked about getting married but it never went further than talk.

Audrey was frightened when her period was late. When she finally got up the nerve to tell Lenny, he shocked her by rejecting the pregnancy. He convinced her that she was ruining both their lives. At his urging, they made the appointment. Abortions were newly legal and Audrey knew nothing about the potential for risks. She was feeling so bad, so scared, that she just nodded as Lenny rattled off the time and place.

She walked through the next few weeks in a trance, going with him to a clinic in Indianapolis where a butcher poked, pulled, and suctioned until there was no more life inside her. She felt violated and ashamed and cried at the least thing. Lenny detached himself until they were barely speaking to each other. Audrey refused to admit her anger and disappointment in him and instead, blamed herself. The episode haunted her throughout her life. Though she eventually told Renita what happened, she never could express how damaged the abortion had left her emotionally. It was like an emptiness that nothing could fill. It wasn't until years later when she was married and trying to conceive that she learned the botched procedure had left her physically scarred as well. She would never be able to bear children of her own.

Recently the memory of the procedure and its devastating results invaded her waking consciousness. Audrey didn't understand what she had been feeling lately. It was like all of this trouble with Bobby, the death of Simone, and the thought of her motherless nephew was affecting her in ways she had never imagined. Her heart had a gaping hole in it that she felt could only be filled if she were able to satisfy her inherent maternal thirst.

She reached up and pulled Renita back down beside her.

"What's going on, Renita?" Audrey looked into her younger sister's eyes, trying to reach into her soul.

"With all that's been going on we still have to do the Renaissance gig. The hotel manager acts like he's doing us a fuckin' favor." Renita's sigh was weighted with exasperation. "It's a drag after what happened to Simone. The crowds have been sparse. It takes time for people to heal after such a tragedy."

Audrey wanted to make her sister feel better, but she knew that even she didn't want to return to the hotel where Simone had been killed. But she had to lend her support. Renita had an obligation, and a contract with the managers of the establishment, so she was in a tricky position.

"Would it make you feel better if Paul, Jules and I attended every show?" Audrey tried to sound bright, wanting to lighten her sister's mood. Renita smiled but she still seemed depressed. She evaded Audrey's gaze.

"What's really bothering you, Renita?" Audrey asked knowing her sister had been hedging, covering some larger issue. Renita had never let a gig worry her in her life. Her maternal antennae started going haywire when Renita suddenly burst into tears. Audrey pulled her close and held her, but Renita pulled away.

"Goddammit, Renita! You're making me crazy." Audrey started crying too. People gawked as the two women cried like they were at a wake instead of at the park. Audrey focused on her sister and all kinds of horrors started swirling through her mind. Was Renita sick? Had she in a weak moment succumbed to the power of the narcotic?

"I was afraid to tell you but I thought I'd better before you hear it from Lloyd." Renita looked at Audrey through red puffy eyes. Her long lashes were dewy and the mascara was slightly smudged.

"I've been seeing Fran."

Audrey wrinkled her face and drew her chin into her chest trying to dredge up memory. Fran? Who the hell is Fran? The blank canvas her face had become gave away her ignorance. Renita looked at her impatiently.

"Franchot, Audrey. Franchot Arnaud."

Audrey blinked several times before wrinkling her brow in disbelief. She looked at Renita like she had gone crazy.

"Are you out of your mind? Renita you swore you'd never have anything else to do with him." Audrey was angry with her sister. Here she was thinking that Renita was dying or strung out on cocaine and instead she was crying over some knucklehead that wasn't worth spit. Franchot Arnaud was the man responsible for introducing Renita to drugs when she was in Europe. Because of him, what started out as the most exciting time of her life had become the darkest. Franchot had been supplying drugs for her and then left her alone when the powder had her in its grip.

It was 1993. Their mother, Esther Morgan Wilson was losing her fight with a lengthy battle with cancer and wanted her children near her. Audrey hadn't heard from Renita in months. She called the hotel daily and her sister wasn't there. Emotion gripped her stomach and pulled at it. She tried to rationalize Renita's lack of response, telling herself it was due to her hectic schedule. But deep inside Audrey was worried. She'd never forget the call she'd received from Lloyd early one morning telling her that she needed to get a flight over there as soon as she could.

Audrey didn't know Lloyd Eckstine very well at the time. He was in her early fifties, tall and thin, with silver waves framing weathered light brown skin. He'd visited Renita a few times when Audrey was at her apartment and she'd heard him in concert. He seemed likeable enough. He showed more emotion in that phone conversation than she'd ever seen him display. Audrey could tell by the tremble in his voice that something was very wrong. She wouldn't let Lloyd off the phone until he told her the truth. Audrey was so shocked at what she heard she almost wished he hadn't told her.

Renita had gotten involved with a man in Europe who introduced her to cocaine. Lloyd had found her on the streets of Paris, delusional and dirty. He'd signed her into an institution that specialized in drug detoxification. Audrey took the first flight out.

She viewed the "City of Lights" through tear-clouded vision. The only recollection she had of the trip was the sight of her sister in a hospital bed, gaunt and bruised from God only knew who or what. She lay there glassy-eyed, looking like a familiar stranger.

Audrey was relieved that Lloyd was there. He eased his lanky frame from the chair he'd folded himself into and in two steps stood next to Audrey. He touched her elbow and guided her into the hall.

"Thank you so much for calling me, Lloyd."

He shook his head and shrugged slightly.

"I would have called sooner but I was so busy looking for Renita I didn't even think to check the desk and see if you'd been trying to reach her."

"What happened?"

An angry pall deepened Lloyd's complexion. He dug around in his pocket for a cigarette, and mumbled a curse when a nurse walked by and shook her head. Lloyd said something to the woman in French and she responded and smiled slightly. Audrey was surprised at the way the foreign language fluidly rolled off the tongue of the musician.

"Let's go outside. I need to talk to you before I talk to Renita." Audrey was smoking back then and she needed a cigarette too.

They walked down the polished corridor, passing a busy nurse's station on the way to a bank of elevators. Everything was beige, white, yellow, and brightly scrubbed——a stark contrast to the dreary sky and drizzly air outside. They spied the area designated for smokers. The space looked like a carport with benches, tiny tables and a couple of trashcans. Bright green shrubs helped oxygenate the space as nicotine addicts infused the air with blue-white smoke.

Men and women stood or sat alone and in groups savoring their smokes. To Audrey, they all looked European——whether they were black or white. Perhaps it was the way that they stood, or how they held their cigarettes, or the way that they laughed.

Audrey breathed in the second hand smoke that embraced her like an errant lover. She hadn't smoked during the long flight and had rushed from the airport to the hospital. Nicotine withdrawal made her itch.

They selected one of the tiny tables. Lloyd shook a Newport out of a half full pack and offered it to her before pushing one into his lips. He lit hers and then his own, each ingesting the drug before speaking.

"I found her on the streets." He said like he still didn't believe it himself. "She had missed a couple of nights work and that's not like her. The hotel staff hadn't seen her. I was worried sick." Lloyd looked down at the cigarette and frowned like it had done him wrong. He put it to his lips and pulled on it angrily, expelling a hot gust of smoke.

"I contacted the police and the American Embassy but no one was able to help me. The only thing they would do was keep an eye out and get back to me. The Embassy promised to get in touch with her family if the situation warranted it." Lloyd looked away from her, glassy eyed. Audrey knew that he knew what they'd meant by that. People go away to foreign countries all the time and end up dead. They had all but verbalized the fear that had hovered over him like a haint ever since Renita had disappeared.

He looked everywhere he could think of letting nothing dissuade him in his quest for her. He'd finally resorted to showing her picture to people on the streets near the hotel. As he'd wandered into the seedier side of Parisian life, he began to get responses from his queries, nods of acknowledgement from street people. Renita had been seen on the streets in the company of a man. They were frequent customers of a local drug dealer. The man that Renita was seen with was Franchot Arnaud. He was known throughout the city as a flutist and also, as someone who romanced women and got them to score anything he needed.

"A pimp?" Audrey turned up her nose and drew away from Lloyd in disbelief.

"Pimp, gigolo, whatever you want to call him, he enticed Renita into using drugs, and God only knows what else." Lloyd took another drag on the cigarette before flicking it away. "People had seen them around but no one knew where I could find them. I was so exhausted from the search and so sorry for what happened to her that I just sat down on the curb and cried."

Audrey searched his face. Deep lines rutted his walnut shell colored skin, accentuating his pain. He was in love with her sister. He was so hurt, talking about it with someone who knew her seemed to help and hurt him simultaneously.

"A little boy saw me sitting there holding her picture. He said he knew where she was. He told me a man had beaten her and left her in the street. The boy led me to an alley between a bar and a tiny grocer." Lloyd let out a ragged sigh and looked down like he was seeing her all over again, broken in body and spirit and discarded on the filthy ground.

"She didn't even recognize me. But she was alive. That's all that mattered." Lloyd smiled the saddest smile Audrey had ever seen. "I sent the boy for an ambulance. Except for her bruises, physically she was okay. I had her brought here so they could bring her out of her catatonia and wean her from the drugs."

Lloyd searched the gray sky while Audrey finished her cigarette. She stubbed it out after one last puff and they re-entered the main building. Lloyd left the sisters alone, promising Audrey he'd go to his hotel and get some rest.

Audrey watched her sister for about an hour before her anger spilled over and flowed onto everything there. She grabbed her sister's hand and talked to her. Renita just looked at the ceiling saying nothing. Audrey couldn't feel sorry for Renita for making a stupid choice and getting herself into this mess. She was tired of trying to coax her out of her dreamy state and started screaming.

"Dammit Renita, Mama is dying. She's at home worrying about you and you go pull some shit like this! What the hell is the matter with you? Mama and Daddy preached to us about drugs until they were blue in the face. Why would you do something like this?"

The hot words penetrated Renita's fog. She looked at Audrey like she just realized she was there. She sat upright in the bed, her swollen eyes frowning with worry.

"Mama is dying?"

That was all it took for Renita to get herself together and leave Paris. As soon as they were back in Ohio Renita checked into Rollman Center and attended sessions during the day and nursed Esther at night. She took care of her mother until she died several months later.

Now after nearly ten years and what seemed like a lifetime repairing the damage, she's taking up with this guy again? It just didn't make sense. Audrey was looking at her like she was some crackpot who had just shot a loaded gun into a crowd of people.

"Audrey, I know you think I'm crazy…"

"You got that right…"

"See that's why I didn't want to talk to your ass." Renita left her place on the bench. Audrey stood up too. She touched her arm but Renita jerked it away.

"Wait a minute, Renita." Audrey knew that she could be insensitive at times, just like Renita could be. They got that from their mother.

"I'm sorry. Please, come sit down and tell me what's going on." She steered Renita back to the stone bench and they sat down. Audrey watched her sister's chest rise and fall as she moved past her anger and prepared to talk about what was on her mind.

"I can't explain it, but lately I've been feeling very…finite."

Audrey didn't want to interrupt. She knew at some point Renita would get around to what she was trying to say. She hoped it would be soon because right now, Audrey didn't have a clue.

"I know exactly what you were talking about earlier." She met Audrey's confused gaze with unwavering eyes. "What you said about aging. I'm forty years old and I don't have anything to show for the forty years I've been on this earth."

"Now I *know* you're crazy." Audrey interrupted. "You're just going through that big four oh depression. Everybody goes there." She touched Renita's hand and gave it a reassuring squeeze.

"Girl, ignore that stuff I was saying earlier. I got PMS and I was just trippin'. Plus, you're not like me. You've recorded and sung with some of the world's top entertainers. You've traveled to Europe, Asia and Africa. You're living the life you've always wanted."

"Audrey, have you ever been to a really fun party and looked up and everybody had gone home and you were still there?"

Audrey shook her head. Never being much on partying, she couldn't say that she'd had that experience. The blank look on her face led Renita to add sarcastically, "Oh, I forgot who I was talking to."

"No, I think I know what you mean. It's like when you're at work and you're so caught up in a project the next thing you know it's dark outside and you're the only one there."

Renita offered her a pitying look.

"Well anyway, I feel like everybody else has moved on to a family or committed relationship but me." She squeezed her sister's hand in return. "I'm lonely and I feel old. I'll never be a girl again. I feel like I'm losing myself." Renita looked wistfully into the distance, past the circles of water and the children romping through them. "When I'm with Fran I feel like I'm twenty-nine instead of thirty-nine."

"Forty."

"Huh?" She focused on Audrey like she'd almost forgotten she was there.

"You mean, when you're with Fran you feel like your thirty instead of forty." Audrey clarified.

"Fuck you, Audrey. You know what I'm talking about."

Audrey laughed.

"So what are you gonna do—-marry Franchot and have six kids?"

"No. I mean, I don't know. I just want to have some meaning in my life before it's too late."

"Well maybe you ought to start going to church." Audrey was only half serious. Her mind couldn't wrap itself around Renita Wilson on the usher board. She thought she'd fall on the ground with Renita's next comment.

"You know, I've been thinking about that. Mama and Daddy raised us in the church but I let the lure of the world distance me from all that." Audrey was surprised when Renita reached over and hugged her tight.

"I should have talked to you sooner, Audrey. I'm going to church next Sunday either here or in Rosemont. I'm going to get back in touch with my spirit."

"Oh hell, now you done turned into Oprah on me." Audrey laughed, but her eyes were full of tears at the thought of her sister realizing what she needed to do for self-healing. Renita laughed too.

"Come on." She said. "We'd better get down to Children's Services before that little boy graduates high school."

Chapter 13

▼

If Marsh didn't know any better he'd swear he was dreaming. He inhaled deeply and Marlena's scented skin awakened every part of him. Her fragrances were custom blended oils of citrus and dried herbs and flowers that a chemist friend of hers created. No woman he'd ever known smelled as good as Marlena. Marsh leaned nearer and breathed in again. This definitely wasn't a dream.

"What are you doing?" There was a smile in her voice. The glow of the moonlight peeked through the blinds outlining her slender curves. He couldn't see her eyes but he knew she was looking at him. He could feel her gaze and it made him weak for her.

"Nothing." He wasn't going to tell her that he had been watching her for close to an hour.

"What time is it?" She looked at the nightstand but Marsh had turned the digital clock/radio toward the window so that its red glowing face wouldn't disturb them. He also didn't want her to know what time it was. She would want him to leave before Toots awakened. Marsh didn't understand why.

He was disappointed when Marlena slid from beneath the sheets and took three steps over to the table and turned the clock around.

"Oh my God, it's almost six o'clock!" She started picking his clothes from the floor and tossing them at the bed. "You gotta get outta here."

"Why Marlena? I'm the boy's father for heaven's sake." He'd leaned up on one elbow and with the other hand caught the jeans that she'd thrown in his direction. "And stop throwing my clothes like that. You act like I'm some guy you picked up in a bar."

"I'm sorry, Marsh. I'm just not ready to talk to Toots about this yet."

"Well when will you be ready?" He watched her pace the room. She stopped to check beneath the bed and the chaise to make sure she'd gathered all of his things.

"You don't trust me, do you?" Though he understood her reservations, Marsh couldn't keep the disappointment from his voice. It seemed she'd never completely recovered from his betrayal of her. Her hunger for him during their love-making had been tinged with hesitance. He'd periodically feel her holding back, keeping her emotions in check. This only excited Marsh further, making him want to please her all the more. She plopped down on the bed and Marsh pulled her to him.

"I'm sorry. I just…"

He put his fingers to her lips, and then tilted her chin up so he could kiss her worried mouth.

"I'm in no rush." He lied. "I know that you need to feel that I'm totally committed to you before you agree to have me move back here. I don't know of anything but time that will ease your mind."

Marsh pulled the ribbon from her wavy brown hair and combed his fingers through it.

"What time does Toots get up?"

"His lesson is at nine o'clock."

"That's almost three hours from now." He rubbed her back. "You got plenty of time to kick me out."

Marlena smiled and leaned into him. Her tension hard shoulders softened. Marsh pulled her closer and she went limp. Her legs spread easily, welcoming his hot hardness into her warm wetness.

It was over quickly. His growing frustration with the situation was beginning to interfere with his enjoyment of what for him was a dream come true. Marsh left the bed and collected his clothing. He pulled the bathroom door hard and then became irritated when an obstruction prevented it from closing. He cast an angry glare downward and saw that he had dropped his shirt in the doorway.

"Shit!" He bent down to pick it up and caught a glimpse of Marlena's slender leg. She stood near the bathroom door, viewing him through teasing eyes. She picked up the shirt and tossed it aside. His tense shoulders softened as she rubbed her hands along his back before encircling his waist. She pressed herself into him and he came to attention once more.

"Marsh, come back to bed…"

*   *   *   *

Though there had been an attempt to mask its drabness with fake greenery and brightly colored artwork, the Department of Family and Children's Services, also known as DFCS, still had the look and feel of an institution.

A glass partition separated the sterile waiting area from the receptionist and other office personnel. Renita sat in one of the gray cushioned metal chairs that lined the wall while Audrey signed in.

Neither of them spoke. The room possessed an eerie big brother aura and the sisters were afraid that any act or word might be recorded. Audrey wasn't sure what to expect. She didn't want to do anything that might jeopardize her chances of making a good impression.

At four o'clock on the dot the door opened. A Vietnamese woman and three tiny children were led into the waiting area by a tall, thin woman with skin the color of warmed honey. Her short Afro was neatly trimmed and nearly all gray. She smiled and touched the woman's shoulder before speaking a few reassuring words in a foreign tongue. The Asian woman nodded; returning a sad smile, she gathered her brood and left the building.

The tall woman looked down at Audrey and Renita with questioning eyes.

"Miss Wilson?"

Audrey gave a slight smile and tipped her head.

"Miss St. James?" She rose and shook the woman's hand. "I'm Audrey and this is my sister, Renita Wilson."

"Renita Wilson, the singer?" The woman's wide mouth opened into a gapped-toothed grin. Her eyes crinkled into a smile. She released Audrey's grasp and held her hand in Renita's direction. Renita grabbed it and smiled.

"I caught you in Tokyo back in 1990, no, it was '92, during your *Souring To New Heights* tour."

"Really?"

"Yes. You were great. We got an autographed copy of the record. I know you don't remember, but my husband Wallace and I took a picture with you, too."

"Thank you, Mrs. St. James. I apologize for not remembering…"

"Don't worry about it, and please, call me Cordelia. I'm glad that you have so many fans that it's hard to keep track. It's better than the alternative."

"Ain't that the truth?" Renita smiled.

"My husband and I took a tour of Asia that year." Cordelia was saying. "We caught you at the Koma Theater in Kabukicho."

"Is that place wild or what?" Renita smiled like they were chums. Audrey liked Cordelia St. James immediately.

"It was something else." Realizing they were completely monopolizing the conversation, Cordelia turned to Audrey, "If you've never been, you should check it out. It's like Mardi Gras 24-7."

Audrey nodded politely.

"If you haven't been to Tokyo's International Forum, you'll have to go there too. It's beautiful." The space between Cordelia's bright smile made her teeth look even whiter.

She tapped a red button on the wall and one of the women in the office area buzzed them inside. Audrey and Renita followed Cordelia down a narrow yellow painted hall splashed with likenesses of zoo animals, to her small office.

The pale blue room was bright and sunny with a bushy fern suspended from a knotted macramé holder near the only window. The wood furniture was old, but clean, polished, and in excellent condition. Cordelia St. James waved her hand toward two tan over-stuffed ultra suede look chairs that were as comfortable as they looked. To the left of her cluttered desk was a beautiful photo stand of carved soapstone that displayed pictures of her and an attractive, heavy-set man who stood nearly a head shorter than she. They smiled like newlyweds on each of the pictures, displaying that rested, vacation look that Audrey missed seeing on her own face.

Audrey and Renita spent a minute looking at the pictures while their host put away the files from her last visit. She grabbed a thin brown folder from a black slotted organizer behind her desk and lifted skinny glasses that hung from a cord around her neck and started reading.

She looked over the rims of the cheaters, her brow wrinkled in thought. Audrey's anxious gaze met her serious one.

"So you're interested in adoption? Why?"

"No…I mean my interest is less about adoption than it is about Simon Denton, the little boy who was orphaned this past weekend."

"Why the interest in *this* child?"

"We're his aunts" Renita piped. "He's the son of our brother, Bobby Wilson."

"You don't mean that football player who ki…who is being held in connection with that woman who was pushed from a hotel window, do you?"

The cordiality was gone. Cordelia St. James' right eyebrow angled toward her hairline. The smile was now a Grinch-like frown. Audrey imagined a greenish tinge beneath the surface of the woman's skin.

"Our brother is innocent. And he used to play basketball, not football." Renita explained soothingly, trying to recapture the initial connection she'd shared with the woman. Ms. St. James scanned the folder that laid flat on her desk.

"It says here that the mother was single. There is no father's name on the boy's birth certificate."

"What?" Audrey didn't believe she was hearing right.

"When the child was born, the mother did not name a father. From what we've been able to determine, the mother has surviving relations on her father's side…"

"But they don't want to have anything to do with Simon." Audrey said. "We want to take him with us and raise him in Ohio with his father."

"From what I gather, Mr. Wilson is hardly in a position to be making those kinds of plans."

"And what position would that be? He'll probably be released before we get through your agency's red-tape." Renita's strident remark surprised Audrey, as did her change in demeanor. She focused red-hot lasers at the woman across the desk. Ms. St. James caught the beam and neutralized it. She pushed the sleeves of her shirt over her elbows and her nostrils flared. Leaning closer to them, she snatched off her glasses and they landed with a thud upon her chest. She crossed her arms in front of her and spoke in sharp succinct sentences.

"This agency has hundreds of children in its care. We operate on a thin budget with an even thinner staff of over-worked, underpaid people who are dedicated professionals in their fields. The work is not glamorous and the pay is barely above poverty level. We screen, check, question and do anything we deem necessary to ensure the adoptive parents aren't some crackpots who want to use these children for things you couldn't fathom. Each time a child is placed with a family, I pray that the family will do right by that child. If the adoptive parents turn out to be monsters, the posse of media, politicians and angry citizens will come after this agency with more venom than you can imagine. So forgive me for not apologizing if our process is an inconvenience for you."

Audrey held her hands up in a capitulative gesture.

"Ms. St. James. We've been under a lot of stress over the past few days. My sister and I are tired." Audrey ordered Renita to shut up with a mere slice of her gaze. "We understand and appreciate your position. Our main concern is the boy. What can we do to help facilitate this process?"

The lines in Cordelia's face eased and she uncrossed her arms and clasped her hands on the desk.

"If your brother takes a paternity test, and the results are positive, the boy can be remanded to his care with you as temporary guardian. He could then make the two of you the legal guardians by filling out the necessary documentation."

Cordelia picked up a pad and quickly scribbled on it before ripping the sheet off its base and handing it across her desk to Audrey. The paper had three phone numbers next to barely decipherable names. She reached inside her desk drawer and removed a thin sheath of forms and pushed them to the edge of the desk in their direction.

"You or your brother, need to fill out these forms. Call the numbers to find out about the paternity testing. My card is attached. You can call with any questions."

*   *   *   *

It was so quiet in the bedroom that they could hear each other breathing. Marsh rolled over, throwing a lazy arm over Marlena, who wedged her butt into his groin. He immediately came to life. She laughed softly and pulled away.

"Come here, woman." He commanded.

"I've got to get Toots up and ready for his trumpet class."

"Why don't we do it together?" Marsh suggested, pulling her back into the warm crevice of passion. Her eyes slid lazily toward the clock.

"If we're going to get him up we'd better do it now." She rubbed his head lovingly and kissed his lips. "Put on some clothes."

Marlena grabbed her housecoat and pulled it around her. She picked up stray clothing from the floor while Marsh quickly washed and dressed in the bathroom. Soon they were walking hand in hand toward Toot's room.

Marlena tapped on the door. Ignoring the KEEP OUT sign taped to the door, she opened it a crack before sweeping it wide into the room. Worry contorted her face. She turned to Marsh who wrinkled a curious brow before looking back into the room with it's neatly covered bed devoid of post sleep dishevelment.

"He's not here." Marlena said.

CHAPTER 14

▼

Audrey felt like she had spent the day being chased up a mountain by a herd of wild goats. The visit with Cordelia St. James had been draining. Now she had to pull some energy from somewhere to deal with Bobby. It was a little after five when she and Renita reached the jail. They wanted to go over the information they'd gotten from DFCS with Bobby before visiting hours ended.

"I need to take a paternity test?" Bobby expelled a disgusted sigh. "It's always some kind of shit these days every time I want to do anything. I doubt if people are lining up to adopt ten-year old black boys. Why can't they just let you have him?"

"They can't just turn the boy over to anybody." Audrey reasoned.

"But I'm not just anybody." He replied. "I'm his father."

"I know, but since Simone didn't name you on the birth certificate, you don't have a voice in the matter as far as the authorities are concerned." Audrey struggled to keep the impatience from her voice.

Bobby mumbled a curse.

"Why'd you never prove your paternity all these years?" Renita asked him.

Bobby shifted his gaze and spoke without looking up.

"I guess I never thought it mattered and I just didn't want the hassle. At first Simone wasn't asking me for but a thousand dollars a month. I increased that over the years, but it still wasn't any money. The way I figured it, it was easier to just send her a money order and not get involved with lawyers and publicity and all that shit." He shifted in the straight back chair, trying to find a comfortable position for his long legs. "Time passed, next thing you know it's ten years later and we're still dealing with the status quo. I was giving her about two grand a month when she died plus I gave them the condo. That was chump change to me. She coulda' really taken my ass to the cleaners if she wanted to."

"Well according to the woman at DFCS since your name isn't on Simon's birth certificate, you have no legal claim to him." Audrey informed him again.

"I still can't believe Simone didn't name me as the daddy."

Audrey and Renita shrugged. Bobby gazed at the folder with dull, unreadable eyes.

"Leave the forms. I'll go over them with Jules when he comes to see me tomorrow."

*   *   *   *

Audrey retrieved Paul's silver Volvo S80, dropped Renita off at the Marriott and then drove around until she saw the signs leading her to Interstate-75 North.

"You look beat." Paul opened the back door and walked toward the car when Audrey pulled into driveway at the rear of the house. She welcomed his embrace and missed it when he pulled away.

"Where's Renita?"

"She decided to stay downtown tonight." Audrey said through stiff lips, pushing away thoughts of her sister with Franchot Arnaud.

"I'd forgotten that she's not a stranger to the ATL. I suppose she's got lots of friends here."

"I wouldn't call this guy a friend." Audrey mumbled.

"What?"

"Never mind." She said.

Audrey couldn't believe that Renita had hooked up with Fran again. She couldn't discuss any of that with Paul without telling him the whole ugly story, so she walked along side him in silence. She knew he wouldn't pry. He draped his arm over her shoulders and led her toward the house.

"Come inside. I'll have Martha fix us something and you can tell me about your day."

They walked through the door and down the short hall to the kitchen. Martha looked at them and nodded before turning her attention once more to whatever she was cleaning in the sink.

"Can I get anyone anything?" She addressed them without turning around.

"Dinner, Martha." Paul ordered. "We'll be in the dining room. I'll fix us something to drink." Paul gave Audrey a slight nudge toward the other room.

"Right away, sir." Martha drifted phantomlike out of the kitchen.

Paul combated the quiet by filling the space with ebullient small talk. Though she paid little attention to what was being said, Audrey added a "Really?" or an "Uh hum," whenever it seemed appropriate to do so.

They stopped in front of the spacious powder room where they washed their hands at twin sinks located near the front of the toilet and bath area. The layout was different from any she'd ever seen with varying levels of burnished tile and chrome everywhere. The forest green wallpaper with tiny magnolia blossoms was a beautiful backdrop to the white wood with gold trim fixtures. The air smelled of flowers. Magnolias? Audrey sniffed. No, a fragrant gardenia scent clung to the air seductively. Audrey regarded the discovery with slight curiosity. There were many subtle feminine touches to Paul's house and even in his demeanor. Audrey wondered if he had a woman in his life or perhaps he merely possessed an appreciation for delicate things. Maybe he needed to balance the machismo his public image often called for with softness. She dried her hands on a plush green towel and followed him to the kitchen.

The table was already set for dinner. Audrey thanked Paul as he pulled out her chair for her. He continued to chatter while he fixed a pitcher of martinis. All the talk was getting on her nerves so she was glad to get the drink.

She sipped from the glass he put before her and felt the day's weariness slip from her head down her shoulders and back and through the tips of her toes.

"You make a helluva martini."

"I know." Paul replied and they both laughed. "Now, tell me what you've been up to today."

Audrey started at the beginning, telling him about her conversation with Lenora Sleighton, the DFCS visit and finally their trip to see Bobby.

"Bobby never got a paternity test?"

"It was a shock to me too, but I told you what he gave as reasons."

"I can see his point. There have been more pro athletes than you could count who've had their names dragged through the mud by some gold digger. If you find one that's not trying to extort millions of dollars from you, I guess it would be easier to pay them a measly few thousand to stay off your back."

"Well," Audrey said. "Bobby seemed to think so. He's going to have his lawyer look over the documents before he makes a move."

"I would have thought they'd have him out of there by now." Paul looked at her over the wide rim of the glass.

"He has a hearing at 1:00 tomorrow afternoon. We expect he'll be released."

"What about the aunt?" Paul's gaze was intense. "Could she help us access Simone's place?"

Audrey shrugged. She still couldn't believe her phone conversation with the woman. She didn't know if she was capable of sitting through a meeting with Lenora Sleighton without hauling off and slapping her. She hated to pre-judge but Audrey had already formulated a negative profile of this woman who seemed as nasty as a bed of maggots.

"I'll find out where Simone lived and we'll talk to the owner or manager about getting her things." Paul said.

By this time the police had surely transferred anything she's left in her hotel room to her home address. Anything they had that supported their case against Bobby, of course, would still be at the station. But they hadn't mentioned anything other than the eyewitness.

"Maybe I can find her son's school and medical records." Audrey thought aloud. "I really got my work cut out on this one."

"Yeah. We can do that first thing tomorrow. We'll most likely need Mrs. Sleighton's authorization."

"Fine." Audrey said. "Let's pay a visit to the heartless dog that would turn her own blood out like that without a thought."

CHAPTER 15

▼

When they called the manager at Simone's Sandy Springs condominium, she seemed relieved that someone was finally calling about their former tenant. According to them, repeated calls to Mrs. Sleighton to collect the rest of Simone's things had gone unanswered. Concerned about any negative press Simone's violent end may have brought to their business, they were eager to release her things to the next of kin. They would get a fee for re-selling the place for Bobby, so they were anxious to dissolve all ties with the previous tenant.

Since neither Paul nor Audrey's names were anywhere on the lease, they would have to talk to the aunt, or lie and hope management wouldn't do too much checking, in order to get Simone's things.

It was eight o'clock and since most people are up getting ready for work, they decided to place a call to Lenora Sleighton. Paul found out from a sleepy sounding man on the other end of the phone that Mrs. Sleighton worked the graveyard shift as a baker at the Krispy Kreme Donut Shop on Ponce De Leon. She'd be home at eight-thirty. Paul grabbed his keys from the peg near the door leading to the garage and he and Audrey left the mansion.

*   *   *   *

The store was on a street in Midtown Atlanta, notorious for drug dealing, prostitution, and every other kind of crime imaginable. Audrey nudged Paul when she saw the green and red neon sign up ahead.

"There's the Krispy Kreme." She said.

"Hers is the next street." Paul said, slowing the car and putting on his right turn signal.

The main street had been littered with discarded trash, some of which was still breathing. People collected in quick clusters to sell drugs or themselves before passing along to enjoy the proceeds of their transactions. Despair hovered around the street like an uninvited guest, blending in with the detritus. So they were shocked when they turned down Argonne Avenue and found a nice, clean, tree-lined street, accessorized by old-fashioned gaslights.

Paul parked in front a beautiful brick and wood-frame Tudor that looked like it had been recently resurfaced. In the wake of another dry summer, the lawn was sparse, but neatly edged. The flowers had dried to brown, their heads curled inward, bowed as though ashamed that their brilliance was gone.

Audrey and Paul made their way along the concrete path. Their footfalls pounded the wooden stairs as they climbed to the spacious porch. She moved closer to Paul when several dogs barked and snarled from somewhere behind the house. Audrey prayed that the animals were adequately secured as they took tentative steps to the front door.

One corner of the gray painted, wooden deck displayed white metal furniture. A thirteen-inch TV with rabbit ears cocked to one side was shoved in the other corner. Potted philodendrons spilled over the edge of their containers throughout the space. Audrey turned the old fashioned crank doorbell and they waited.

After what seemed like an eternity, but was really just a minute, they heard shuffling from inside. Cloudy gray eyes peered at them from the other side of the screen door.

"Yeah?"

"Is Mrs. Sleighton in?"

"Who wonts tuh know?"

"My name is Audrey. I called her about Simone earlier…She's expecting me." Audrey lied.

The man looked around her at Paul, giving him a suspicious once over before being swallowed into the bowels of the dark, musty house. They heard him holler, "Lori!" Then a few degrees softer, "Lori——there's a couple of colored people at the door."

Audrey and Paul looked at each other with raised eyebrows.

"People still use that term?" She asked mumbled to him.

"People still use that term and all the others as well."

Audrey shivered. Hearing backwards racial terms was not that foreign to her; nevertheless, she was never prepared for the ignorance.

They heard the rumblings of an argument from within the house cussing and then coughing, as Lenora Sleighton flip-flopped her way to the door. She was average height but nearly as wide as she was tall. She regarded Paul and Audrey suspiciously, sizing them up with a wrinkled brow. A cigarette clung to her bottom lip and danced up and down when she spoke.

"You the one called me?"

"Yes." Audrey replied.

"You didn't say you was coming by here."

"I'm sorry to impose, but I wanted to know if you would sign a statement allowing us to get Simone's things."

"Why do you want Simone's things?" She still hadn't opened the door. She wasn't looking at Audrey now, but Paul. "Don't I know you?"

"I don't think so, Ma'am."

"I've seen you before. I never forget a face."

"I'm Paul Radford, you may have seen…"

"Oh, you're the boy with that talk show on cable." She started fiddling with the locks on the screen door. "Come on in."

They stepped over a pair of mud caked work boots and a nasty undershirt into a room lit only by the light of an old floor model television. Lenora Sleighton still smelled of work. If the sugary doughnut smell hadn't been mixed with her perspiration and cigarette smoke, and didn't emanate from the vile creature before her, it would have made Audrey crave a sticky sweet honey glaze. Instead, it made her slightly nauseous. The filmy drawn blinds added to the room's dreariness, making it seem like daylight hadn't reached the Sleighton household. Their hostess offered them a seat. Audrey sat on the end of a scratchy plaid chair. The cushions on the matching orthogonal couch wheezed when Lenora Sleighton plopped down next to Paul.

"I used to watch your show sometimes." She was saying to Paul. "It's not often you hear the blacks with the right point of view these days."

"I beg your pardon?" Paul gave her a slight smile. Audrey wondered what the woman was talking about, and what Paul was thinking.

"You talked about how you had to pull yourself up by your own boot straps and how blacks rely too much on handouts to get by."

"You sure that was *my* show?"

"Aren't you the one…you know what, I think that mighta been that other boy's show. You know, the one run for President…Keyes, that's his name. It's hard to keep up anymore. Everyone has a talk show these days." She leaned in closer to Paul. Audrey suppressed a laugh when she saw the look on Paul's face.

He was doing a good job of holding it together, but she could tell the woman was irritating the hell out of him. Paul looked about as much like Alan Keyes as she did.

"I've seen you though. I never forget a face." Lenora put her hand down the top of her uniform and scratched a floppy breast.

Paul tried to look away as flaccid, stretch marked flesh popped forward, moving around like a venous pink bubble as the woman satisfied her itch.

"You have been on TV? I'm right about that?" She coughed without covering her mouth spraying errant strains of God knew what into the thick air. Audrey made a mental note to swing by the CDC and get a tetanus shot before she left Atlanta.

"Yes. I do have a syndicated talk show." Obviously repulsed by the pink glob of breast tissue and the germ spray, Paul pressed his back so far into the sofa Audrey thought a spring would pop out. To his credit, his face remained an unreadable as a poker players.

"I knew it!" She clapped her hands delightfully, displaying a haggled yellow grin. Lenora Sleighton was excited to have a celebrity in her house. "So what you doing, one of those exposé things?" She smoothed the greasy strands from her face and straightened the top of her dress.

"Not exactly. Right now, I'm trying to help a friend of mine who's in a bit of a jam." Paul gave her a killer smile that worked on the big woman like a charm.

"I'll do what I can to help. But of course you do understand that I don't make a lot of money. I tried to give Simone and the boy what I could, but it was hard..."

Audrey thought she would gag when the woman squeezed a crocodile tear out of her bovine face. The ash on her cigarette drooped and then fell onto the greasy carpet. Audrey had seen enough.

"Here are the statements we had drawn up." Audrey pushed the papers toward the woman. Mrs. Sleighton took them and scanned the documents briefly before looking from one to the other of her guests.

"How bad do you need my signature on these papers?"

"What do you mean?" Paul was smart. Audrey knew he knew what she was getting at, but he was going to make her tell them what she was after.

"I told you I don't make a lot of money. Simone took me through hell..."

"So what is it you want?" He asked her.

"Ten thousand dollars."

"Thank you for your time, Mrs. Sleighton." Paul made a move to stand but Lenora stopped him with a fleshy hand.

"I can get a law clerk to file a petition with the court for twenty-five dollars and get all of this taken care of, Mrs. Sleighton. We came to see you out of courtesy to you and in memory of your niece." He told her.

Paul stood all the way up and Audrey followed suit. They were headed for the door when Lenora stopped them again.

"Now I didn't say I wouldn't sign. But my time should be worth something."

Paul took out his billfold.

"I'll give you five hundred dollars to sign both documents."

Lenora Sleighton coughed and nodded greedily as Paul extracted the cash from his wallet. He and Audrey took the signed papers and left the musty house after muttering disingenuous thanks.

"Why'd you pay her all that money?" Audrey asked him when they were in the car.

"That was a bargain. Her release is going to save us a lot of time and aggravation."

"I think we should have gotten a paralegal to do it for twenty-five dollars."

"That would have been good, except for one thing." Paul snorted. "I don't know no damn law clerk."

They cracked up laughing as Paul pulled the car into the thickening traffic toward I-75. Paul exited on Roswell Road and drove a couple of miles and made a right turn at a black sign with gold lettering affixed to a massive stone. Tuxedo Canyon was a condo community of pastel pink stucco homes with rust colored Mexican tiled roofs. There was a beautiful waterfall in the center of the parking area with so many flowers covering its banks the water was barely visible.

"Swanky." Audrey said like Granny Clampett. He laughed but Audrey made a mental note that Paul had driven directly to Simone's community without asking for directions. Maybe he'd found out how to get there earlier. Or, maybe he had been there before.

They parked in front of the manager's office and went inside. A twenty-something blonde looked up from her filing, held her hands out to make sure her nails were perfectly shaped before addressing them. The manager was out showing a unit; she told them before directing them to a comfortable waiting area.

Minutes later the door opened and a petite woman in a peach colored pantsuit entered. Her long, light blonde expensively cut hair contrasted the cheesy orange lipstick that matched her tanning bed skin. The File Queen said something to her and she looked over at Audrey and did a double take when she saw Paul. She walked over with her hand extended for Paul to shake.

"I'm Mindy Meyer. And, you're Paul Radford!" Paul nodded.

"I love your show." Mindy's eyes swept over him hungrily.

"Thank you." He beamed, holding her hand in his. "It's always nice to meet a fan of the show."

"I have two of your books and found them truly inspiring!"

"If you have them here I'll sign them for you."

"I don't...but you know what? I don't live too far from here..."

Oh, brother! Audrey thought. She cleared her throat and glared at Paul. Embarrassed, he averted his gaze before addressing Mindy once more.

"I was wondering if you could help me with something, Mindy." He sounded as weak as an overcooked noodle.

"Sure, Paul. Anything."

They fawned over each other for another minute or two. Audrey could have gotten down on all fours and rubbed her ass on the carpet until it was as red as a baboon's and neither of them would have noticed. Mindy Meyer struck Audrey as the type who'd turn a smile or even turn a trick if it led to a commission. But Mindy wasn't trying to sell a condo and Paul certainly wasn't trying to get Simone's things.

They needed to get back downtown to Bobby's hearing. Paul could come and pick this up on his own time. Audrey pushed the papers toward Mindy.

"We need to get Simone Denton's things." She said.

Mindy barely glanced at the papers. She touched Paul's hand and led him toward the door.

"Her Aunt picked up her clothes and jewelry." Mindy said. "I had the rest of her things packed yesterday. Let me take you to the storage area."

Audrey remembered the aunt saying that she hadn't taken any of Simone's things and wondered which of them, the Aunt or the condo manager, was lying. They followed her to the building behind the office and waited for her to unlock it.

The furniture had been rented. The only thing left of Simone Denton was crammed into a huge garbage bag and three small cardboard boxes. Audrey grabbed a box and Paul lagged behind before lifting the bag and the other two boxes, giving himself ample time to get Mindy's phone number while Audrey was out of earshot. When they finally had everything packed into the trunk of the car, they headed south on I-75 to the Courthouse.

CHAPTER 16

▼

Audrey waited with Paul in front of room 11C. They were a little early. Audrey looked around for a vending machine so she could get some mints or something to settle her jumpy stomach. On her way down the hall, she met Renita and Lloyd.

"You doin' okay?" Lloyd held her at arms length. She nodded and he embraced her warmly. He opened his arms and included Renita in the circle of comfort.

"Don't ya'll worry about a thing." He said. "If anybody can get him out of this mess, Jules can."

He released them and nodded in Paul's direction. The two men shook hands. The quartet stood quietly in the busy hallway as people pushed passed them on their way to court or to freedom.

The door to the courtroom opened suddenly, and some of the people standing in the hallway shuffled inside. Renita and Audrey looked at each other through wet, glassy eyes and walked toward the courtroom.

Paul led the way to a section of benches and they took their seats. Audrey stifled a gasp when she recognized Bobby as one in a group of men seated behind a Plexiglas screen. He looked slightly disheveled and irritable sitting there waiting his turn on the docket.

Judge Florence Lincoln looked on passionlessly as public defenders stood before her and pleaded cases for clients that they hardly knew. Judge Lincoln doled out decisions in an assembly line like manner as one defendant after another paraded before her and then, marched past.

Audrey's stomach lurched and she and Renita linked hands when a whiny voiced bailiff announced 'Robert Morgan Wilson'.

This was Audrey's first time seeing Jules at work. Transformed from the goofy klutz who used to be her office neighbor, Jules addressed the court with Masonesque charisma. This was only a hearing, so she could just imagine what he'd be like during a trial. She felt herself flush with a feeling that she couldn't name as she watched him. Renita gave her hand a comforting squeeze. They were happy and relieved that Jules was on their side.

After both the defense and the people made their arguments, the judge set bail at one hundred thousand dollars. The trial date was set and the next case was called. Jules held his hand out for his client to shake. Bobby pumped it for a quick second before returning to his place in line behind the glass. Another guard appeared through a side door and led Bobby out of the room.

A handful of reporters stopped Jules outside the courtroom. Bobby Wilson hadn't played ball in years but he was still known to die-hard basketball fans. The story of Simone's death and Bobby's arrest had made the national news. With all of the sports figures that had been in the news in recent years charged with violent crimes, this case just added fuel to a fire that never seemed to go out. He answered their questions briefly before cutting them off and turning his attention to his client's family and friends.

"You're Paul Radford!" Jules was still the same groupie as always. He extended his hand. "Jules Dreyfus."

"Glad to meet you." Paul replied, shaking his hand. "Thanks for taking Bobby's case."

"These folks are practically family." Jules responded. "I listen to your radio show from time to time over the Internet and your book *Using What You Got To Get What You Want* is poignant and inspiring. You've really walked through the fire and triumphed over incredible odds. It's a pleasure to meet you."

"Thank you, Jules. If I can just reach one person living in a hopeless environment and help them to overcome their surroundings, it's made anything I've had to endure worthwhile." Paul nodded at the knot of reporters. They had given up on Jules giving them anything more and filed out of the courthouse.

"It's a good thing Bobby's no longer in the NBA. They'd latch on like pit bulls and never let go."

"Isn't that the truth?" Jules replied, shifting his eyes in the directions the reporters had gone. They stood silent for a moment, not knowing what to do or say next.

"Sit back guys and relax. It'll take a while to process Bobby and get him released." Jules told them.

"We'll wait." Renita said. But neither Audrey nor Jules seemed to hear her, as they were too busy looking into each other's eyes. She held out her hand and he enclosed it in his.

"Thank you, Jules." She said.

"I didn't do that much. They don't have a strong case against Bobby." He squeezed Audrey's hand reassuringly.

"But what about the witnesses that said they saw him on the same floor where Simone's room was?" Renita asked.

"I haven't seen any evidence showing that Bobby was the only person who visited her that night. It would help if that lady he was with that night would come forward."

"Yeah, but how likely is it that a woman, who's probably a prostitute, will come into a courtroom and testify that she was on call that night with Bobby?" Renita questioned.

"I admit it *is* a long shot." Jules agreed. "But we'll prevail. I don't know who's the biggest worry wart, you or your sister." He yawned and stretched.

"I'm going to take care of the bail." Jules smiled at them, then walked down the dimly lit hallway and disappeared into a doorway on the right.

The four of them killed time by looking at the pattern of the floor tiles, checking the big, white-faced wall clock over the entrance to one of the courtrooms, and pacing. Jules had been away from them for over an hour, but when he returned, Bobby accompanied him.

His sisters ran to him and they all hugged. Like cockroaches, a swell of media came from cracks in the walls and out of drains, pushing their mics and their questions at Bobby. This time Paul didn't escape the onslaught. He was questioned about his friendship with Bobby and if he believed in his innocence. Jules intervened, while Paul helped them push through to a service elevator, away from the noisy throng.

"You seem to have some experience with this sort of thing." Jules said, giving Paul a grateful pat on the back.

"I guess you could say that. I know another way out of here." Paul touched the black elevator button marked LL and the car descended to a deserted floor with a warehouse feel to it. They stepped out and Paul pointed to a narrow stairwell.

"Those stairs lead to the backside of the parking deck. Bobby, here's the key to the Hummer. You go out first. They won't be looking for you to come out alone."

Bobby grabbed the key from Paul and made a dash for the car.

CHAPTER 17

▼

"It's good to have you back, Mr. Fixx." The man in the dark suit held the door and Marsh slid onto the leather seat. The driver grabbed the heaviest suitcase and the sedan shimmied when he placed it into the trunk. The driver finished loading the bags and merged into traffic.

Marsh arrived at Greater Cincinnati Airport on Tuesday afternoon. His partner, the ever-efficient Ernest Pressley, had sent a car for him. Pressley had transitioned easily and had everything running smoothly at the Midwest branch of Fixx Law. Marsh's goals accomplished, it was time for him to go home.

He was glad that Audrey had extended her stay in Atlanta. This way he could freely bask in the glow of the time he'd shared with Marlena without the guilt. After this weekend there was no question in his mind where he needed to be. His son was headed down a dangerous path. Marsh's stress level rose as he thought about the fear he felt when the boy was missing.

He had turned the neighborhood upside down until he located Toots at a park with a group of lanky, disheveled adolescent boys. They rocked to the lazy beat pounding from a boom box that took up a quarter of the bench where they sat. The air was thick with the musky smell of refer and the sound of profanity and laughter as the boy's swapped lies about one thing or another.

A boy with reddish yellow skin and hair cut in rings that resembled crop circles jerked the knob that controlled the sound when he caught a glimpse of Marsh striding toward them. Young heads jerked in Marsh's direction. Most of the teens scrambled to their feet and stumbled up from the bench and off into the distance. A few of the older ones lolled defiantly for a moment before following the others.

His friend's desertion and fear of his father drained the color from Toot's face. His throat bobbed up and down nervously. Marsh wanted to laugh but he suppressed the cocktail of feelings——the joy at finding his son, the elation that he wasn't dead or hurt, the humor as he watched the boy's clear eyes dart back and forth trying to think up a good lie to tell his father. He was still holding the blunt that one of the boy's had passed him when Marsh approached. Marsh slapped the cigarette from his hand and crushed it beneath his shoe.

"I thought you said you wasn't getting high, Toots."

"It's not refer, Dad. It's bidis."

"I don't care what it is, you ain't old enough to be smoking nothing, boy." He jerked his son up from the table and lifted his head so he could look in his eyes.

"Where the hell have you been? Your Mother's worried sick."

The sullen guise of the first night had returned and Toot's eyes burned defiantly into his fathers. Bravado from the weed and foolish adolescence jutted his thin chest outward. He boldly held his father's gaze.

"You don't give a damn about me or Mom." Toot's lips pulled downward and his forehead wrinkled in anger. "Why don't you go back to your girlfriend and leave us alone."

The back of Marsh's hand connected with the boy's face. He grabbed Toot's by the shoulders and gave him two hard shakes before closing his eyes and letting the anger flow from his head down into the parched grass beneath his feet. Toot's eyes were full of tears. The boy averted his gaze so his father wouldn't see the sign of weakness. When they rolled down his face his anger nearly turned them to steam. Toots looked at the ground. Marsh's heart turned into jelly.

"I shouldn't of hit you, son."

Toot's was silent.

"I'm sorry." He pulled the boy to him. Toot's was stiff, unyielding. Marsh continued to hold him until the youngster gave in. It was right then that Marsh made up his mind. Whether he and Marlena reconciled or not, he was coming back to Massachusetts to be with his son. He'd done this damage to his family and only he could repair it.

Audrey's last message to him had said something about Bobby being in a jam and that she'd give him the details when they spoke. He hadn't called her back. He didn't want to get his head filled with thoughts of Audrey and what she might be thinking or feeling. The truth was, he just didn't want to care and he didn't want to lead her any further than he already had. He should have felt bad for his behavior, but Marsh had dreamed of getting his family back for too long to let anyone or anything mess this up for him.

The car flowed with the light early afternoon traffic. Marsh had been so busy organizing his thoughts he was home before he knew it. They pulled to a stop at the end of the long driveway and the driver helped Marsh bring his bags inside.

"Thank you, Henry."

"You're quite welcome, Mr. Fixx." He tipped his hat and pulled the door closed on his way out.

Marsh took a deep breath and released it as he looked around him. He was going to miss this beautiful property. He would have loved to bring his family here. But that would never happen. Besides, his business associate, Ernest Pressley, had already moved in. With the Midwestern branch in his partner's capable hands, Marsh could rest assured that everything would run smoothly. His corporation owned this house, and the Mercedes. Both would be at Ernest's disposal.

The telephone rang.

"Hey, baby. I was just thinking about you guys, too." Marsh smiled into the phone, tickled at the little things that people take for granted. Having Marlena call him once more was better than anything he could imagine.

"I've got a few things to tie up here. I'll be flying out on Friday." He paused, listening to the music of her voice. His heart swelled with joy when she finally expressed her feelings to him. He responded in kind.

"I love you too…"

*　　　*　　　*　　　*

The air was filled with the spicy, greasy, goodness of dinner when Paul opened the door to his home. Martha seemed almost pleasant as she went from one of them to the other setting plates of food and filling water glasses. They hadn't spoken that much on the ride out and now, sitting before Martha's table, plates heaping with fried chicken and every side dish imaginable, they gorged themselves on her sumptuous country cooking.

They were on their second pitcher of lemonade when Bobby cleared his throat and tapped his water goblet with his fork. Every one of them shifted their focus from the food to hear what he had to say.

"I want ya'll to know that I appreciate the support over these past few days." He held up his hand to stop them before anyone could respond. "I brought all of this on myself and you guys…well, let me just say that your standing by me has meant a lot. I've been a real butt hole in the past and I wouldn't have blamed ya'll if you had left me in there to rot."

"Bobby, there's no point in beating yourself over the head about this." Audrey said. She marveled at how her brother had matured recently. "We'll make it through this and be home in a few days. Jules is out now trying to get leads on that woman you were with. As soon as she gives her statement, they'll dismiss the charges."

"Well, that's just it." Bobby averted his eyes, focusing on the artwork on the dining room walls. "The lady I was with that night was Jules' woman."

"What?" Paul left the table and walked over to the window. Audrey could see his jaw tighten even though he wasn't facing them. He turned suddenly. Coming back to the table, he confronted Bobby.

"You're saying that you were with the man's woman who's trying to get you off a murder rap?" He drew back in his chair, slamming his napkin onto the table. Paul's eyes pierced Bobby's like hot lasers. "How fuckin' low is that?"

Audrey, as well as everyone else, was shocked at Paul's reaction. He'd been pretty even keeled through this whole thing. Watching him now, arms akimbo, shoulders tight, and nostrils flaring, was quite a turn. Audrey couldn't remember ever seeing him angry and she'd never heard such profanity come from this man who had spent so many years perfecting his speech.

Bobby's head snapped around and he drew himself up taller in his seat. He crossed his arms in front of his chest, eyeing Paul like he was deciding which way to hurt him first. The room had taken on the feel of high noon in a Western movie. Everybody, including Martha, prepared to duck beneath the heavy oak table to find shelter there. Though danger was apparent, the intensity that flowed between the two big men kept everybody else glued to their seats.

"I don't need none of your sanctimonious bullshit right now, P." Bobby's gaze withered his lanky friend who decided to keep any remaining commentary to himself. He returned to his chair like a scolded child. Bobby kept a trained eye on the man across from him for a few chilly seconds. Once he relaxed, a palpable though inaudible sigh shook the walls of the dining room. Movement returned to a room that had been as still as a painting.

"Anyway," Bobby picked up where he'd left off before the interruption. "I'm not trying to piss Jules off, but if he thinks a statement from that woman would get me out of this shit…"

"You don't have a choice." Renita said. "Maybe you can tell Jules you didn't know she was with him until you saw the woman go to his table afterwards."

"Everybody saw them come in together and all during the banquet they sat next to each other." Bobby replied.

"So why did you get with her if you knew she was with Jules?" Paul was trying to suppress his distaste for Bobby's actions.

"Because I could." Bobby shot back.

Paul could hold back no longer.

"That's why we get such a bad rap as pro athletes and as black men. I got so tired of that shit when we were playing ball…brothers acting like they have no self control."

"You was just mad back then cause nobody wanted your ugly, stuttering ass."

The low blow seemed to cut Paul in half. Everybody looked at Bobby like they couldn't believe he had made such a wicked comment. Audrey could see the repressed anger pushing toward the surface as Paul decided whether to let the remark slide. Audrey was beginning to wonder if they should start looking for cover again…or just leave. But it was Paul who finally capitulated, his brown eyes withering under Bobby's evil glare. Embarrassed and hurt, he shifted his eyes away from his friend's threatening gaze. Bobby's behavior was just too much for Audrey to take. She caught a glimpse of Martha. The servant's eyes sliced Bobby with ice-cold abhorrence. Her hand moved inside of the big pockets of her uniform. The white apron shifted as her hand went deeper into the folds of fabric. Audrey imagined her producing a gun and putting and end to the feud once and for all. She stood by the door, waiting. Martha had obviously reached a position of employee loyalty far beyond any Audrey could imagine.

"The important thing is to get you out of this trouble." Renita reasoned. "All this infighting isn't doing anybody any good."

Bobby shook his head. "P man, I'm sorry. That was real fucked up of me."

"Hey, don't sweat it man. You're under a lot of pressure." Paul's smile never reached his eyes.

"I'll give Jules a call this evening." Bobby said. "But there's one more thing I need to tell you, Audrey. You and Paul have been working hard to see about Simon. I know that you have even mentioned adopting him yourself." The silence lingered a touch too long as Bobby tried to collect his thoughts and search for the right words to speak on a difficult subject.

"What is it, Bobby?" A wrinkle creased Audrey's forehead as she raised her eyebrows in concern. When Bobby spoke, the words flooded out and ripped through Audrey's mind like a torrent before breaking her heart.

"Audrey, Simon is autistic."

CHAPTER 18

▼

It felt as though someone has taken a knife and plunged it through Audrey's heart. In all of the years she'd known that Bobby had a son, she'd never considered that he was anything but a beautiful, healthy little boy. The word reverberated in her brain…AUTISM. As she sat in the room with her sister and brother and Paul, feeling the weight of her tender heart, a question popped into her mind. What is autism? Was the child deformed? Is he aggressive or even violent? Or is he heavily medicated, spending his days in a vegetative state? Should he be institutionalized? Their brother had never told them there was anything wrong with Simon so Audrey imagined the boy must be in pretty bad shape and it hurt Bobby too much to talk about it. Or maybe he was ashamed. Maybe he just didn't care.

A flood of emotion overwhelmed her. Tears sprang to the rims of her eyes and spilled over onto her cheeks before she could stop them. Renita ran to her, comforting Audrey as she shook with sorrow for the little boy who may not even realize that he'd never see his mother again.

*　　*　　*　　*

Audrey's face was swollen and tears had left dry ridges down her cheeks. She'd awakened after a bad dream where she'd seen a small boy, wafer thin, huddled in a corner crying. The visualization was so real it shook Audrey awake. She sat upright in bed waiting for her beating heart to settle down. She looked at the glowing amber numbers on the digital clock. Three-forty five a.m. was too early to be up and about, disturbing the others.

She left her bed and went to the bathroom. She watched her reflection as if the glass possessed the answer to a secret code. Audrey splashed water onto her face and brushed her teeth. The best way for her to deal with problems or worries had always been to work her way through. She decided to create a to do list. She felt compelled to meet Simon and talk to whatever professionals she could to learn about him and his condition. She was sure there had to be information on the web and books at the library on autism. The people at DFCS would be a good resource, too.

Audrey went to the closet to get some clothes and nearly broke her neck stumbling over something in the middle of the floor. She looked down at the three cartons she and Paul had retrieved from Simone's Sandy Springs condominium. Falling down on her knees like the box was the answer to a prayer, Audrey pulled the lid off the first container and tossed it onto the floor.

The box was full of books—-heavy books, the subjects ranged from child psychology to neurological disorders in children. There were books about autism and books written by people who'd raised autistic children and even a couple of books penned by people who had the disorder. There were also three books on epilepsy. Did Simon have that too? Audrey began to tear up. That poor little boy. Discovering that he may have additional problems should have driven her away, but instead, it made her all the more determined to help him.

She dried her eyes with the back of her hand and looked inside the deep carton. Audrey didn't know where to begin. She finally selected a book with a white cloth cover. Black lettering etched out its title, *Inside The Autistic Brain*. She learned the definition of autism: A developmental disability manifested by self-centered mental activity, withdrawal and language deficiencies. Audrey squinted in confusion. That could have described half the people she'd known throughout her life. She continued reading. The cause of autism is unknown though it's thought to have a genetic basis. The book was filled with case studies and Audrey read a few of them before going on to some of the other titles.

Audrey looked at the clock. It was a little after five. She left the bedroom and went to the kitchen to get a bottle of chilled water from the refrigerator. She still wasn't completely at ease in Paul's home and felt like she was intruding on Martha's space whenever she opened the refrigerator. She snatched a plastic bottle of water, went back to her room and closed the door.

She took the lid off the next box. It was filled with spiral bound notebooks. The pages were rumpled by use or moisture or age. Audrey pulled back the worn yellow-brown cover. It was a journal. Folded between the cover and the first page was an age-yellowed handkerchief. Audrey lifted it gingerly and brought it to her nose. She squinted, trying to remember where she'd smelled the scent. When no memory was forthcoming, she dropped the hanky into the box. She focused on the journal once more. The squiggly handwriting looped and slanted like an organized mass of spaghetti. The letters huddled together like they harbored a horrible secret.

Audrey hesitated. A person's journal is a private matter, full of feelings or actions not meant for anyone else's eyes. She remembered a time in her youth when she had given both her sister and brother a few sharp raps upside the head for reading about her deepest thoughts. She'd even gotten rid of a lover for rummaging through her dresser drawer and finding her diary, then later using what he found there to try to analyze her.

But Simone was dead. There might be something in these pages that would lead to Bobby being freed. The first page was dated August 17, 1995. Audrey read:

Took a day off work. Simon's first child psychologist's visit was at 9:00. There were so many questions! I had to go all the way back to before I was pregnant...How many sexual partners have I had? (Ha! That's a good one. I lied and told them three.). Did I have a family history of neurological problems? (Yeah if you count my neurotic aunt and whacked out cousin, I would say so). I told them No. Was it a planned pregnancy? Where was Simon's father? How did he react to the pregnancy? Did I know anything about his health? I wasn't about to tell them who Simon's father was. Nor would I tell them what his reaction was to the pregnancy. It was a bad situation. Their questions brought back the joy and pain that tied me to the man who fathered my son.

I fell quickly and madly in love with him. We were both stoned out of our minds the night Simon was conceived. I was happy when my period was late. I thought he would be too. He slapped the hell out of me when I told him I was pregnant. I was so hurt when he did that. But the slap didn't hurt as bad as the words. He called me a slut...a scheming whore. It was like I was twelve years old all over again with Auntie Lee. He said that I had slept with half of Atlanta and now that I got caught I was trying to use this to trap him or get money from him. I swore that I wouldn't do anything like that to him. When we started seeing each other I'd stopped dealing with all those other guys. He didn't believe me.

"So what you think Ahma do...marry you or some shit like that?" he asked. Then he started laughing." You bitches kill me with that shit. Hangin' around, trying to get lucky. You ain't nothin' but a fuckin' gold-digging prostitute." That wasn't even half of the terrible things that he said. None of it was true. I really loved him. I'm ashamed to admit, I still do. He told me that I better get an abortion or he would kill me...

There was a knock on the door. Audrey slammed the notebook shut. Quickly collecting the books, she put them back like she'd found them before getting up to see who was there.

"It's me." Paul said softly.

The hot aroma of breakfast invaded the space when Audrey swung the door open. Her stomach rumbled and a wave of nausea washed over her.

"I just wanted to make sure that you were alright after last night."

"I'm okay." Audrey tried to look bright, though her heart was about to beat out of her chest remembering the chilling text in the journal. *"...he would kill me..."*

"Martha's got breakfast ready." Paul was saying. "Why don't you join us?"

"Let me take a minute to freshen up and I'll be right there." Audrey pushed the door shut after Paul walked away and let out the painful breath she had been holding. She was hoping that she would find something that would help Bobby; instead, it seemed the words Simone had written would make his prosecution a surety.

She wanted to forget she had ever looked inside the cartons, but it seemed like the boxes were calling her, the lids, animated lips, forming her name. The last thing she wanted was something to eat, but if she didn't go out there soon, Paul would be back. She didn't want to tell him about the contents of the boxes and hoped he had forgotten that they were there. Audrey pushed the heavy containers inside the large closet and used her foot to smooth the impressions the boxes had left on the carpet. Simone's plastic trash bag of stuff was in the back of the closet, which was a decent sized space. Audrey could comfortably review the contents without anyone seeing her. A switch on the inside wall lighted a seashell shaped sconce that bathed the area in soft light. When she returned to her secret project, she would stay inside the closet. If anyone came in the bedroom she could quickly turn out the light and no one would suspect a thing.

CHAPTER 19

▼

Audrey was surprised to find Bobby and Renita at the breakfast table when she entered the dining room. She thought Renita was with Fran and that Bobby was out in the streets trying to make up for lost time after being locked up. Upon hearing the upsetting news about Simon, Audrey had retired to her room the night before and stayed there. Renita wanted to come with her, but Audrey was too upset for her sister's company. She called Audrey's name from the other side of the locked door for the longest time before giving up. Audrey felt guilty at first, but then she realized that she needed some time by herself to absorb this new development. She'd talk to her sister and brother later. This morning her siblings looked up from their plates and smiled.

"What can I get you?" Even Martha seemed to have grown a heart sometime during the night. Her words sounded as comforting as a mother's. As Audrey put in her request for orange juice she wondered if Martha had children. The woman was a curiosity. Each time she drew near the hairs on the back of Audrey's neck swayed to attention. Martha sat a frothy glass of orange juice and a saucer of zwieback and peach marmalade in front of Audrey before she could take the thought of the maid's personal life any further. Audrey thanked her and spread a bit of the jam onto the dry sliver of toast and nibbled it. She swallowed the morsel and her stomach accepted the bread like it housed a nest of hungry sparrows. The plate was soon empty and Martha replaced it with standard breakfast fare. Audrey ate pancakes, ham, eggs and southern fried corn until she was too full to move. For a second she thought she detected the slightest smile on Martha's face.

"I thought about going down to DFCS this morning." Paul was the first to broach the subject that was weighing on all of their minds.

"They won't talk to us until they get the results of the paternity test." Audrey told them. "I believe they already have a signed document from Lenora Sleighton relinquishing her rights.

"I called Jules last night and told him what I did." Bobby threaded his fingers and rested his elbows on the table. "He took it pretty good, considering. I guess the two of them wasn't that tight."

Audrey remembered her conversation with Jules the other day in the hotel restaurant and how he had assured her there was nothing serious between him and the willowy blonde.

"He said he wouldn't have a problem getting a statement from her." Bobby continued. "According to Jules, the DA's office will most likely drop the charges against me before the week is out."

"What a relief!" Renita released a sigh. "This shit has been killing me and I can't wait to get back home."

"But what about Simon?" Audrey was surprised to hear that Renita planned to be on the first thing smoking after Bobby was released.

"Audrey, I know you've gotten emotionally attached to Simon, but you're not equipped to raise a handicapped child." Renita ran her hand along the cream-colored organza tablecloth as she spoke, avoiding Audrey's eyes.

"How do you know what I'm capable of, Renita? I'm not going to walk away from him just because he has a problem. I thought I'd at least study the condition before I make a final decision." Audrey was irritated by Renita's statement and by her attitude. She was dismayed by all three of them. How could they behave as if Simon doesn't matter? People constantly walk away from children, treating them worse than they do their pets. Audrey felt like she had something to give to Simon. No matter what DFCS decided to do, she vowed she would make a positive contribution to the young boy's life.

"You say 'he has a problem' like he's having trouble with his math homework, Audrey." Renita had stopped fidgeting with the tablecloth, her gaze even with Audrey's. "This is some serious stuff. You're a single woman, living in another state. You live in a home that barely has enough space for you and that cat of yours. You don't know what services are available in Rosemont that would address his needs. And what about Simon's feelings? What if he doesn't want to leave Atlanta? What about relationships he's formed here? What if he just doesn't like you? What if he hates cats?"

"You know what, Renita? You always see the negative side in everything!" Audrey pounded the table making the silverware jump and water spill over the edges of some of the goblets. "This is our nephew. I would think that you would be trying to think about someone other than yourself for a change…"

"*Me* think about *myself?*" You're not doing this for Simon. You're doing it for yourself." Renita charged. "Hell, you've never even met him. How could you possible have an attachment to a kid you don't even know? You want to become a mother so desperately that you're being irrational. It's pathetic!"

Audrey jumped up from her chair with such force that it tipped over and crashed to the floor. Paul grabbed her and Bobby grabbed Renita who was making her way to the buzz saw that was her older sister. She was prepared to either dull the blade or get sawed in half by it. Luckily the doorbell rang. Audrey could hear Martha, who had probably been listening to them the whole while, speaking with someone at the door. A few seconds later, Jules was standing in the dining room looking surprised at the two angry women trying to hit each other while the two rangy men held them back.

"Uh, if this is a bad time, I can come back." Jules looked from one to the other. The women relaxed and the men released them. Without acknowledging Jules, they took their seats, careful not to look at one another.

"Have a seat." Paul offered.

Martha was standing in the doorway.

"May I get you something, Sir?"

Jules turned around in his chair and faced Martha.

"I'd like a cup of coffee, please."

She filled a cup from the silver urn on the buffet and set it before Jules. He dressed the liquid with sugar and cream before taking a sip.

"That's good coffee."

Martha nodded and disappeared.

"I've got some news." Jules moved to open his briefcase then changed his mind. He sat it on his lap and drummed his fingers on its knobby ostrich skin for a second. They watched him expectantly, waiting for him to continue. "I've got the results of the paternity test." He sipped from the cup again.

"Well…?" Bobby asked anxiously. Jules sat the cup on the saucer, laced his fingers and looked Bobby in the eyes before speaking.

"You're not the boy's biological father, Bobby."

CHAPTER 20

▼

"You mean to tell me that all this time, all the money, everything, was wasted on a lie?" Bobby leaped up from his chair and punched the wall so hard he dented it. "That bitch! Now I see why somebody killed her ass!"

Bobby was pacing the room, fists balled, hot steam flowing through flaring nostrils. Audrey thought about the diary again and the last entry she'd read. Was Bobby capable of killing? Had he killed Simone? Even though he had an alibi, could they be certain that he was with the woman at the exact time of death? Was this his first time learning that he was not the father of Simone's son? Maybe he found out about it that night and was just pretending that Jules' news was a revelation to him. Audrey wanted to say, 'was that somebody you?' But instead she said, "How can you say that the time and money you spent was a waste, Bobby?"

"Cause he ain't my son, that's how." Bobby shot back. "Why the fuck would I spend thousands of dollars on a kid that wasn't mine?"

"But he could have been yours." Renita said. "And the money helped him. Isn't that worth something?"

"Yeah, it's worth plenty…several hundred thousand dollars when you include the condo. I was paying that bitch more than thirty thousand dollars a year and she lied to me."

"Well you could have taken the test ten years ago and maybe we wouldn't be here like this." Audrey said.

"I don't need you to remind me how I've screwed up everybody's vacation." Bobby said sarcastically, shooting Audrey a withering glare.

"What*ever*." Audrey mumbled.

"Look. This isn't helping anything." Paul reasoned. "The important thing is that Bobby got out of this okay and that everything worked out for the best."

"Really?" Audrey asked. "What about Simon? Has everything worked out for him?"

*   *   *   *

Audrey went to her room and slammed the door. She couldn't believe what she was hearing from them. Her head was still pounding from the harsh words exchanged with Renita when Jules comes in and cavalierly drops this bombshell like he was reporting that it was sprinkling outside. While she could understand Bobby for being angry at Simone's betrayal of him, it was his own fault for not getting the test when the baby was born. He'd had his own selfish reasons for not taking responsibility for his part in the situation, thinking he was getting over by paying Simone a nominal amount of money. Now he was whining about paying her what was, for him, chump change. Audrey couldn't give him an ounce of sympathy. When you act stupid, stupid things happen to you.

The cap had been that remark by Paul. Everything had not worked out for the best. Nobody seemed to care that a little boy had lost his mother, and now it seems, his father, in the course of a few days. Audrey pictured him going from one foster home to another or worse, wasting away in an institution. She didn't care if everybody thought she was crazy, she would go down to that DFCS office and she wouldn't leave until she was satisfied that Simon's best interests were being addressed. She would also fill out and sign adoption papers and apply for temporary custody.

It was just after 9:00. Audrey grabbed her bag and pulled out her address book. Cordelia St. James answered on the first ring.

"Ms. St. James, it's Audrey Wilson. I was wondering if you'd had time to read the lab information on my brother Bobby in relation to the Simon Denton case."

"As a matter of fact, I've just completed my review and notes."

"So you know that my brother is not Simon's father."

"Yes." Cordelia St. James paused. Audrey swallowed. She was about to change her whole life with her next statement. She prayed to God that she was ready.

"Ms. St. James, I'd like to adopt Simon and take him to live with me in Ohio."

"You are aware that Simon is autistic and is subject to occasional petit mal seizures?"

Audrey visualized the raised eyebrow on the light skinned face of the reedy woman on the other end of the phone. She hadn't realized that there were different types of seizures until she'd read some of Simone's books. It was a relief to learn that Simon was not subject to grand mal seizures where the body writhes and convulses. That would totally freak her out. People affected with petit mal seizures go into a dreamlike state without warning. There was a section in one of the books about nutrition, medication, and lifestyle effects on the disorder. Simone's three boxes were like the mother's legacy to the son who desperately needed all support he could get.

"I know about the autism and I suspected he might be epileptic as well. I'm trying to educate myself, but I have to admit, I just found out about his condition recently."

"And you still want to adopt him?" She asked.

"More than ever." Audrey replied.

"There's one other thing." Cordelia St. James said. "Simon has been non-verbal since we picked him up. We don't know if he's in shock or if he just refuses to speak because he doesn't know us. According to his history file, he can speak, mostly monosyllabic. He also knows sign language. Since he's been in house, he refuses to do either."

"I can learn some simple signs so that I can communicate with him." Audrey suggested.

"That's an excellent idea." The woman on the other end sounded pleased by Audrey's determination. Cordelia St. James promised to start the paperwork and they set up a meeting for ten o'clock the next day.

Audrey felt better than she had in days. She knew in her heart that she was doing the right thing. Her mind drifted back to the argument she'd had with Renita. They were in their forties and Audrey could count the number of times they'd quarreled. It didn't happen often, but when it did…

In spite of the anger and hurt feelings, Audrey couldn't help but remember the things her sister had said. Even though she felt the way Renita did it was tacky and mean, the validity of her points were without question. There was so much to consider, most notably, Simon's feelings about a complete change in everything he'd ever known. What if he hated her? What if she didn't like him? One thing was certain; Audrey had a lot to learn and a lot to do. First she'd draw up a list of all of the things to consider and she would begin preparation for bringing Simon home.

CHAPTER 21

▼

Jules tapped lightly on the door, and then a little louder. He asked her to let him in but she didn't answer him. Audrey didn't want to talk to him or any of them. She waited until she heard the activity in the house subside, realizing that each of them had left the premises to go about their day. Life goes on.

Audrey decided that this would be a good time to resume her search through Simone's journals. She opened the closet, hit the light switch and sat cross-legged in front of the box. She picked up her reading where she'd left off—August 17, 1995.

> *It's been months since he's called me. I've got to look out for my baby and myself so I do what I have to do to survive. I'm not trying to hurt anybody. I need money and I figure with all these high rollers coming into the club, I'm going to get one of them to help me. There's a guy that I hook up with whenever he's in town, another NBA player. He's nice in a crude kind of way. I told him that Simon was his son. He was mad at first but then he just started sending checks. I thought for sure he was going to want a paternity test. I was prepared to persuade him otherwise but I never had to. He's not too bad a guy. I hate to have to do this to him but I need the money. Maybe one day, he'll forgive me.*

Audrey wondered what she meant by that. It must have been during this time that she told Bobby that Simon was his son. Back then Bobby had a few commercial endorsements and was under contract with Cleveland. He had plenty of money and Simone knew it. He had been too stupid to make her take a test figuring if he threw her a few dollars she'd shut up about it. It worked. The problem for Bobby was, Simon wasn't his son.

August 18, 1995

Simon has been diagnosed with autism. When Dr. Hylbert gave me the news, I couldn't help it, I just cried and cried. Simon is the sweetest little boy. He's so loving, and he's smart too. To look at him, he seems totally perfect in everyway. Why does he have to have this terrible thing?

He started out like any normal baby, maybe even a bit advanced. But his third birthday came and went and he still wasn't talking. He just grunts or uses an occasional word like "milk" or "juice" or "eat" when he wants something.

I met this girl, Amy at the club. She told me that she works at this child development center during the day and that I should take Simon to a specialist there. She also told me that I should apply for Medicare because Simon's therapy could cost hundreds of dollars a month. That's how Simon and I got involved with the Marion Center and Dr. Hylbert.

The day that Simon got the diagnosis was one that I'll never forget. The doctor tried to be consoling but the news was devastating. He told me that we were very fortunate to live in North Fulton were the services provided were excellent and that Simon would get the best of care. Though I was still crying, that did make me feel better. Maybe I could find a doctor who could cure him.

I was crushed when Dr. Hylbert told me there was no cure. He said the best that I could hope for was to find a situation for Simon that would stimulate his ability to learn. The doctor gave me a bunch of referrals to other analysts who could help Simon with any developmental difficulties. There were numbers for speech and occupational therapists, behavioral specialists and even support groups for families on how to cope with raising children with neurological disorders. It was overwhelming. He was trying to talk to me further, but I couldn't stop crying. He gave me a prescription for Prozac and told me to take it at night before bed…to relax. I didn't take it though. I don't want to relax. I want my little boy to be all right.

Audrey let the book drop into her lap and wiped away a tear. Simone's hand written squiggles of emotion moved from the page and tugged at her heart. She felt as if she knew the girl. She felt bad that Simone had loved and cared so much for her baby and now was dead.

She wanted to get a greater insight into this young woman who raised her son alone, saddled with the heartbreak of knowing that he was different from many other children. Audrey decided to take all of the notebooks from each box and put them in chronological order. The best way to get to know Simone was to start at the beginning.

*   *   *   *

Jules had a room in the same downtown hotel where Renita was staying with Fran, so she accepted a ride with him. She had always liked Jules. He frequented the Spice Rack, the club where she sang in Rosemont, and they talked often. Well, he talked. Renita mostly listened. Jules was still in love with her sister and when his love would come down on him, he'd come to the club and sip on the notoriously weak drinks and talk to Renita between sets. She told Audrey about the first couple of visits but her sister seemed so disinterested that Renita no longer bothered talking to her about Jules. Besides, he never said anything new or interesting that she could use to pique her sister's curiosity.

"I've never seen Audrey act this way before." He kept his eyes on the road maneuvering the car through the light mid morning traffic.

"She's got her mind made up about adopting Simon. It's ridiculous, Jules. She's never even met the boy. He's autistic and he's not even related to us. His mother was some loopy booty club dancer and one can only imagine the kinds of things she exposed that little boy to. Why would Audrey court those kinds of problems?"

"Because she has a wonderful, loving heart." Jules said with a breathy far-a-way voice.

Renita narrowed her gaze. "What a sap!" She thought. Jules thought Audrey walked on water. Renita looked at him like he was crazy and kept on talking like he hadn't spoken.

"My sister is not being rational. Up until five days ago, she was a single woman looking forward to partying in Atlanta, now she wants to be some sort of den mother? It just doesn't make sense. Audrey doesn't have the kind of lifestyle that would accommodate a child. She's got that small condo, she's always working so who would watch Simon while she's was working?"

"Is that what you guys were fighting about when I came in?"

Renita nodded. Jules rummaged around in the compartment next to his seat for a box of Chiclets. He popped one into his mouth and pointed the yellow box in Renita's direction. She waved it away.

"What about you?"

"What about me, what?" She looked at Jules like his brain had just run out of his right ear. "I know you're not suggesting that I baby sit this kid."

"Why wouldn't you help your sister out?"

"Because I think she's wrong." Renita pouted.

"That's a lame ass thing to say. How many times has she helped you when she thought you were wrong?"

Renita twisted her mouth and looked up at the roof of the car trying to keep from feeling like a jerk. Jules was right. Throughout her life Audrey had always stuck by her, no matter what stupid things or people she got tangled up with.

"Maybe you're jealous." Jules said.

"Jealous? Stop this car!" Renita stiffened with anger. Jules kept right on driving. "I said, stop the mutha fuckin' car, Jules."

He slowed the car and exited at Howell Mill Road. He made a right turn into a small park that was tucked behind a Texaco station and stopped the car. Renita opened the door, hopped out of the car and started walking. She walked around a small track twice before she came back to the car and propped her rump against the passenger side door. Jules had been sitting with his door open, his feet in the gravel and sparse grass. He walked to the other side of the car and collected Renita's hand in his own.

"Audrey is taking a big step, a step that requires a lot of courage. You're absolutely right, she does have a small place, she never had kids, but she did help raise you and Bobby for years while your mother worked after your father died." He looked into Renita's eyes. She skirted her gaze ashamedly.

"She'll have to find a school, tutors, specialists, and God only knows what else in order to help that boy to lead a normal life." Jules continued. "She may not have a big house or a lot of money or time, but she has a lot of love and a lot of heart. I think any child would be lucky to call her Mom."

"You're right, Jules." Renita felt the tremble in her voice and swallowed the emotion before it had a chance to overwhelm her. "You're right about everything that you said. I envy her for taking a stand for something that she believes in when I don't have the guts to do half of what I should be doing. I always told Audrey that I never wanted children and it was true. But I've changed." She pulled her hand away and rubbed the back of her neck. She looked into the distance, squinting at the noonday sun.

"A part of me wants a family too. But I'm afraid to trust a man, or myself with that responsibility." She locked her eyes on his. "It's hard for me to imagine making that kind of commitment. Audrey isn't denying herself. She's following her heart."

"So, are you going to help her?"

"She's my sister. Of course I'm going to help her." Renita muttered.

Jules pulled her to him and hugged her like a brother would. He patted her back and rubbed the soft twists of her hair until she broke the embrace. They got into the car and continued moving toward the city.

CHAPTER 22

▼

Suddenly ravenous, Audrey opened the door, stepped out of the closet and stretched. She looked at the dial of the clock and realized she had been in the closet reading the journals for more than five hours. Looking out of the window she could see that there was plenty of daylight remaining. She thought about getting a sandwich and eating on the patio.

She had taken in a lot of information and needed time to sort things out. It was quiet in the big house but Audrey was certain that Martha was around somewhere. As if they'd installed a motion detector at the entrance to the kitchen, Martha appeared as soon as Audrey's foot touched the earth toned tile floor.

Audrey asked if she could fix her whatever she had prepared that day and that she'd take the meal outside. In nearly no time at all, Martha was rolling a brass cart out to the umbrella-shaded table where Audrey was sitting. She'd prepared a honey glazed chicken breast and three-bean vinaigrette salad. There was a basket of warm bread and a container of butter and jam. Martha poured a tall glass of lemonade before disappearing inside the house. Audrey had to admit, she could get used to this kind of service. Coming home from a hard day's work to a clean home and prepared food was definitely the way to go.

The first mouthful tasted like heaven. The chicken was sweet and tender, melting in her mouth like butter. The salad was so fresh Audrey could taste the distinct nuances of every vegetable and each ingredient of the dressing. When she pulled back the napkin to expose the bread, the steamy aroma gave her a feeling close to rapture. The perfect balance of sweet and tart, the lemonade was delicious.

With her hunger satiated, Audrey tried to organize her thoughts regarding the journals. It was almost as if Simone was taking her on a journey. Like she knew that someday, someone might read her writing. It was a fascinating account and Audrey was caught up in the woman's story.

Simone lost her parents at a young age and went to live with her paternal aunt and an older cousin in southeast Atlanta. She'd braved the torture meted out by her adolescent cousin until he'd gone to juvenile detention and later to prison for a series of increasingly serious crimes. After the boy got sent up, Simone's aunt had yet another reason to take out her dissatisfaction with the world on Simone. Thinking about the horrific abuses made Audrey's heart pound with emotion.

Simone had been raised in a horribly abusive environment where her aunt sold pieces of her flesh to help smooth out an uneven cash flow situation. Lenora Sleighton had, for all intent and purpose, been the young girl's pimp. After she turned Simone on to sex, she then labeled her "boy crazy".

Lenore had weekend card parties where participants drank, smoked, and played cards from Friday nights until the wee hours of Sunday mornings. Players had to tip the house so it was a good way for Lenore to make a little extra money on the side. The players were mostly men and the cheap wine and liquor would loosen their tongues and what little morality they might have ordinarily shown.

> Every time I think about those card parties I get mad. Those rolled up bills Auntie Lee would slide inside her bra before the drinking and smoking began. She made me fix them sandwiches and refill their drinks. She pretended she didn't see them putting their hands up my dress when I brought them their food. I tried to stand as far away from the table as I could or serve it on the side that Auntie Lee or a lady was on. But then she started encouraging me to take the food to the person who ordered it.
> "You should be glad that a good man wants to show you some attention." She told me when I complained.

Led by greed, and her hatred of the child she felt unjustly saddled with, Lenora began charging men to touch the young girl while she slept. Lenora would mix a thick, fruity flavored concoction in the blender, loaded with alcohol and give the drink to her niece so the child wouldn't waken during the night. At first it made Simone feel special when her aunt made her these delectable treats. She looked forward to the nightly ritual when they shared these special moments before bedtime. She'd go to bed at night feeling happy and loved for the first time since her parents died. Simone was hurt and confused when she learned the drinks were full of liquor. The evil aunt introduced Simone to sex and alcohol when she was hardly more than a baby.

Simone described the horror of waking up one night to find one of her aunt's guests in her tiny bed. He covered her mouth with one hand and stuck the other between her legs, ignoring her cries he poked at her until she was sore. When she later told her aunt about it the woman had slapped her face and called her a lying little whore. The next night, Simone went to bed with a steak knife under her pillow. When one of the men came to her bed, she lashed out at him but he grabbed the weapon before she could use it. He slapped her so hard that for a few moments she couldn't hear. While she lay there on the brink of consciousness, the man mounted her and forced himself inside her as she lay there trembling, too afraid to cry.

> *I heard the door open and was so glad to see Auntie's face. She checked me down below and then started screaming every kind of cuss word at that man. But as I listened I realized she wasn't mad at what he did to me. She was mad because he had only paid to feel me up, not go all the way. She told him that if he didn't give her twenty-five dollars, she'd call the cops. Twenty-five dollars. That was all I was worth to her. Twenty-five dollars.*

Audrey thought about the woman she'd met in the smelly, unkempt house and felt like doing a drive-by on the sick bitch. How could anybody hurt a child that way? How could Simone grow up to be a normal person or have faith in anyone or anything after such a betrayal? Audrey's contempt for the aunt grew with each page that she read.

Simone was a light sleeper after that. She refused the sweet tonics her aunt would mix that made her so sleepy. Reluctantly, she began to go along with the routine. In her aunt's words she was already *"spoiled"*. No man would want a girl who'd gone all the way with a man. She took every opportunity to reinforce the growing feelings of insecurity in the girl. By the time Simone was twelve she was a prostitute. Every night the men came. When Simone tried to refuse them, they would beat her. They had already paid Lenora, so they didn't want any resistance from the child. She soon found it easier to let them have their way than to fight. She started drinking the sweet, blended drinks again to ease the pain.

When Simone turned sixteen, she and her aunt had a huge fight. Simone refused to keep doing all the work and giving the money to Lenora. That's when her aunt put her out. Simone started selling herself on the streets of Atlanta.

One night a woman in a white limo rolled up and Simone got into the car. She'd had sex with women before, so to her, a jane was just another john. This client obviously had money to be driven around in the luxurious car so Simone looked forward to a good payday. Full of liquor and weed, Simone was ready for whatever freaky request came her way.

But the woman didn't want to have sex. Her name was Portia. She told Simone that she was looking for girls to work as dancers at her new club down-town. Simone would share an apartment with some of the other girls and she would get one meal a day provided by the company. She would not get a salary but any tips she made were hers to keep. *'The harder you work, the more they'll like you. The more they come to see you, the more tips you will make.'* The woman had told her. Simone saw it as an easy, less dangerous way to make money. No more living on the streets and being at the mercy of the elements of her profession. She started working for Portia that night.

Simone enjoyed her work at the club. She only had to take off her clothes and dance. The men were not allowed to touch her unless she wanted them to, and when they did, they paid handsomely for the privilege. The only thing that Simone didn't like was the times when Portia's Picks were in town. These were the powerful corporate executives, land barons, and magnates of industry who were willing to pay any price to have a beautiful girl in their bed.

Simone would grit her teeth and smile, doing and saying whatever the man wished so that he could feel as powerful in bed as he did on Wall Street.

> *I tell them incredible lies.* Audrey read. *These men are so pitiful you would think they would be ashamed to face their wives and kids after the things they do. But they just keep coming back and back and back. And I just keep smiling and telling them how good they are and how big they are and that it's never been this good for me...*

Audrey had welled up at the thought of a young Simone being used by her own aunt. How awful that a mere child would be put in a position to prostitute herself to survive, and then thinking that it elevated her in some way by working for this Portia character. She was repulsed at the thought of the girl being with men she couldn't stand for money and having the mindset that she had no other choice.

But as the girl grew into a woman she started controlling what she could of a bad situation, asking for a larger share of the take from these high-powered men, and later picking the ones she could tolerate and rejecting the others. Business-men were not her only clients. She also became acquainted with rock stars, movie stars, and athletes.

To Simone, the businessmen were old and boring. The rock stars and Hollywood-types were so basted in alcohol and drugs that sometime in the course of the evening Simone would end up cleaning vomit, excrement or urine from her clothes and skin. But she liked the athletes. They were young, in great shape, and many of them seemed to get off on her having as good a time as they did.

In her writing, Simone rarely used names when referring to her clients. Audrey's eyes became more focused on the words whenever Simone mentioned a professional basketball player. Though she felt like a voyeur, she wanted to see if anything in the description of the client or the way the words were written that would tell her that Simone was talking about Bobby. She physically described the men, but in Audrey's experience, white people described people of color slightly differently than black folks described each other. It seemed like every man Simone was with was described as *"tall, muscular black man,* or *his smooth black skin..."* To Audrey, that sounded about as generic as a media description when a black man committed a crime. Were the men light or dark skinned? What about hair and eye color? Were their tresses long and dreaded; pulled into braids; faded, or completely shaved? There just wasn't that kind of depth in her account of her clients. Perhaps she'd done that intentionally.

"Are you finished with this Ma'am?"

Martha stood before her like a phantom. She started collecting the dishware before Audrey responded, stacking them onto a cart.

"Thank you Martha but I would have brought them inside."

"No trouble at all, Ma'am."

Audrey waited for the spooky old woman to finish her task. Once she was back inside, Audrey extended the chair into the reclining position, relaxed and looked into the clear blue sky. She thought about how it seemed so unfair that there where some people who lived in almost sinful opulence while so many others lived lives that were ugly and harsh where getting a decent meal is a struggle and where nobody loves you at all.

*   *   *   *

Renita hated explaining herself. Fran was looking at her like she had betrayed him. Perhaps his feelings were warranted. He'd re-entered her life at a time when Renita was at a crossroad. She was only using Fran as the walking stick that helped her along a bumpy course. Renita was terrified of aging and seeing Fran reminded her of the time she'd wasted. She wanted that time back. She needed to recapture a part of herself and she had used Fran to do it. It was funny how things sometimes worked out. Lloyd was still angry with her for re-involving herself with the man who caused her so much pain. As she sat next to the person who'd led her to a figurative cliff and gave her a nudge, she felt neither love nor hate for him. And she didn't feel like she'd recaptured something lost either. Franchot Arnaud was nothing more than a one-night-stand who had outlived his expiration date. If she had been as mature a few years ago as she was now she could have saved herself a lot of heartache.

"You come in here and say you're leaving." He searched her eyes for under-standing, but found no emotion in her flat gaze. "What the hell do you expect me to do?"

"I don't expect you to do anything, Fran." She rose from the bed, took a few steps, and then whirled around to face him. "What did you think was going to happen? I live in Ohio and you live in New York. We both came here to work a gig. You knew this was temporary."

"You are holding a grudge from the past, *n'est-ce pas?*" He tone was a blend of anger and pain.

"No, that's not it, Fran."

"You know how I feel about you, *Cherie.* I am opening my heart to you like I have never done with any woman." He moved toward her, dragging her back against him. He wrapped her in his arms and whispered in her ear, "I love you, Renita."

She doubted it. But the fact that he said it let her know just how desperate he was to remain in control. She loved the way he said her name. The heat of his nearness and the thrill of his smell——a pheromone that tickled every erogenous zone, made her want to get back under the rumpled bedclothes with him.

If nothing else, he knew he still had a sexual power over her. That's why he leaned in to her, letting her feel the intensity of his desire. He kissed her, removed her clothes and pulled her back to bed. She'd do it one more time. He was such a skilled lover. What could one more time hurt?

CHAPTER 23

▼

"Oh, there you are." Paul always seemed happy to see her. Audrey was still on the patio, looking out into the greenness of Paul's sumptuous landscaping, thinking about the diaries. She hoped he had some news about Simon.

"Guess what?" He said.

The sun had set and Audrey looked up at his clear, smiling face and sensed he had something good to report.

"It seems that Simon's age, and the fact that he has no mother and father, are instrumental factors in insuring that you get to adopt him." He stopped for a second, enjoying her relieved sigh as the worry lines softened and fell away from her face.

"They will have you complete a background package when you meet with Mrs. St. James tomorrow. It will take a few weeks to check everything out, so you'll probably want to go home to start getting some things in order."

Paul lifted her up from the chair and hugged her; then he kissed her softly on the lips. They looked into each other's eyes for a moment. He kissed her again, deeply. Audrey felt his hands moving over her, awakening parts of her that she had sealed off, saving for Marsh. But Marsh had not only chosen not to make the trip with her, he hadn't returned any of her calls. She suspected he had been with Marlena and she knew he'd lie to her about it when they finally spoke. So she accepted Paul's attention, relaxing and letting him take her to a place where there were no worries about her brother, her sister, or a dead woman and her little boy.

Paul was leading her down to the softness of the lush lawn, and she was letting him, when an abrupt sound behind them tore them from each other's arms. They looked into Martha's cold eyes. She stood a few feet away from them, her thin arms crossed in front of her bony chest. Paul dropped Audrey and turned his full attention to the domestic.

"There's a visitor." She said, before turning and walking in the other direction. Paul followed after her like he was tethered to her waist. Audrey scrambled from the ground, dusted herself off and sat on the edge of an ornate iron settee. She barely had time to absorb what had happened between her and Paul, when he was standing before her once more. He seemed a bit irritated.

"Jules Dreyfus is here to see you. I'll send him out here." Paul said abruptly.

"Sure." Audrey told him. What did Jules want and why was Paul suddenly acting so funky? She wasn't going to waste her time trying to figure him out. She wasn't fooled by his attention. Paul was just horny or predatory. He knew that Audrey was dealing with a lot of issues and was trying to play the concerned friend role hoping she would drop her guard, and her underwear, and he'd be right there to give her what she needed. She kissed him because she wanted to. If she slept with him, it would be on her terms, not his.

She pushed all thoughts of Paul out of her mind when she saw Jules. He wore white linen slacks and a soft white shirt with a few of its buttons undone to reveal his sun kissed chest. The slight summer breeze tousled his hair softly. He looked down at her and smiled. Audrey hoped he had come out here to console her too. A girl could never get too much male solace as far as she was concerned. Jules sat down and took her hands in his.

"How are you feeling?" He asked, looking into her eyes with genuine concern.

"I'm good." She smiled. He released her hands and touched the tiny braids like the little plaits were the most amazing things he'd ever seen on a woman.

"I got the statement from Heather and they're dropping the charges on Bobby."

"That's great!" Audrey said. "Thank you so much for all that you've done."

"I only did my job."

"But you could have told me to take a flying leap when I asked for your help but you didn't." She looked at him squarely. He was about to say something and Audrey didn't know why, but something in his demeanor made her anxious.

"I'd planned on going back to Rosemont tomorrow."

"I can't tell you how much I appreciate you for supporting me, Jules." Audrey was barely able to get the words out. She was literally and figuratively on the edge of her seat waiting to hear what was on his mind.

"How much longer are you going to be here?"

There was something behind the words that made her think he not only meant "here" in Atlanta, but "here" at Paul's house.

"I don't know if you've heard, but I'm strongly considering adopting Simone's son." Audrey waited for him to fall in line with the others and tell her that she was making a mistake. But he didn't.

"I did hear and I think it's great that you would consider something so unselfish. If there's anything at all I can do, you let me know." He pulled her hand to his mouth and kissed it. "I'll even stick around a few more days if you want."

"That's really nice of you, Jules."

"I think what you're doing is an amazing thing and I truly admire you for it."

"Thanks." She smiled. "You know Bobby will be out of here as soon as he's given the green light by the court and Renita is ready to leave too. While I can use all the support I can get, I can't ask you to extend your trip again. You've already helped us so much."

"It wouldn't be any trouble for me. I'd just need to make a few calls"

Two brown doves cooed in the dogwood behind them before taking flight and disappearing into the distance. Audrey followed their course long after they were gone. Without turning she knew that Jules was watching her. He was still in love with her. She cared for him too, but she didn't want to lead him on. The truth was she would love for him to remain in Atlanta until she got everything straightened out with the adoption. Paul was helpful, but she didn't trust him. He was such a shameless skirt chaser. For all of his sanctimonious spouting at Bobby's expense, he was just as much dog as he was man. Audrey knew that his concern for her and the situation was more self-serving than anything else. There was something sneaky about him. He always flirted with her when the two of them were alone, but when her family was around, he kept her at arms length. When Martha interrupted their embrace earlier, he'd pushed away from her, giving Martha the impression it had been she who'd made the advance. Jules didn't want to say it, but she knew he wanted to ask her to leave this place, especially since her family would no longer be there. Audrey didn't want to be here anymore either. She faced him.

"Yes." The word slipped out like her brain was tired of the vacillation.

"Yes?" Jules looked at her hopefully.

"I would like for you to stick around while I'm here. It will only be another day or two. The DFCS caseworker is pushing through the paperwork and also compiling a referral list of doctors and different services I might utilize once we're back in Ohio. I'll have to go there and get everything prepared and then come back here in three or four weeks to get Simon and bring him home."

"That settles it then." Jules clapped his hands together like a kid whose parents had agreed to take him to Disney. Audrey didn't clap her hands, but she was happy too.

*   *   *   *

Lloyd banged on the door a second time before Fran yanked it open with so much force it smashed into the wall and stayed open. He scowled at Lloyd and then stepped aside so the gangling man could enter. Lloyd ignored Fran, knowing that with little provocation he could wrap his hands around the man's neck and snap it like a twig. The only thing he cared about was getting Renita as far away from him as possible.

"Renita you ready?" Lloyd was accompanied by a bellman pulling a tall brass luggage cart. Lloyd nodded in the direction of the zippered designer luggage and the man started loading the bags onto the caddy.

Fran had gone onto the balcony. The sheer white curtains billowed into the room, accenting his angry mood. Renita walked outside and put her arms around him. He stiffened. She pulled away and looked up into his eyes.

"Are you going to be alright?"

Fran snorted, looking down his nose disdainfully. "What do you think I'm going to do, Renita, fling myself over the railing? Why don't you just get out of here while that old man out there still has breath in him."

She shifted her gaze into the darkened room. Lloyd Eckstine, his head held high and shoulders back, glowered at them. The heat of his glare made Renita nervous. Fran turned and looked down at her. His face was a kaleidoscope of emotions. He couldn't understand why she was leaving the city now and why she chose to go with Lloyd, a man Fran saw as a second rate has been. He took every opportunity to demean him, commenting on his age, his deteriorating musical talent and his net worth. Renita would allow a snipe here and there but Fran always knew when he'd reached his limit with her and he'd curtail the verbal assault.

He leaned onto the railing once more, his jaw tight and brow furrowed, looking out on the city of Atlanta. It was a steamy evening with occasional hot gusts that brought little relief. Renita was ready to get about the business of going. She'd turned to go back inside the room when she heard the words slice through his thin lips with enough vinegar to make her wince.

"I won't forget this, Renita." She'd never heard her name spoken with such venom. "You haven't heard the last of this, believe that. For your sake, you'd better hope I never see you again."

The menacing, barely audible words sent a chill through Renita. She stepped away from him and into Lloyd's arms. Franchot could be a very evil person. How stupid she had been for letting him into her life once more. She hoped to God that he would just let this go but she knew there was nothing in his heart for her but vengeance. The question wasn't if he would retaliate, but when.

"I'm ready Lloyd. Let's get out of here."

She examined her make-up in the bathroom mirror and then checked the room one last time to be sure she wasn't forgetting anything. Her heart pumped uncomfortably in her chest as she caught a glimpse of Fran from the corner of her eye. He remained on the balcony. The sheer curtains swirled in the sticky breeze illustrating the sense of foreboding that haunted Renita as his threatening promise played itself over and over in her mind.

CHAPTER 24

▼

Audrey spent Wednesday night reading the journals. She had been in Atlanta a week now and would most likely be leaving Friday or Saturday after getting all of the information from DFCS. At home she could get everything organized and prepared for Simon's arrival. Just thinking about having the boy with her filled her with a nervous excitement. She was looking forward to bringing him home and happy to think of sharing her life with someone who needed her.

Audrey didn't know if she'd be allowed to take Simone's things with her so she'd better get as much of the reading done as possible. Paul had either forgotten about or didn't care about the bag and the boxes. That was good. She still hadn't told anyone about the writings. At first she'd thought she might find something there to implicate Bobby, so she'd held back. After Bobby was released she felt uncomfortable about letting her family know that she was reading someone else's private thoughts. It didn't matter now because Renita and Bobby would be leaving soon. She didn't think Paul gave a damn what the boxes held. She would tell Jules about the diaries when she talked to him tomorrow.

She opened the closet door and went inside. Audrey had gotten through the first few years in the diaries. The more she read she could see Simone's progression. In spite of all of the heartache and desperate situations the girl found herself in, the earlier writings showed that Simone had a great spirit and held out hope that things would get better. The later writing was not like that. Maybe it was her work with Portia. Whatever the difference was, increasingly the words were edged with despair. Audrey read:

November 23, 1998—I was too sick to go to work tonight. I hope I don't have pneumonia. It's all his fault. I hate him! And I hate this time of year. The only thing I wanted was to spend Thanksgiving with him. I was going to cook dinner and we'd have a real Thanksgiving—like a family. He told me that we could spend Sunday night together and we'd discuss the menu.

So last night I got a sitter for Simon, packed my overnight bag and put on the new outfit I'd spent a small fortune on and headed for his place. But when I got there he wouldn't answer the door. I waited outside in my car all night. At about 4:30 or 5:00 it started raining. I continued to wait.

When he finally opened the door, it was to let that whore out. They were so busy kissing and feeling each other up they didn't even notice my car at the far end of the driveway. I know I shouldn't have done what I did, but I wasn't thinking clearly. I ran up on them. I must have called him everything I could think of. What the hell did he ask me to come over there for when he knew he was going to be with someone else?

He slapped me and started cursing at me telling me if I didn't get off his property he'd call the cops. I knew he wouldn't do that because he couldn't take the negative publicity. He certainly doesn't want it to get out that he's got a disabled illegitimate son. He's scared to death that I might tell somebody and tarnish the reputation that he spent so much time and money building.

I don't know when the girl left. He and I stood in front of the house screaming at each other. Out comes his shriveled up bitch of a mother looking at me like I was crazy. Maybe I was. She said 'Don't you have sense enough to know when a man don't want you?' I looked into her beady little eyes and told her to mind her own fucking business. That's when he hit me in the head so hard I blacked out.

He left me sprawled on his lawn. The rain woke me up. I lay there on the grass. My new outfit is ruined...

Well, Audrey thought, whoever the father of Simone's baby was, it certainly wasn't Bobby. The man she wrote about was living in Atlanta. He sounded like he may have been a city official or someone of position who's standing might be damaged if it was discovered that he was lived a less than pristine existence. Audrey read on.

The entries became less frequent with time. It seemed Simone only wrote when she felt really bad. Audrey wondered if she felt bad all the time and just didn't bother writing or if the times she wrote about were those moments when she was at her wits end and had no one to turn to who would really understand.

Christmas, 1999—This is the last year I'll be spending my Christmas waiting for him. I don't know what it is. Why can't I walk away from him? I guess a part of me feels that he still loves me. He must—-we have a baby together. That must mean something to him. Or maybe that's the problem. Maybe he loves me but he can't stand the thought of Simon and the fact that he's not perfect. Well, I won't give up my son for him. Simon is the only thing that I have. I won't abandon him. But the way this life is, somebody might make that choice for me. I have to make a plan for my boy. I don't know what he would do without me. I don't know if anyone else would love him enough to have the patience.

It's very hard. Sometimes, when he throws a tantrum or when I'm trying to work with him on his language, it gets so frustrating. I cry at night when he goes to sleep in my arms. I cry from exhaustion and from the fear I have that he will one day be in this world without me and no one will love him and take care of him.

I look down at his beautiful golden brown face smoothed out by the peace of sleep and think, how perfect he looks. He is the happiest kid I've ever known. He gets pleasure out of the smallest things. When we go out in public he is so happy that he makes loud noises trying to express himself. People give us strange looks or terrified looks or worse, pitying looks, when they realize that something is not quite right with him. I just come out and tell them that he's autistic. The responses are always the same. They fall silent like if they say anything they'll catch it or something. I wish they would just ask me, 'What is that?' or 'What does that mean?' But they just stand there like statues.

But I love little children. They ask a million questions about Simon. The children are not afraid of their curiosity. It's amazing to see the confusion fade and the clarity that brightens their clear eyes when I explain Simon's condition to them in a way that they understand. If things had been different, I would have been a teacher. I love little kids and I think I would be a good teacher. But it's too late for dreams now.

My goodness. Audrey thought as she put the notebook down. The more acquainted she became with Simone she realized that she was not only a good mother, but a good person who just had a lot of bad breaks. Audrey wished that she had known her. She wondered if they would have liked each other. Was she as honest in her walking around self as she was on the pages of her diaries? Probably not. That's not the kind of honesty that the average person has the confidence to portray continually. Surely she felt the need to hide her pain just to make it through the day without breaking down. Audrey continued reading.

New Year's Day 2000—I've reached the end of my rope with him. There was a big party at the club tonight. Portia wanted us all to work the holidays and there was no talking her out of it. I had a dreaded feeling as I dropped Simon off at Mrs. Carter's last night but I went to work anyway.

He came in with his entourage. I felt sick to my stomach when I came out to dance and saw him in the crowd. He acted like he didn't know me. I felt he could at least be decent to me; wish me a Happy New Year or something. I wanted him to like me. I tried to talk to him. I asked him how his mother was doing. That was a mistake. He looked at me like I was a piece of shit, like he couldn't believe that I would get personal with him. He leaned over and whispered something to the man sitting next to him and they both laughed. But all while he was laughing his eyes had that evil look that told me he was mad. I was scared. He had told me before not to speak to him in public.

It was almost four o'clock in the morning when I woke up. He was outside my house pounding on the door. He demanded that I open the door. I was too scared not to. I cracked it open and he pushed the door wide with one hand and grabbed my throat with the other. I couldn't breathe and struggled to free myself from him. He put his face close to mine and whispered, "Stay the hell away from me, do you hear?" I shook my head. "If you ever approach me again, for any reason, I'll see to it that you never see that kid again." I was terrified. I was used to him beating my ass so that didn't faze me. He had never threatened to take my Simon from me.

After all the years of running after him, and wishing and hoping that he would do the right thing, it was that act that broke the chain for me. As bad as I want him, Simon is my heart and my life. I'd do anything to protect him.

He called me a few filthy names, said I was just a piece of trash titty shaker and that the best thing for Simon would be if I weren't in his life anyway. That hurt me more than anything he's ever did or said. For the first time I had to ask myself, by continuing to chase this man, am I doing my son more harm than good?

The entries after that were the sparse, sporadic scribblings of a young woman who had lost a piece of herself. She dabbled in drugs and talked about suicide. Audrey closed the notebook and put it into the box with the others. She felt sorry for Simone and most especially, for Simon.

CHAPTER 25

▼

Audrey heard the telephone ring and a moment later Martha was knocking on her door telling her that she had a call. She looked at the clock. It was fifteen till seven. Who on earth could that be? Perhaps Marsh was finally calling her. No...he wouldn't be calling at this hour. She grabbed the extension on the nightstand and put it to her ear.

"Good morning. It's Jules."

"Hey." The heavy silence on her end of the phone was surely a disappointment to him. If he'd expected her to be excited by his call, he'd expected wrong.

"I thought I'd come and take you to breakfast and we could discuss what you want to do about the adoption."

"That's really nice of you." She perked up. "I have a meeting at ten with Simon's case worker."

"If you want, I'll go with you."

"That would be great." She released a huge sigh and felt the stiffness in her shoulders loosen. "I would really appreciate the support."

"What do you say I come out there and get you and take you out to this great breakfast place that I know about before heading over to DFCS."

"Sounds good to me. I'll be ready in thirty minutes." She said and they ended the call.

Audrey showered and put on a pair of olive colored linen slacks and floral print top. She twisted the braids into a bun with little tips spraying out like birds of paradise. Large gold hoop earrings, a gold bangle and matching necklace completed the look. She was putting on her lipstick when the doorbell rang.

Martha's hand was raised to knock on the bedroom door when Audrey opened it.

"I heard the door. Is it for me?"

"Yes. It's Mr. Dreyfus." She stepped aside so that Audrey could exit her bedroom.

"Is Paul awake?"

"Mr. Radford left at 6:30. He had to go downtown to his office." The way she said it made Audrey feel like a bum for sleeping until seven. The housekeeper seemed to warm to Audrey when she decided to continue with the adoption in spite of the news of Simon's autism. But after Martha had busted her and Paul kissing in the garden, she'd become as evil as a snake. Audrey didn't have time for Martha's moods. She pushed past her and headed for the front door.

"You look really pretty." Jules eyes twinkled as he looked at her. He held the car door open and Audrey slid onto the leather seat and waited for him to get in and close his door.

"You look cute." She replied. He was wearing a pair of tan Dockers and a light green Polo shirt and a pair of Espadrilles. Jules looked like a lawyer on vacation.

"Cute? What is this cute? What am I a Dachshund or something?"

"So what do you want me to say?" She asked, laughing.

"I want you to tell the truth. I spent a lot of time perfecting this look and Audrey, I gotta tell you, I was expecting something a little more along the lines of 'You look fine as hell.' Or 'Damn Jules, I had forgotten how goddamn hot you really are.'"

"You're crazy." Audrey cracked up laughing.

"I'm waiting…" He still hadn't started up the car. His eyes pierced hers. She grinned at him, amused by his pretend conceit. With a few silly phrases he had taken her away from the oppressive stress of the past week.

"Jules, you look fine as hell. As a matter of fact, you are the finest man in all of Atlanta."

"Okay, that's enough. My ego is sufficiently inflated." He started up the car and pulled out of Paul's driveway. Audrey laughed and glanced over her shoulder. She thought she detected the heavy drapes at one of the windows inside the house move slightly. She could feel Martha watching them as they pulled onto the street.

Jules turned the radio to 91.9 FM and they listened to the blend of traditional and contemporary jazz as the car trudged through the heavy morning traffic. They snaked off the exit and merged onto the street. A gleaming white convertible Ford Focus with a ten thousand dollar rim job cut in front of them. The driver and passenger, two white boys who looked about fifteen, bobbed their heads as Ludacris rapped about his sexual exploits. The boy's sound system was cranked so loud Audrey thought the windows would shatter. On the other side of them a girl with golden brown skin and shiny black hair sat in a candy apple red convertible, bobbing her head as Lisa Left-Eye rapped into eternity. From behind them they heard somebody else add Nelly to the mix. Two middle-aged blondes in a purple customized Ford truck turned The Dixie Chicks up full blast and rolled their windows down, sharing the wealth.

"Check this out." Jules nodded his head directing Audrey to look behind her. Nelly had been the contribution of a white man with a head full of long silver hair. He had to be pushing sixty—old enough to know better, and sitting next to a girl that Audrey hoped was his daughter. Jules and Audrey cracked up laughing, tripping at this town that seemed to have a little something for everybody.

They sat in the bottleneck of traffic headed into downtown Atlanta, in the middle of dueling stereo systems backed up by the brass section—a multitude of harmonizing car horns. The scene was a steamy parking lot set to an urban orchestra. Drivers and passengers ignored the battle of the bands or took them in stride, turning their own music up or off, depending on their level of appreciation for rap, country and whatever other music was thrown into the mix.

A pedestrian made the mistake of trying to cross the street at, of all places, the crosswalk and somebody hit him. The incident clogged traffic even further. The whine of an ambulance wailed in the distance. Audrey wondered how the emergency vehicle would cut through the gridlock. It seemed like they were never going to get to the restaurant. Jules suddenly veered the car into a nearby Waffle House and killed the engine.

"Well, this is special." Audrey said. She'd never eaten at the establishment but she remembered seeing the yellow awnings with black block lettering near every exit as they traveled up and down I-75 on family vacations when she was a child. The restaurants hadn't changed much. The outside looked like a cross between a ghetto fish shack and 1950's diner. There were enough vehicles parked out front to fill a car dealership. The buy here pay here kind.

"Sorry, but at the rate we were going we'd be sitting in that mess at least another hour." He looked at the snarl they'd escaped with a wrinkled brow before turning to face the restaurant once more. "Hopefully the food is good and the coffee is hot."

"Well there's a convenience store next door." Audrey quipped. "We can stop there for antacids after we eat."

"Deal." He opened the door and she walked into the cool air and greasy smell that emanated from the restaurant.

A buxom woman standing behind the cash register wearing a shiny brown uniform beneath an orange and yellow striped apron beamed and welcomed them to Waffle House. They smiled and returned the salute before looking for an open table.

Two male cooks worked hard at a grille behind a semi-circular counter packed with patrons who sat like fixtures. Wide hips spread over the sides of the bar stools sturdy enough to support any burden hoisted upon them. A table was finally available and Jules led Audrey through the rows of stiff brown, orange and yellow Formica seats. The décor with its bright colors and early 60's motif took Audrey back to a time long ago. She wondered if she would have been allowed to eat in this very restaurant thirty or forty years prior.

A thick-thighed waitress with pink cheeks and an uneven grin approached their table with a pot of coffee and two white cups.

"Good morning!" She bubbled. "My name is Tillie. Ya'll wont some coffee?"

"Yes." Jules said. "Two coffees please." He grabbed a couple of menus from a metal holder and passed one to Audrey as Tillie filled their cups from the pot that she held. The deep aroma of the brew was like a welcome wake-up call. Audrey sipped, enduring the slight scald to her tongue, letting the drink work its magic on her nerves.

Tillie returned with their silverware and her pad ready to take their orders. They ordered Belgian waffles and eggs. Audrey requested bacon and Jules, a t-bone. The waitress thanked them and turned to fill the water glasses of the people at the next table before taking their orders to the cook.

Audrey thought this would be a good time to bring up the subject of Simone's journals.

"Paul and I went out to Simone's condo and got the rest of her things the other day."

"I would have thought that her family would have seen to that." Jules sipped his coffee, then added another packet of sugar and stirred.

"Simone's aunt didn't want to have anything to do with her. The management at her building said the only thing her aunt took was clothes and jewelry. A garbage bag and some boxes with her records and books were left behind."

"You find anything interesting?"

"A box with books about autism and seizure disorder and two boxes filled with diaries dating back from when she was about sixteen years old." Audrey said before raising her cup again.

"That *is* interesting." Jules said, intrigued.

She answered his next question before he asked it. "I haven't told anyone else about the books. I hesitated to read them, feeling I was invading her privacy. When I did start to read them it was because I thought I might find something that would exonerate Bobby. Now I want to get anything that might help me with Simon and I want to know the truth about what happened to his mother."

"Did the diaries give you any insight?"

"Probably more than I needed to know." Audrey proceeded to tell him about how Lenora Sleighton had led her niece into a life of prostitution and how the girl ran away and became a stripper. She ended with Simone's pregnancy and childbirth and how the father of the baby had rejected them both.

"Who is he?" Jules asked as Tillie brought their food and placed it before them. She heated their coffees and refilled their water glasses before toddling off to the next table. They dug into the waffles and chewed, agreeing that the coffee was weak but the food was good, considering the cost. Audrey could see why the place was packed.

"She never mentions the guy's name." Audrey said after swallowing some water. "He treated her horribly and she stuck around for years hoping that he would be an active part in their lives. According to her writing, he teased her, keeping her on a string for years and she just let him play yo-yo with her head until he got tired and kicked her to the curb—-hard."

"Wow." Jules said. He worked his tongue to dislodge a stubborn piece of meat trapped between his teeth and jaw before washing it down with a few long gulps of water. "So how did she get Bobby involved in this?"

"Apparently, he was one of her contacts from the Platinum Club. When he was playing ball it was one of his hangouts I suppose."

"You didn't mention any of this to him?"

"Not one word. I didn't even say anything to Renita."

"Why are you playing this so close to the vest?" He pushed the food around his plate before scooping a forkful into his mouth.

"I don't know. At first, I was scared that I would find something to incriminate Bobby and then once we realized he hadn't done this, everybody started leaving and there was no one to tell."

"What about Paul?"

"What about him?"

"He helped you take Simone's things to his house." Jules reasoned. "He's not curious about the contents?"

"I guess not. Or maybe he looked inside and thought they were all books and wasn't interested in Simone's reading taste. He didn't know her, except through Bobby so why would he care about her boxes?" Audrey was stuffed and pushed the plate away.

"I was just curious. I guess you're right." Jules checked his watch, and then looked out the window.

"It looks like traffic has slackened a bit. We'd better get down to that office." Jules grabbed the check and threw a few bills onto the table. They paid for their meal at the register and left the restaurant.

CHAPTER 26

▼

Traffic was better but still not good. They made it to the DFCS office with less than ten minutes to spare. At ten sharp, Cordelia St. James opened the door to the waiting room and greeted them warmly. Audrey introduced Jules as her attorney. Cordelia extended a bony hand before leading them inside.

Once they were seated in Cordelia's office, she handed Audrey a fat yellow envelope explaining that it contained an outline of Fulton County adoption policies and procedures. Audrey opened the envelope and peeked at the daunting two-inch thick stack of guidelines. She hoped she wouldn't become overwhelmed before she even started. Jules pried the papers from Audrey's trembling hand. He pushed a pair of readers onto his nose and scanned the documents for a moment.

"I'll read these and highlight all pertinent information for you." He smiled at her and then looked across the desk at Cordelia. "I'm sure that everything will be fine."

What a godsend, Audrey thought. Her initial hesitance about Jules' involvement was swept away; his support was needed more than she could have imagined. She hadn't expected the feelings of anxiety about the adoption that nearly gagged her.

"There is also an application in there that I need you to fill out and get back to me as soon as possible." Cordelia gazed at her squarely. "I won't be able to proceed with the adoption without that form."

"How long does the whole thing generally take?" Audrey asked.

"If everything goes well, anywhere from thirty to ninety days." Cordelia smiled reassuringly. "For older kids, and especially children with disabilities, that time can be reduced significantly."

"Can I see him?"

"Sure." Cordelia smiled. "He's in the Activity Center.

*   *   *   *

Jules held her hand and they walked outside through a neat, grassy play area. They passed colorful swings, slides and a jungle gym, on their way to the center's annex. A lump formed in Audrey's throat as she imagined playing with Simon. They would race on the swings, pumping their legs to see who could go the highest. She snuck another quick look at the play area as they moved past it.

The DFCS Activity Center was a bright brick building with yellow trim. An unexpected veil of panic enveloped her and her feet felt like they were moving through mud. What if Simon didn't like her? What if she didn't like him, or worse, felt nothing?

Cordelia moved her long legs quickly and they had to step lively to keep up. Jules trotted ahead to reach the door before she could open it and held it as the two ladies walked through. They followed a painted paw print wall to a glass enclosed room that held about fifty children. They were busy with computers, video games, cards, and chess sets. Some of the younger ones ran around the room like they had rockets in their sneakers. Though they were all involved in some activity there was no interaction between them.

The adults stood outside and watched the swirl of activity for a few moments.

"You okay?" Jules asked Audrey. She nodded her head. She was anxious to get a glimpse at Simon and hoped they could talk for a few moments.

"There's Simon in the blue and white shirt." Cordelia said. They followed her gaze. It led them to a small boy sitting in front of a computer screen. From where she stood Audrey thought he looked much younger than ten. He was completely focused on the screen in front of him.

"Can I talk to him?" She looked at Cordelia, her eyes twinkling hopefully. Cordelia smiled encouragingly.

"Audrey, children with autism have special abilities. I like to call it autistic intuition." She touched Audrey's hand trying to reassure her. "Simon will most likely figure you out before you do him."

"What do you mean?" If she was trying to comfort Audrey, she was going about it the wrong way.

"All I'm saying is that your genuine concern will reach him even if it seems like your words don't."

A nervous smile danced around the corners of Audrey's mouth. She touched the handle and turned it. Noise spilled out into the hallway when she opened the door. Audrey walked in the direction of the computer lab. There were no doors on the inside of the area, just transparent partitions that separated activities and groups. Simon sat in a room with seven other children; the youngest looked about four, the oldest, around twelve. Audrey was amazed that a boy of about four seemed very PC savvy, clicking the mouse with skill. She could faintly hear a computerized voice encouraging the boy, rewarding correct responses.

Audrey walked past his pod and slowly approached Simon. She didn't say anything to him. If he noticed her, he didn't acknowledge her in any way. Audrey observed him from a few feet away.

His smooth olive toned skin was creamy and unblemished. Long full lashes that any girl would die for dressed lucky lids that never pulled back to betray eyes that remained trained on the computer. His hair was brown, kinky and in need of a cut. He was slight for his age, looking more like six or seven than ten.

Audrey took a few tentative steps until she stood beside him. Simon continued to work the screen as if no one was there but him. She started to call his name, but thought better of it, choosing instead to let him break the ice if and when he felt the need.

She looked at the screen. Simon was playing some sort of phonics game. The player was to choose the correct suffix or prefix and a little bell would ring and a computerized voice would praise the player each time he answered correctly. Simon was right every time.

Audrey wondered if the people at the center had tried communicating with Simon using the computer. The way he was answering these questions, it was obvious he could read. She felt excitement stir in her at the possibility of being able to reach Simon. This proved the boy was educable and that was a huge relief.

She stooped down next to him, still not talking. Audrey detected the slightest flicker as Simon snuck a glance at her before returning his focus to the screen. Audrey smiled. She had a feeling that a good deal of the boy's behavior was very conscious. Perhaps he chose not to communicate verbally because he knew he didn't have to. Audrey began to see this as a challenge that she would welcome. She felt so excited at the thought that she reached out her hand and gently touched the little boy's shoulder.

A sudden piercing scream slashed the roar of youthful play. Audrey's surprise melded into fear when she realized the source of the siren was Simon. He ran from his seat over to one corner of the room. He pressed himself into the crook of the wall, crouching, with his arms wrapped around himself protectively. Cordelia and a Para-professional burst into the room, the latter consoled Simon and got him quieted down. Cordelia searched Audrey's face with concerned eyes. Panic and confusion wrinkled Audrey's brow.

"What happened?" Cordelia asked.

Tear gushed from Audrey eyes, burning her face like acid rain. "I touched him." She sobbed. "I didn't mean to scare him."

"It's okay, dear. You'll never learn where the boundaries are unless you broach them. Once those boundaries are discovered one must challenge those until the two of you reach a common ground." Cordelia touched Audrey's shoulder. "Listen, autistic children are very conscious of their space. Simon will let you in, it will take a little time but you'll get there."

Audrey searched desperately past Cordelia, beyond the glass walls for Jules who was looking in, pacing like a caged tiger.

"I told him to wait." Cordelia said. "We needed to stabilize Simon before we can allow anyone else in."

Audrey looked through moist lashes at Simon. He'd left the corner and was walking around an imaginary circle on the floor. He was babbling and shaking his hands like he had washed them and didn't have a hand towel to dry them on. Some of the other children had become agitated by the commotion. A few of them were acting out now too while others kept about their tasks as if nothing had happened. The center had changed from a tranquil sea of constructive activity to a roaring typhoon of chaos. Audrey couldn't pretend the scene wasn't disturbing.

"Let's go back to my office." Cordelia was almost yelling to be heard over the ruckus. "We'll have some coffee and talk."

Fear rooted her to the spot. Cordelia put her arm around Audrey, shaking away the paralysis. She felt herself moving toward the door; Simon's shrieks and the noise of the other children rang in her ears. Her stomach burned with a feeling of helplessness.

Jules ran to her and pulled her into his arms. Once she'd assured him that she was okay, they followed Cordelia out of the building to her office.

CHAPTER 27

▼

"I know that had to be difficult for you." Cordelia St. James sat behind her desk searching Audrey's eyes, trying to detect her mood. "This is not going to be an easy undertaking and while I'm sorry that you had to experience that, it's a part of what you'll have to expect when you adopt Simon."

Audrey didn't know what to say. She was suddenly terrified at the prospect of dealing with a child with special needs when there was so much that she didn't know. Cordelia had said *when* you adopt Simon, not *if*, like it was already a done deal. What was she getting herself into? A simple touch had caused the boy to go into total meltdown. She wasn't equipped to parent a handicapped child. Renita was right; her own selfish arrogance had put her in this situation. Who did she think she was approaching a handicapped child who didn't know her?

"I can imagine what you must be thinking." Cordelia was saying as if reading her thoughts. "Even under the best setting, adopting a child is daunting enough."

"Can we talk to some parents of autistic children?" Jules asked. Audrey shot him a quick glance. He was able to remain levelheaded through the whole ordeal. "I'm sure these kids have good and bad days like anybody else." He said.

"You're absolutely right." said Cordelia. "But even on a good day many autistic people are sensitive about their private space and some don't like being touched."

"So if he doesn't want me to touch him how will I be able to raise him?" Audrey finally found her tongue and forced out the burning question. If she couldn't reach him, how would this work? This whole thing was a mistake.

"He has to get to know you. It's going to take time. He's still waiting for his mother to come and get him. There's no way we can get him to understand that she's never coming back. We haven't been able to communicate with him like we'd want to, but he responds well using the computer."

"I noticed that. He knows how to read." Audrey stated.

"What? How do you know that?" Jules asked.

"I saw him playing this phonics game on the computer. He created sentences and finished stories. He never missed one time."

"Some autistic people have extraordinary memories." Cordelia said.

"So."

"Simon has memorized all of the right combinations and he's completing the exercises by rote."

"But isn't that a big part of what learning is…memorization?" Jules contributed.

"True. But comprehension is the key and that's where most autistic people have problems. Even when some have a general understanding of what is read, few are capable of complex thought."

Audrey and Jules slumped in defeat. Cordelia smiled soothingly.

"On the other hand, many people with conditions in the autism spectrum possess cognitive and creative abilities that are far beyond the norm. This isn't a hopeless situation. It requires patience and it's important to educate yourself as much as possible." She looked down at her watch.

"I'm sorry, but I have another appointment in a few minutes. In light of what happened today I think it would be a good idea to give this some more thought. Weigh all the pros and cons and see if you can get a support system in place. It's important that you have family and friends who will be there when you need a respite. You'll be exhausted a good deal of the time."

They rose to leave but Cordelia stopped them before they left her office.

"Mr. Dreyfus, you asked about talking to parents of autistic children?" Her eyes darted from one to the other before continuing. "Our son Jonah is twenty. He was diagnosed when he was three and a half. If the two of you want, you can join us for dinner tonight."

"I had no idea…uh, thank you." Audrey said, glancing at Jules who gave the social worker a grateful smile.

"How about eight o'clock? Cordelia's brow wrinkled. Jules and Audrey nodded in unison. "Give me a call here at the office before four thirty and I'll give you directions."

*   *   *   *

The mail that had piled up and the wilted, scrawny leaves of her plants made it seem as if Renita had been gone much longer than a week. It felt good to be home. She touched the power button on the remote, filling the house with music from the sound system.

Renita plopped down on the sofa and started going through the mail. The few items of interest were opened and inspected; the rest were tossed into the trash bin or onto the cocktail table to deal with later. She rose from the couch moving fluidly toward the bathroom humming to the music while she pulled off her clothes.

She took a long hot shower, dried off and then wiped the steamy glass clear. Her body seemed different, more alert. Her small breasts looked fuller, the nipples ripe and swollen to attention.

"Damn girls, settle down." She coaxed. "Ya'll can't be telling my business." Renita ran through a mental Rolodex of paramours trying to think of one who might be lusty enough to satisfy her itch. She fanned herself with her hand before she started the process of oiling her body. She sprayed on a cooling floral fragrance before pulling on her panties.

She put on her make-up before selecting a flowing, multi-colored skirt and peasant blouse. The gleaming, deep brown skin of her shoulders seemed more alive than usual. Renita felt a weird current running through her. Fran violated the peace in her mind with a sharp visual of his angry face and his rancorous parting threat. Remembering him standing on the hotel balcony, the sheer panels billowing in the hot, foreboding wind made her shiver. Renita knew that he was planning his revenge. She shook away the chill and finished dressing. She liked her vision in the mirror and decided she'd treat herself to an early dinner. She had to go downtown anyway.

She and Audrey had made up after the screaming match they'd had the other night. The stress of dealing with Bobby being suspected of killing Simone and Audrey's ridiculous plan to adopt a ten year old autistic boy that wasn't related to them had taken its toll. Sure she felt sympathy for the little boy but her sister was thinking with her heart and not her head. What would she do if the whole thing proved too much for her? It wasn't like Simon was a handbag or a sweater and she could return him. Renita felt bad for not being supportive, but she would have been lying if she hadn't voiced her concerns. In the end, she just wanted

Audrey to be happy. Renita finally threw her support behind her sister. She would have said or done anything to close the rift between them.

She had promised her sister that she'd go by her office and make sure that everything "looked all right". Bobby was back in town and the office manager they'd hired was professional and efficient. There was no reason for Renita to go by Audrey's office. Audrey didn't say it, but Renita knew what she really meant was *go by my office and see what the fuck is going on with Marsh.* He hadn't called Audrey the entire week she was in Atlanta. Audrey tried to play it off but Renita knew that she liked him a lot and was, at the very least, disappointed that he hadn't taken the time to call.

Taking one more approving glance at the glowing creature that looked back at her from the mirror, Renita grabbed her purse and keys and pulled the door closed. She got in her car and drove into downtown Rosemont.

*   *   *   *

A short yellow man with stiff hair and Garfield pop eyes came out of Marsh's office. He rolled his big eyes around Renita's petite curves before offering her his hand and a toothy smile. Though he wasn't attractive he walked with a sexual swagger that Renita found hard to resist. Confidence was the ultimate aphrodisiac.

"What can I help you with?" He said it like he was hoping she'd say something nasty. Or maybe she just took it that way cause she was so horny. Renita reconsidered her initial impression. He wasn't really *that* pop eyed; hell some people would say he had bedroom eyes. As she accepted the smile and offered one in return she tried to remember if there was some saying about men with big eyes, or maybe that was big feet. She glanced at his slick leather shoes and felt her nipples hardening. They seemed to take on a life of their own, shooting like hot bullets trying to tear through the filmy fabric of her blouse. Renita knew her body well enough to know what it was telling her. She tried to stay focused on the reason for her visit.

"I'm looking for Marshall Fixx." She pulled her hand from his grip, smoothing it over her breasts trying to calm them. Renita knew the little man was going to ask her out and she knew she would go with him.

"Mr. Fixx moved back to our East Coast branch. My name is Ernest Pressley. Why don't you come into my office?" He hadn't stopped showing those long, sparkling teeth. "I'm sure that I can take care of you."

"What? Marsh is gone?"

"Yeah...just this weekend. I'm heading the Midwest offices now."

"But he...uh, never mind." Renita turned to leave.

"Wait a minute. You sure I can't help you with something?" Ernest Pressley took a step in her direction. His voice cracked with disappointment.

"No, I'm sorry I bothered you." Renita stumbled out of the office and headed outside to her car. How could she tell Audrey that Marsh had left and hadn't even had the decency to tell her? She felt her anger rise as she turned the key in the ignition.

"That lowdown son-of-a bitch." She said aloud. The car screeched recklessly into traffic. Renita ignored the expletives and the blare of horns from the cars behind her.

CHAPTER 28

▼

After they left the DFCS office Audrey wanted to get back and finish reading the last few pages of Simone's journals and weigh the day's developments into her decision to go forward with the adoption. She needed to be alone to properly sort everything out. This was going to be harder than she'd ever imagined. She didn't feel it right to just abandon the boy. What kind of person would she be if she walked away from him before she even gave it a chance? She told Jules she was tired and had a bad headache.

"Go get some rest." He'd said. "I'll be back out here at seven sharp." He kissed her lips lightly and gave her hand a squeeze before she exited the car. She waved as he backed out of the driveway. Martha opened the door and Audrey slipped into the coolness of the mansion.

She went to the bedroom and laid her purse and jewelry on the dresser. She hadn't seen or talked to Paul since he punked out on her that day in the garden. She wondered what was going on with him. He had been so helpful at first but lately he'd been distant. Audrey was glad that Jules had stepped in when he did.

She grabbed her briefcase, remembering how her sister had laughed at her for bringing it on vacation. "I can see you're going to be a lot of fun." Renita had said. She missed Renita. She was glad they had mended the gaping hole the fight had torn in their relationship the other night. She'd give her a call later that evening. Right now she wanted to plot exactly how she could make this work. If she couldn't get it to fly on paper, she'd never make it work in the real world.

Audrey pulled out a yellow legal pad and sat down on the bed. With her pencil, she scored lines the length of the page making two columns. In the first, she wrote the names of her family and close friends. Then she included the names of any associates who might be able to assist, including her next-door neighbor Mrs. Mashburn and her office assistant, Dorothy Lofton. Next to each name she noted ways that person could assist her. The page was soon filled with everything from baby-sitting and help with homework to fill-ins for field trips and social events.

She started a new page and jotted down everything she could remember of her conversation with Cordelia St. James. She added the names of the agencies she would need to contact in Ohio and the types of professional services the case-worker had said would be helpful to Simon. She also noted classes that would be beneficial, like learning sign language and maybe even CPR.

As soon as she got home she would plan a dinner and inform invitees that the dinner was a solicitation of help with raising her son. Her son. Wow, that was the first time she'd put the two little words together that would create such a huge change in her life.

She picked up the phone and dialed Cordelia St. James' office. Cordelia was busy but took a few moments to hastily give Audrey directions to her house and her cell phone number. After hanging up, Audrey felt like she'd accomplished a lot since her meeting this morning at DFCS.

She raised her arms and stretched them over her head before leaving the bed and going to the closet. She grabbed the journal from the top of the box she'd opened, brought it to the bed and started reading.

March 27, 2002—I saw him on television today. He was discussing his new book and...

"What are you reading?"

Audrey was so startled she fell off the bed.

"I didn't mean to scare you." Paul said with a laugh, reaching down to help her up. "I just hadn't talked to you in a while and thought I'd see how you were doing."

She was so tired when she'd come in she'd left the door ajar. The closet door was open too. The three cartons sat on the closet floor, the lid to the side of one. Something had told her not to discuss the journals with Paul and now here she was—busted. How long had he been looking over her shoulder before he'd announced himself? Her best bet was to play it cool.

"I finally opened those boxes we got from Simone's." She tried to sound casual. "It's just some books and stuff."

"Looks like some kind of diary to me." Paul said. "Let me see that."

Audrey moved the book away from his reach. Think fast girl, she told herself.

"There's a boxful," she said. "Get your own." This was the only one of the notebooks she hadn't read and she wasn't about to give it to him.

Paul reached into the box and pulled out one of the diaries. He'd kept his back turned to Audrey as he scanned a few of the pages. Audrey observed him silently. The book trembled slightly in his hands a moment before he steadied it. He stared at the print without speaking. Audrey's heart pounded so loudly she was sure he must hear it. When he finally spoke, his tone sent an eerie chill down her spine.

"This is interesting." He said. "When did you say you started reading these?" His eyes burned into her. She gazed back with doe eyes that she hoped would not reveal her fear.

"Just now." She lied. "I had a meeting today with the DFCS worker and thought there might be something in the boxes that would help me understand Simon's condition." That part was true. Paul's gaze shifted. He suddenly closed the book and placed it onto the box. He turned in a deliberate manner like he was being guided by remote control.

"Martha will be fixing dinner soon. You will be joining us, won't you?" A smile, devoid of humor, never reached his cold eyes.

An alarm suddenly sounded in Audrey's head. The last entry she had read ran across her mind like the scrawl on a cable news channel. *I saw him on television today. He was discussing his new book...* She already knew from previous reading that the man in Simone's life lived in Atlanta. Paul lived in Atlanta. He'd authored several books and he had a talk show. He was still waiting for her answer. *I'm staying in the home of a killer*, Audrey thought. Panic pounded her chest and she struggled to keep her face composed.

"Thanks but I have dinner plans." She didn't want to talk to him anymore. She looked at the clock on the dresser. It was nearly six o'clock. She still had to shower and change. She jumped up from the bed urgently. "I need to be getting ready."

A low rumble bubbled up from somewhere in the back of Paul's throat that he tried to pass off as a laugh. He still had that crazy looking smile plastered on his face. He took a couple of steps back toward the door like he didn't want her out of his eyesight. He stood for a second before walking away without saying another word.

Audrey closed the door and took the journal that was on the bed and shoved it into her valise. She went to the closet and knelt before the box that Paul had taken the notebook from. Careful to set that book aside, she shuffled the journals in both boxes so that they were no longer organized chronologically. She snatched one out at random and spread it open on the bed. She put the book Paul had looked through on top of the open box.

She heard the doorbell ring ten minutes after she'd showered and dressed. Paul was standing at the front door talking to Jules. He looked normal, like the Paul she'd known for years. But now she'd been enlightened by Simone's detailed account of the unsavory underpinnings of Paul's sterling persona. Now that the mask was cracked, Audrey felt like running in the other direction.

"Well," Paul said. "Here's our girl now." He smiled at Audrey. He was a devil in the guise of a trusted family friend.

"You seem a bit flustered." Jules smiled at her, his hair was still damp and she could smell his shampoo and aftershave. He had on a big tan shirt and baggy-legged olive-green slacks that tumbled fluidly over the tops of soft leather sandals.

"Just rushing to get ready." Her voice wavered thinly into the air. She needed to relax until they were safely out of the house. She changed the subject.

"You look, like totally hot," she said in a mock valley-girl way. "What ever happened to those buttoned-down shirts and wing tips?"

"I have a confession to make." Jules looked from Paul to Audrey, issuing an easy grin. "I invested in a personal dresser."

"A what?" Now she'd heard everything.

"I always admired guys who had a flair for dressing so I hired a professional dresser to help me put the right combinations together."

"I've had a dresser for years." Paul said. "In my profession every detail counts and I've never had a fashion eye. As a matter of fact, I couldn't coordinate my way out of a wet paper bag. You should have seen me a few years ago..." He quipped in simulated self-deprecation.

Audrey felt like slapping that Hollywood grin right off his face. What a fake! She clutched her stomach. He was making her sick. But she couldn't let him know that she knew he was a treacherous, murdering louse. She ignored the nausea, laughing a bit too loudly. She waved a cavalier hand as Paul continued to relay tales of his lack of fashion sense. Audrey even played along with the discussion, but all she could think about was getting away from him.

"You guys know Sears has had that same thing for years." She injected.

"Really?" Jules blinked questioningly.

"Really. It's called Garanimals." She quipped.

"Cute." Jules tapped her on the butt and she squealed. "Let's get going. See ya' round, Paul."

"Later." Paul held the door open for them.

Once they were safely inside the car and headed down the street, Audrey pulled the notebook out of her valise and told Jules what she'd read and Paul's reaction when he'd caught her with the journal.

"I knew there was something wrong with you." Jules' eyebrows knitted together in concern. "That's it. You're not staying there another night."

"I'm not going to argue with you." Audrey looked out at the traffic still heavy with people leaving work late and going about their evening activities.

"All kinds of things have been running through my mind. Is he Simon's father? Did he kill Simone? If he did, why?" She wondered out loud.

"I don't know the answers to any of that, all I know is that after our meeting with Ms. St. James we're getting your things and moving you out of there."

CHAPTER 29

▼

They slowed the car when they approached a sign announcing *Rolling Glen Plantation* in an Atlanta suburb called Lithonia. Jules made a left turn and followed curving streets leading to the last house in the subdivision. It was a sprawling ranch style home built on a five-acre lot. A lush magnolia was the centerpiece of the tightly manicured lawn. Neat rows of white edged hostas flanked the stone walkway leading to the main entrance. The smooth flagstone path separated plush green grass from beds of hearty, multicolored flowers that preened haughtily on either side of the ornate glass and oak door.

The air was filled with the mouth-watering aroma of barbeque grilling. Jules pushed the buzzer and a few seconds later the door was opened by a dumpling shaped woman with islands of splotchy rosacea coloring her fair skin. Wispy hair that still had hints of its original red peeking beyond the predominant gray strands, fell from a loose bun on top of her head. She smiled at them politely.

"Miss Wilson and Mr. Dreyfus?"

They nodded and the woman stepped aside so they could enter. The spacious foyer, with highly polished wood floors, opened onto a sunken living room that was surrounded on two sides by glass. Beyond the expansive pane was a stone patio, lush greenery, and a shimmering pool reflecting the remnants of daylight that waned into the early evening.

"Please make yourselves comfortable." The maid told them. "Mr. and Mrs. St. James will join you shortly."

Audrey and Jules eyed each other, both impressed with the elegant comfort of the home. They didn't have time to sit on the soft white sofa before Cordelia St.

James and the portly gentleman Audrey had seen in the photo in Cordelia's office entered the living room. Cordelia extended her hand.

"Audrey Wilson, Jules Dreyfus, this is my husband, Wallace St. James." Cordelia was absolutely radiant. Audrey didn't know if it was the love of a good man and owning a beautiful home or a good line of cosmetics, but Audrey wished she had some of whatever it was. Cordelia towered over the rotund Wallace St. James, who exuded the same resplendence as his wife. Audrey had never met a couple that complimented each other more.

"Welcome, welcome." Wallace St. James had a smile that was nearly as broad as his stomach. His highball glass was filled with something that looked like a red slushy. He waved it around as he spoke. Glancing over his shoulder, he motioned for them to follow him onto the patio.

"What would ya'll like to drink?" He tipped his glass in the direction of the bar. "Eric makes a mean Maui Wowie."

They walked through the glass doors onto the patio. The outside was dressed for a Hawaiian luau, complete with strategically placed flaming torches and fake pig dressed with tropical fruits and flowers as the table's centerpiece. A youngish, blonde man wearing a black and white uniform tended a full bar at the side of the pool. In keeping with the tropical theme, Audrey requested a mai tai; Jules asked for scotch and water. They sipped the drinks, looking around at the beautifully landscaped grounds.

"Are you expecting others?" Audrey asked taking in the lavish display.

"No, you're it." Their host said. "We like to make dinners an event. It keeps things interesting and it sure beats the hell out of meatloaf."

"Wallace is quite the romantic." Cordelia said.

"Your place is *really* nice." Jules said, regarding Wallace. "If you don't mind my asking, what do you do for a living?"

"I work for the State Department. If I tell you any more than that, I'm afraid I'll have to kill you." He dissolved into belly-busting laughter, slapping Jules on the back so hard some of his drink sloshed onto his hand. Cordelia shook her head and handed Jules a cocktail napkin.

"Honey, please…see, this is why we never have company." The fact that she was completely mad about her husband was apparent and refreshing.

"I think I'll try a Maui Wowie next round." Jules said good-naturedly. Cordelia smiled.

"This palace is the property of the United States Government." Wallace told them. "Did ya'll check out that sign at the entrance to the subdivision?"

Audrey remembered the sign, *Rolling Glen Plantation*. She and Jules nodded.

"I figure if Uncle Sam was going to keep me on the plantation, I was going to let white folks work in the fields and we'd run everything else." He said, not giving a damn if he'd offended Jules. "My entire executive staff is African American. All of the flunky jobs are held by whites." He laughed again.

Jules nodded before raising his glass to his lips.

"I made it clear when they hired me that I'm not from the Moteesa tribe." Wallace eyed Audrey like they shared a private joke.

"Moteesa?" Jules said. "I'm afraid I'm unfamiliar with different African tribes."

Wallace, Cordelia and Audrey erupted into laughter. Jules looked from one to the other completely confused.

"It's not African." Audrey was laughing so hard she was blinking back tears. When she'd finally pulled herself together, she continued. "More tea sir."

Jules' face remained blank.

"More tea sir." Cordelia said and then scratching her head and using a southern accent, "Mo Tea Suh? Moteesa. It's kind of a Black Thing, meaning you're not going to be disrespected."

Jules flushed, shaking his head in understanding before crumpling into laughter.

"Hey, you all right with me." Again, Wallace slapped a meaty hand onto Jules' back. "Sometimes the best way to fight ignorance is with humor. What else can you do? I sure as hell ain't gonna cave in to their nonsense. And believe me, I've seen plenty of it." He sipped from his cocktail glass. "They gave me grief about my hiring methods at first, but by the time I got finished sighting all of the examples of them doing the same thing, they backed off."

"He only gets away with it because he's the best at what he does." Cordelia beamed proudly before sipping from her wine glass. It wasn't lost on Audrey that they still hadn't mentioned the type of work that Wallace did. She'd glanced at Jules when Wallace made the statement about his hiring practices and noticed that it didn't faze him in the least. But then why would it? Jules was one of the few people she'd ever met who seemed unaffected by race. It had been she who couldn't deal with an interracial relationship and had stopped seeing a man that she really liked because their union made her self-conscious.

"Jonah is in his room dressing." Cordelia offered. "He had to work late today."

"Boy is so particular about what he wears," Wallace said with pride. "He should have been out here by now."

"Here I am." They all turned to see a thin young man with a baby face and innocent smile of a child. At nearly six feet tall, he'd obviously taken his height and honey colored skin from his mother. The facial features were a younger, slimmer version of his father's. Cordelia's eyes twinkled as she introduced him. Jules and Audrey shook hands with the clean looking young man.

"Let's sit down." Wallace said, leading them to the table. He pulled out his wife's chair before taking his place beside her. Jonah sat on the other side of his father. Jules slid Audrey's chair away from the table and helped her into it before sitting down.

A slender, gray haired man of average height with patrician features appeared from somewhere inside the house and filled their water glasses.

"We'll serve ourselves from the buffet tonight, Henry." Wallace said. "If you'll bring the dessert cart out that will be all for the evening."

"Thank you, sir." He said and then addressed the table. "Enjoy your dinner." He said ceremoniously before heading back into the house.

Audrey hoped this wouldn't be the night that the white staff decided to get back at Massa' by adding some deadly spices to the meal. Wallace St. James displayed such virulence about the majority society she wondered how his household staff was able to remain professional. Perhaps they were paid so well that they didn't care what he thought about them.

She and Jules collected their plates and followed Wallace to a table banked heavily with food. Appetizers included a variety of fresh fruits, cheeses, smoked salmon dip and an assortment of salads. There were entrées of grilled chicken, fish and ribs. Audrey's mouth watered, She selected a bit of everything that she saw, careful to keep the portions small. She didn't want to get so full that she'd be unable to partake of the luscious desserts Henry left close enough to the buffet to tempt.

The table was quiet for a few moments while everyone settled themselves and their heaping plates at the table. Wallace rushed through the blessing, ignoring the raised eyebrow of his wife. The food was delectable but Audrey spent just as much time observing Jonah as she did her plate. She didn't want to be rude, but wasn't he really the reason they were there? She wanted to ask him a million questions.

She noticed a deliberation in everything that he did. It was as if he were running through a mental list of behaviors and consciously choosing the correct action. He'd taken his plate to the buffet and selected mostly vegetables and fruit. He took his time with his plate, slicing his food into tiny pieces before putting it to his mouth.

"So, Audrey," Wallace said. "Delia tells me that you're considering adopting the son of the poor woman that got killed at that hotel." His knife and fork were poised over his plate. His gaze held hers. He listened intently, still working the remnants of his last mouthful.

"Yes. Initially I was doing it because I thought he was my brothers'…well, let's just say I want to be a mother and he's lost his, so I thought, why not?" She decided against getting into Bobby and his mishandling of everything from the first news of little boy's birth to Simone's death.

"Usually people want to adopt babies. Older children, especially those with special needs aren't even considered." He stated. "It's important to have a strong support system in place."

"I'm working on that." Audrey mumbled. She was starting to feel the strain once more of the whole thing. If the very thought of everything that she had to do was making her this tired, what would it be like when she was actually raising Simon?

"It's going to be an arduous undertaking," Wallace was saying.

"That's what I keep hearing." She looked at her hosts and then at Jonah. "Can I ask you some questions?"

"You can ask us anything." Cordelia said.

"I mean you, Jonah." She looked at his smooth face. He had been totally absorbed with his dinner. When she said his name he looked at her and smiled.

"How old are you?" She asked.

"I'm twenty years old." He said in the voice of a child. "My birthday is March eighteen and then I'll be twenty-one."

"What do you like to do?"

"What do you like to do?" he repeated, his eyes looked past her like he was really considering the question. "I like to play with Kenny. We go to the park sometimes and sometimes we go fishing. Last time, I caught a fish this big." He held his hands about a foot apart.

"Kenny is the neighbors son." Cordelia interjected. "There's a stocked lake on the property that we love." Audrey smiled at her and then addressed Jonah once more.

"Do you like your job?"

"I like my job. I won a present for attendance and I won another present for um, um," he looked off for a few seconds and then smiled. "I won another present for customer service."

"Jonah works as a stockman at Kroger." Wallace said after reaching for his water glass. "Tell her about your promotion son."

"I got a new job managing the grocery inventory. That means I'll be counting all of the grocery that is received and keeping track of it as it's sold on a computer." The boy said. "That starts next Monday."

"That sounds like a very big job." Audrey was encouraged.

"It *is* a very big job, and it's important too." Jonah stressed.

They all laughed. Jonah seemed pleased that he was making everyone happy. He was still laughing after everyone else had stopped. Wallace eyed him like only a father could before Jonah stopped snickering and turned his attention to his plate.

"Jonah has excellent math and organizational skills." His father beamed. Audrey wondered if it was hard for him having a son with diminished capacities. It seemed that in many cases men left the burden of child rearing up to the woman. She supposed most men wanted his son to be an athlete or possess the sharp mind of a scholar. How involved would a man be if his son couldn't play catch or throw a pass?

"How do you get to work?" Jules asked Jonah.

"Sometimes Mom takes me. Sometimes I take the bus." Jonah said. "I have to be careful when I take the bus because sometimes I fall asleep on the bus or I forget to get off at the right stop."

"That happens to everyone." Jules smiled reassuringly. "One time I fell asleep on the bus and woke up all the way at the end of the line."

"That happened to me too, Mr. Dreyfus." Jonah picked up his water and drank down the entire glass. He belched loudly and quickly put his hands to his mouth. "Sorry."

He snickered. His mother gave him the 'mother eye' and he stopped. "One time I got on the bus and fell asleep and I didn't know where I was. I was very scared. The bus driver called my Mom and she had to come and get me."

"I bought him a pocket alarm and set it to go off at five minute intervals to keep him awake." Cordelia said. "He has a phone now too, so we can keep in touch throughout the day. I try to drive him as often as possible, but there are days when he has to get around on his own."

"We don't want Jonah to be totally dependent on us." Wallace added. "When we first found out that Jonah was autistic it was devastating. I'll be the first to admit that it was harder for me to accept than it was for Delia. She was great. She immediately started reading, attending counseling and talking to doctors."

"That's when I went back to school part-time and got my masters in social work with a duo concentration in child psychology and neurological disorders." Cordelia said. "Education has always been my way of dealing with challenging situations. We immediately enrolled Jonah in speech and occupational therapy and even a few experimental therapies; some were helpful, some not."

Audrey listened to them for the next hour as they talked about their support structure. They had an extended family utilizing the services of their parents and siblings when they needed a breather. Their family and friends were a big help in allowing them to get away when the stress of raising a child with special needs overwhelmed them. They traveled, and when they couldn't get away, they made evening meals an adventure. The St. James' believed in enjoying life to the fullest. Audrey came away from the evening feeling more assured in what she was doing. Would it be easy? No. But she wanted to adopt Simon and she knew that she had plenty of love to give him. She would have to take some time off to prepare for all the changes that were coming to both of them. She looked forward to the future with the nervous excitement of any expectant parent.

"Thank you so much." Audrey and Jules hugged Cordelia, Wallace and Jonah St. James at their front door and headed for the car.

"How are you feeling?" Jules asked her.

"Pretty good." She leaned over and hugged him. "Thank you for doing this for me."

"You know how much I care about you." He pulled her closer. "Tonight wasn't about giving a ride to buddy who's down on his luck or something. I want to be included in the circle of support for Simon. I want to be a part of your life."

CHAPTER 30

▼

Audrey didn't know what to say to him so she didn't say anything. She already had a man waiting for her in Rosemont. She didn't think Marsh would go for some weird three's company *trois*. She would not re-involve herself romantically with Jules and she knew that was what he wanted, no matter how sincere his desire was to help Simon. Perhaps he'd detected that he'd frightened her by his forwardness. They were silent all the way out to Paul's.

Jules pulled up in front of the sprawling grounds of Paul's East Cobb home and turned off the engine.

"You want me to come in with you?" He asked.

"No, it shouldn't take me long to get my things. I don't have much." She left her valise and purse in the car and trotted to the front door and rang the bell. It was nearly midnight and she felt like a kid who'd missed curfew as she waited for the door to be opened.

Martha's frown was so deep it pulled her chin down to the loose wrinkles of her neck. She stepped aside and let Audrey enter.

"Is Paul here?" Audrey asked.

"At this time of night, I should hope so." Martha muttered as she trudged off to bed.

Audrey didn't have time to deal with Martha's attitude. She was going to thank Paul for all that he'd done, but she was tired. She had a lot on her mind and Martha had pissed her off.

"Whatever." Audrey said, dismissing the old woman's evil attitude. She was sick of Martha, Paul, Atlanta and the whole scene. "Let me get my stuff and get outta here." She said to herself.

Jules was still staying at a suite at the Marriott and they had agreed that Audrey would sleep on the pull out couch. They would be in Atlanta at least another day or so. She'd come back for Simon after she got everything settled at home.

Audrey took her toiletries from the bathroom shelf and put them inside her overnight case. She pulled her suitcase from beneath the bed and clicked it open. She'd packed most of her things from the dresser before going to the closet. The garbage bag was open revealing a jumble of clothes and shoes. Simone's three cartons were gone.

*   *   *   *

Renita felt sick as a dog. She'd run to the bathroom several times but was rewarded with gagging dry heaves that produced clear, bitter tasting fluid that made her feel even worse. She never got sick so these queasy feelings she had over the past two days were baffling.

She scratched at an old mosquito bite on her arm.

"I hope I ain't got West Nile Virus." She said to herself. Then she thought it might be food poisoning. When she got back in town she'd gone to her favorite seafood restaurant. Perhaps she was having a reaction to the mussels. Remembering the meal caused her stomach to lurch and her head to swim. Clutching herself around the waist, she made her way back to the bedroom. She glanced at the glow of the digital clock on the nightstand. It was three-thirty a.m.

"Shit!" It would be hours before she could call her doctor's office and who knew if they could even see her today. The way she was feeling, she'd never last another five or six hours.

She went back to the bathroom and looked in the medicine cabinet. A half full bottle of antacid tablets stood next to an ancient box of Band-Aids and an old prescription for antihistamine spray. Renita grabbed the container of antacids like a hungry man going after food, and smuggled them back to her bedroom.

She chewed two tablets and then let another dissolve in her mouth. Relief was immediate and comforting enough to let her relax the grip she had around her waist.

Maybe it was her guilty conscience making her sick. She had spoken to Audrey briefly last night and hadn't told her that Marshall Fixx had left Rosemont. She wanted to, but Audrey was talking so fast about everything that was happening in Atlanta that Renita found it hard to get a word in. And this was a biggie, not really something that she wanted to just drop on her without being there to console her. But she knew she would have to find a way to talk to Audrey about this before she came home.

Her sister was sharing a suite with Jules at his hotel. She'd been feeling more and more uncomfortable around Paul. Renita pressed to find out why, but Audrey said she would fill her in on that later. What she really wanted to talk about was Simon.

Audrey had just returned from having dinner with the DFCS caseworker. Renita knew that it was selfish of her, but as soon as Audrey started going on and on about her plans to go forward with the adoption, Renita found her irritation level rising. How could Audrey seriously consider bringing that boy here? Hell, he wasn't even related to them. She said he'd had some kind of fit and it had almost made her change her mind. Renita wanted to shout, "Maybe that was God trying to tell you something." But she bit her tongue.

Audrey had prattled on about the visit to Cordelia's house, her husband and their grown autistic son. If that wasn't enough to make her reconsider what she was doing, Renita didn't know what would. It was storming in Rosemont the night they talked. Thunder rumbled in the distance and lightening crackled as they spoke. Renita used the inclement weather as an excuse to get off the phone.

Renita was glad that Audrey had turned to Jules in her time of need. Lord knew she could use all the support she could get since she'd decided to go forward with the adoption and since Marsh picked such an inopportune time to show his true colors.

A tickle of nausea wriggled inside her and she uncapped the bottle of medicine and gulped another pill. She closed her eyes and sucked another tablet, trying to relax while she waited for the discomfort to pass. When the queasiness refused to leave her she rolled from the bed and padded on bare feet to the kitchen. Renita rummaged through the cluttered cabinets until she located a tin of tea bags. She filled the kettle and sat hunched over in her seat as the waited for the soft rumble of heated water to whistle the signal of readiness.

The hot drink helped her physically, but her mind was troubled. What on earth was wrong with her? She was rarely sick and with so many recent friends and acquaintances coming down with every illness in the book, Renita began to think that her number was finally up. She thought back to a conversation she'd had with Audrey when they were in Atlanta about turning her life around. She hadn't prayed in so long that she couldn't remember how to start. God knew that she had been away too long and this sudden showing of piety would certainly not fool Him. A sharp cramp stabbed at her. The queasiness twisted her gut like kneaded dough. Renita's fear and discomfort overcame the feelings of hypocrisy as she fell down on her knees and lifted her head upward in prayer.

CHAPTER 31

▼

As far as Audrey was concerned seeing that the boxes had been removed from the closet meant only one thing, Paul had killed Simone and he wanted to make sure she hadn't left anything behind that would tie him to her murder. When she told Jules her thoughts, he wasn't persuaded that Paul Radford was involved in any way shape or form. They argued all the way downtown.

"So you accept this as coincidence?" Audrey asked.

Jules nodded. He'd had room service bring up a pot of coffee and a tin of biscotti. They sat nibbling the cookies, sipping from plain china cups and trying to make sense of everything that had happened recently.

"I don't buy it. What other reason would Paul have for moving the boxes unless he was trying to hide something?"

"Who knows?" Jules stopped for a second to wash down the sweet bread with a sip of coffee. "Maybe he didn't want that clutter in his house."

"It seems awfully funny that he would care about a few boxes that were left by someone who he claimed he didn't even know." Audrey didn't care what Jules said. Paul was acting more and more suspicious. She was glad she'd left his house and that she'd had the foresight to take the last journal with her.

"Let's read the last journal." Jules suggested. "It may hold the key to everything."

"You know, it's funny." She mused. "When I first started reading Simone's diaries I was afraid that I might find something to incriminate Bobby. In all honesty, I don't know what I would have done if I had been the one to uncover evidence that my own brother was a killer." She pulled the book from her valise and looked at the ominous manual like it was a snake poised to strike. "Now I'm afraid for Paul. I've always admired him. He's built a fortune out of nothing. I don't want to be the one to bring him down."

"Honey, you're not bringing him down." Jules grabbed her hand and laced his fingers in hers. "If he's involved in Simone's death he brought himself down and he's got to pay for what he did."

Seeing that she was still reluctant to open the book, Jules released her hand and pulled the journal away from her.

"Give me the damn thing. I'll read it." His blue-green eyes pierced her dark ones. He pulled the cover back and started reading aloud.

May 27, 2002—I saw him on television today discussing his new book. His talk show is going into syndication. I know it's sick but I feel happy that he is so successful. Just knowing that the father of my baby is such an important man gives me chills! But I have to admit I got mad the longer I listened. The interviewer said that he was widely regarded as the most sought after motivational speaker in the nation charging fees of up to one hundred thousand dollars per engagement.

That's when I exploded. All these years I've been struggling to support us, lying to a man for child support for a kid that don't belong to him. His own father hasn't given a dime in years, so I have to shame myself by putting my baby on a man who I know is not his daddy. Bobby gives me a lot of grief, but he put us in this nice condo and he pays the child support on time. But it's humiliating. I put up with getting cussed out by Bobby Wilson so Simon and me could get enough money to pay our bills and provide the services that Simon needs while his bastard of a daddy is living the high life. Well, I'm not taking this shit anymore. I'm going public. By the time I finish with his black ass he won't have a dollar to buy a Coke.

"She doesn't mention any other names here..." Jules flipped through the pages, he looked at Audrey like she had a screw loose. "How do you figure she's talking about Paul?"

"Because he's a former pro basketball player, turned motivational speaker turned author who has a talk show. There just ain't that many brotha's out there that's got it like that." Audrey curled her lips impatiently. She was convinced the mystery man was Paul and therefore, past trying to figure out who. Now she wanted to know why. Audrey sought concrete proof of Paul's guilt or lack thereof, so she could put closure on this whole thing and satisfy her own mind.

"You want to finish reading, or shall I?" She asked, reaching for the notebook. Jules smacked her hand playfully and jerked the book out of her reach.

"I'll finish." He turned his eyes to the journal and started reading from the next page.

May 28, 2002—I drank a whole bottle of bourbon before I got the courage to go to his house. I was too afraid to drive in that state, so I took a cab. The damn thing cost me thirty-five dollars one way and I had to get the cabbie to wait because I didn't think it very likely that <u>he</u> would bring me home.

I sat outside the compound thinking about the last time I'd come there. That time he'd left me laying face down in the mud as thunder and lightening crashed over my head. It hurt like hell to come back there but I was determined not to take any more crap from him and make him pay for all the years he'd done me wrong.

The cab driver was fussy and was irritated that I could barely understand what he said because he had some kind of accent. He pointed at the front of the car and told me the meter was running. I reached into my purse and gave him a fifty. That shut him up. He put on some headphones and turned on a portable CD player. I opened the door and approached the house.

As usual, his old witch-faced mother opened the door. Imagine, making your own mother wear a maid's outfit and clean your house. How fucking warped is that...?

"What? Martha is his mother?" Audrey was incredulous. She snatched the book from Jules like she had to see what he'd read for herself.

"You still don't know if she's talking about Paul." Jules looked at her and shook his head. "Jeez Audrey, you could never be a juror, that's for sure."

"It's just so obvious that she's talking about Paul." Audrey was pensive for a moment. "But why would he turn his own mother into a maid?"

"Why would his mother put herself in that position?" Jules wondered, moving closer to the journal. "My mother would pop me in the head if I even thought about asking her to do that."

They looked at each other bewildered at human nature and the things that people do that seem to make no sense at all. Audrey looked down at the book and started reading where Jules had left off.

She always hated me. She thought I just wanted her son for his money, but she's wrong. I love him and I wouldn't do anything to hurt him. Well, at least that's how I used to feel. But as I continue to deal with Simon all by myself it just makes me kind of mad that he doesn't care and refuses to acknowledge him in any way. Simon doesn't deserve that. He's a beautiful, bright boy who just happens to have a disability. That gives his father no right to treat him like a thing instead of a person. To tell the truth, treating him like a thing would be better than pretending that he doesn't exist.

I told her I was there to see P...

"See I told you." Audrey said, slamming her palm against the book.

"That still doesn't prove anything." He nudged Audrey with his elbow. "It could be someone named Peter, or Patrick, or Philip…"

"Let it go Jules, okay?"

"Just finish reading." He rolled his eyes and expelled an exasperated breath before turning his attention back to the notebook.

> *I told her I was there to see P. She told me that he wasn't in and if he were he wouldn't want to see me. I told her I'd wait. That's when he came from somewhere in the back of the house and shoved me away from the door. I knew that he would behave like this and I told him that he was being filmed from the car across the street, and then I pointed to this delivery truck that just happened to be parked on the street. My cabbie friend had exchanged the music for a newspaper. He was peeping from behind it looking at everything that we did so P. caught himself before he did anything stupid. I told him that I was going to sue him unless he started taking care of his damn kid.*
>
> *The look on his face was priceless! He was craning his neck to get a closer look at the truck. Then he looked at me like he wanted to kill me. He started calling me all kinds of names like he usually does. I pulled the big button on my blouse and pushed it to his mouth and said, "Speak into the mic, please." That really pissed him off. It was all I could do to keep from laughing. He started to hit me but I moved out of the way and pointed to that truck. I was praying that they wouldn't pick that moment to drive off.*
>
> *He asked me how much I wanted. When I told him a million dollars, he didn't care about being recorded or what the cab driver might hear. He started calling me every name in the book. I told him to just have my money by the end of business tomorrow or I was going to the press.*
>
> *Knowing him, I wouldn't be surprised if I started having a streak of bad luck. Well, he can try something if he wants to. For the first time in my life I feel empowered. I guess once I woke up and realized that he not only had been disrespecting me, but disrespecting our son, I just don't give a damn anymore. I got me a gun from Stephanie, a girl at the job whose old man is a gunrunner. I know how to use it too. If P. gives me any shit I'll blow his fucking head off.*

"Wow!" Jules exclaimed. "Simone was certainly no pushover. I guess all the hard knocks helped her in a sense."

"Yeah, but now she's dead and my brother came very close to being sent up the river for a crime he didn't commit." Audrey said. "Not only that, he's been paying child support for years for a child that's not his."

"That was pretty evil of her to do that intentionally." He agreed. "But in a situation like that, a man should always get a paternity test."

"Bobby, in his wisdom, felt it was cheaper to give her twenty or thirty thousand dollars than give her hundreds of thousands, so he never got tested." Audrey shook her head, still not understanding her brother's reasoning.

"He was really getting reamed! In addition to paying child support he was footing the bill on the condominium where Simone and her son were living." Jules said. "He's making arrangements to have it sold."

"I don't feel sorry for Bobby. He's gotten a hefty deduction from the interest on the property and he claimed Simon on his taxes. Simone didn't really hurt him at all." Audrey fingered the page. She was anxious to go on but Jules held his hand on top of the sheet as he continued to muse about Simone and her reasons for making the choices that she'd made.

"Still, for a woman to do that to a guy…She must have convinced Bobby that he was the child's father or he wouldn't have gone along with it. But on the other hand, think about all of the guys who father children and don't take care of them." He scratched his head and issued Audrey a sidelong glance. "And I hate to say it, but if you believe the media, pro basketball players seem to shoot their seed just as often as they shoot the ball."

Audrey cast Jules an annoyed frown.

"Can we just read the rest of this thing so I can get some sleep?" She wished she had read all of the journals before talking to Jules about them. Now instead of her being able to read them and interpret the writings for herself, she had to wait for Jules to have a sidebar after every entry.

He finally removed his hand and Audrey read aloud from the notebook:

May 29th—I got a call this morning from some fancy pants law office telling me that the transaction had been completed. I was to go to Wachovia Bank on Roswell Road and see the branch president. P. had set up a fund for Simon for which I was custodian. They needed the name of a beneficiary in the event of my death. Even though P. had done what I'd asked him, I knew it was just a matter of time before he'd make me pay for backing him into a corner like that. That's the way he is. Having a beneficiary was a smart thing to do. There was only one person I could think of that I could trust to take care of my son if something happened to me. I'll have to tell him the whole story and he's not going to like it. He'll get over it though. My main concern is taking care of my boy. I'm going to take care of P. also…once and for all. That stinking bastard can't be trusted. As a little extra insurance, I opened a safe deposit box. I'll use it to keep the tapes, documents, and notes on all of his criminal activity. The upside to hooking is that men talk far more than women do. There are people we know in common who have given me information about P and they didn't even realize who I was. I know about his

holdings in the Platinum Club and his involvement with the drug dealers and gun
suppliers that do business there. If he fucks with me, everybody will know.

"So she's got a safe deposit box at the Wachovia on Roswell Road that con-
tains information that would tie Paul to criminal activity! You go, Simone!"
Audrey raised her fist in the air and pumped it. "And all this time I'm thinking
Simone is broke and she's sitting on a million dollars!" She let the journal drop
onto the bed.

"We need to find out if she left a will." Jules said. "Otherwise that money's
going to be tied up in probate and depending on the laws of the state of Georgia,
may revert to the state, or back to the originator of the fund."

"That would be real jacked up." Audrey frowned. That being the case, Paul
would have more than enough motive to want Simone out of the picture.

"It won't be too hard to discover how Georgia law deals with this situation."

"But she said she named a beneficiary." Audrey picked up the journal again
and traced down to the part that supported her statement. "I wonder who that
was and if she ever got around to doing it."

"We're going to have our hands full tomorrow doing research." Jules said
looking at the clock. "Let's get some sleep. We can read the rest of the diary
tomorrow."

CHAPTER 32

▼

Audrey was sprawled onto the let out couch; the pillows had been tossed onto the floor and the covers twisted around her like clinging kudzu, evidence of her tormented sleep.

CNN projected violent images from the Middle East on the television. The sound was turned down low. The air conditioner hummed lightly in the dimly lit room that was otherwise silent. Audrey leaned over to glimpse at the clock on the nightstand and saw the note on white hotel stationery propped up with her name scrawled in Jules' handwriting. She reached for it and held it open.

——Consulting with a lawyer friend on Simon's trust and Ga. State law issues. Back by 10:30…J

It was almost nine o'clock. Audrey rubbed the sleepiness from her eyes, yawned and headed for the bathroom. She brushed her teeth and took a long hot shower and dressed in a flowing colorful skirt and matching top. She needed to touch base with Cordelia St. James and check in with Renita, Mrs. Mashburn and her office manager.

Audrey put on her watch and gold hoops and moved her make-up case to get the garnet bracelet. It wasn't there. She left the bathroom and checked the dresser, the nightstand and the bed. Nothing. She pushed away the panic that arose at the thought of losing the keepsake. It was the first piece of jewelry her mother had given her and the most special. Now it was gone. It couldn't be.

Tears sprang to her eyes and her heart pounded. Audrey tried to calm herself. She had to think rationally and then maybe she could remember where she'd left it. She sat down on the bed and retraced her steps. Where had she seen the brace-let last? Had she worn it to Cordelia's house? No, she had left it on the dresser at Paul's. But she didn't remember retrieving it when she'd gone there to pack her things. After she'd discovered the disappearance of Simone's boxes, she was so distracted she had gotten careless with her packing and failed to check the room one last time to make sure she was taking everything. She would have to go back to Paul's to get her bracelet.

Martha answered the phone on the first ring. She told the maid she'd left a few things there and asked if it would be okay if she stopped by. With Martha's assur-ance that the visit was okay, Audrey grabbed the square white stationery pad and wrote a quick note to Jules, grabbed her purse and went downstairs to get a taxi.

*   *   *   *

Renita had called Audrey's cell phone several times last night but each time got her voice mail. She was getting the same thing now. This time she didn't leave a message. Irritated, she slammed the phone onto the receiver.

"That girl won't keep her phone on to save her life." Renita muttered. She was exhausted from a fretful night where she couldn't seem to find a comfortable spot on her bed. Her irritable stomach woke her up for the third morning in a row and wouldn't let her rest. She would make a doctor's appointment and perhaps Dr. Beavers could give her an antibiotic or something to get rid of this thing that had been dogging her for days.

Renita mumbled a curse when she felt her stomach churning again. She just barely made it to the bathroom in time for the toilet to catch the Chinese food she'd eaten for dinner last night.

*   *   *   *

Audrey paid the cab driver and the yellow car pulled slowly out of the drive-way as Audrey rang the doorbell. Martha opened the door and stepped aside to let Audrey enter. She seemed strange somehow, even for Martha. Audrey remem-bered what she'd read in Simone's journal and thought about this person being Paul's mother. She caught herself examining the diminutive woman's face in an attempt to match her features with those of her alleged son. Audrey couldn't make a connection. She smiled nervously and brushed past Martha, walking in the direction of the bedroom. A sharp pain sliced through the back of her head as she put her hand on the knob. Suddenly, everything went black.

CHAPTER 33

▼

The slicing pain jabbed her awake. She tried to put her hand to her head but found that her hands were taped behind her back. She lay in a contorted knot on the floor of a one-room space that looked like a storage area. A broad band of tape covered her mouth so close to her nose it partially obstructed her breathing. She looked around the dim, unfamiliar room licking at the tape until it began to loosen. The adhesive tasted terrible and caused her mouth to go dry.

Her feet were not tethered and she struggled to stand. The pain in her head made her rethink that plan. Instead she tried to wiggle out of the tape handcuffs. The few minutes of the activity left her exhausted with nothing to show for her work but swollen hands. After a brief resting period, Audrey was ready to try again when she heard voices. She closed her eyes, feigning unconsciousness just as the door to the shed opened.

"Oh my God, Mother, what have you done?" It was Paul. He bent down beside Audrey and touched a spot in the back of her head and she nearly cried out from the pain that his touch sparked.

"She'll be alright. You oughta be thankin' me." Audrey heard Martha's thick sounding pumps stop near her head. She sensed the woman's presence above her as she joined her son. The phony accent was gone. "I couldn't let her ruin you. I knew we hadn't heard the end of Simone. The little whore is determined to have the last word. Even if it's from the grave."

"Forget about Simone, Mother. Did you at least get the journal from Audrey before you knocked her out?" He asked.

"I checked her bag and it's not in there."

"Couldn't you have found another way to search her bag without going upside her head? Now we've got to come up with a reason why my maid would knock a former houseguest over the head." Paul was exasperated.

"If we get rid of her we don't have to come up with anything. If anyone asks we'll simply say she left here yesterday and we haven't seen her since." Martha explained.

"But what about the taxi. They'll have a record of her trip here."

"Oh."

"Is that all you have to say?" Paul had lost the little boy voice and now sounded more like he had when he'd argued with Bobby the other night. Audrey heard what sounded like a slap across the face.

"You watch your mouth, boy."

"Yes, Ma'am." Paul muttered in a juvenile tone.

Audrey heard pacing and then an abrupt stop.

"We'll say she was a prowler."

"A prowler? Nobody's going to believe that."

"Why wouldn't they? She had moved out. We had no idea she was here. I heard someone in the house and I got my gun. I didn't know it was a former houseguest until too late. I'm an old woman. I won't get convicted."

"I think it might work." Paul was sanguine. Audrey heard the snap of his fingers. "Yeah, you were working in the house and didn't hear her come in. She was snooping around out back and surprised you and you shot her." He was touching Audrey's head. "We'll have to come up with an explanation for this nasty bump."

"The hell with the bump, we have to get that book." Martha's voice sounded closer. She had stooped down next to Paul.

Audrey eased her eyes open. The woman squatted next to her son. She rubbed his head comfortingly before kissing him full on the lips. Audrey's eyes became round as saucers. She slammed them shut and thought she must be dreaming. She kept her eyes closed and waited for the pounding pain in her head to lessen in intensity.

"They're all alike you know. All those bitches are the same, love." Martha said coquettishly. "They just want to take everything we've built. But I won't let them. Nothing is going to stop us. You are going to be the most powerful black man America has ever known. It's your destiny." There was a pause. Movement.

"Don't pull away, love." Martha said in the seductive tones of a woman much younger. "You know that I've done all of this for you. It pains me to pose as your maid but it has been through this guise that I have been able to get next to folks and hear what they really think during parties and other occasions when they think nobody's listening. That's how we got the goods on Senator Gamble. He won't be re-elected next year. You'll move right into his office in Washington."

"Are you sure, Mother?"

"Has Momma ever lied to you before? Don't you ever forget that I brought you from this very house we're standing in, to that mansion on the hill. The exploratory committee has all but assured your nomination. You'll hold the Senate seat for two terms and then, victory is ours!"

Audrey heard movement and then what sounded like a struggle.

"Stop pulling away from me!"

"But Mother…"

"Hush, boy. I gave you my whole life so you sit still till I'm finished."

"But Ma…"

"Ma, nothing! You have to take care of your physical needs and you can't trust those whores. None of them. When the time is right, Momma will pick the right girl for you. Someone who can support you properly…stand by you when you take the helm. But you have to do what I say."

"But I'm doing everything that you tell me." Paul whined.

"You can do better. You have a weakness for bad girls. I've got to keep them away from you or everything will be destroyed. You have to remember that none of them will ever love you the way that I love you."

Audrey could hear the sound of kissing again. Breathing, moving. Her stomach soured and she wished she could tune out the sounds of their sick relationship. She wished she could get up from the floor and run away. But she was far too weak and the pain was excruciating. Even if she could run, they would catch her before she reached the door. She didn't doubt for a moment what they would do to her when they did. There was so much property on Paul's estate that they could drop her in a hole and nobody would ever find her. She heard more movement, a step or two and then short quick steps. They were standing now.

"What's the matter, love?" Martha cooed in the voice of a girl in love.

"Can we do this later, Mother? What did you do to her anyway?" Paul asked.

"I hit her in the head with a hammer, baby." She replied like it was the most natural thing in the world. "Then I drug her out here to the shed. She wants to expose us, just like Simone wanted to. I had to stop her. If I hadn't, who knows what she would have done?"

"But she said she just came to get the rest of her things. You should have let her check the room and while she was doing that, you could have gone through her bag to see if she had the journal." Paul was frantic. He paced the space like a nervous cat. "It's going to be hard explaining that bump on her head."

"Will you shut up about that fucking bump?" Martha shouted.

"But what if she's dead?"

"Well she's not dead. Not yet, anyway. We'll think of something."

"We already thought of something. We have to kill her. If we don't, she'll go blabbing to everybody and they'll hate me. They'll hate me just like when I was in school. I can't take them laughing at me again, Mother."

"Don't worry, dear. Mother will take care of it like she always does. I won't let anything destroy what we've built. And nobody's going to laugh at my baby."

"Well, what if they don't buy the prowler story?"

"Ssshh!"

Audrey heard the sound of lips on lips again, and then the rattling of paper.

"Here love, have some candy."

"Oh goody! Jordan Almonds! Thank you, Mommy." Paul's voice had become childlike once more.

"Did I ever tell you why I gave you these candies when you were a boy?"

"No, Ma'am."

"I remember cleaning up after them filthy whites while they walked around living high like the world owed them everything. While I cleaned Mrs. Hoyt-Grafton would sit on her wide ass and read or watch TV and eat this candy. Before I left at night I would fill my pockets from the bag in her pantry and sneak them home for you and the girls."

She held her story for a few moments like she had gone back in time. Martha began again.

"I just didn't have the energy to give ya'll what you deserved. I wanted my kids to have something pretty in this ugly shack we lived in. I wanted you to be happy if only for a moment."

"We were happy, Mother. This is still my favorite candy." Paul gobbled the treat like a young boy.

"You trust Mother, right?"

"Yes, Mother."

"Have I ever let you down?" Martha asked him.

"No, Mother." He said between chomps on the pastel confection.

"Come here, sweet boy."

Overwhelmed by the pain in her head, Audrey was mercifully lulled into a state of unconsciousness and spared of hearing the disgusting sounds of what happened next.

*   *   *   *

Renita sat upright on the table in the cold room waiting for her doctor to return. What the hell was taking so long? It was freezing in here and Dr. Beavers was taking her own sweet time. The receptionist had worked her in on short notice so she shouldn't complain. Renita hated going to the doctor and when she did go she wanted everything to be as quick and painless as possible.

She rubbed her arms to melt the chill bumps before hopping off the table and selecting a magazine from the rack on the wall. She rejected two outdated copies of *Time* and a worn *People* before choosing *House & Garden*. She flipped through the pages of *H & G* distractedly before tossing the magazine onto the table just as the doctor opened the door. The dumpy, pink skinned nurse who had taken Renita's blood earlier was with her.

"Sorry to keep you waiting." Dr. Harriet Beavers, with her short cropped curly gray hair and dazzling lab coat, entered the room in a swirl of white. She pulled Renita's chart from beneath her arm and whipped a pair of thin, wire-framed glasses from her coat pocket. She took a moment to read the page before glancing at Renita over the rims of her glasses. Renita could read nothing from the stillness of her face. The nurse looked out of the window. Something was wrong.

"What?" She asked. Dr. Beavers was usually much more chatty than she was today. Renita looked her doctor in the eye. She held her breath and waited. Renita was sure she wasn't going to like what she was about to hear.

"You're pregnant." Dr. Beavers said.

Renita opened her mouth, but no words passed her lips. Her eyes rolled back and she fell to the right side of the table. The nurse and Dr. Beavers moved quickly to catch her before she hit the floor.

CHAPTER 34

▼

Audrey's eyes creaked open. The concrete floor of Paul's shed was sticky with her blood. She listened. Silence. Her mouth was parched and her head throbbed. She didn't know what time it was or how long she'd been there. With any luck, Jules had gotten her note and was en route. But what if he did come to get her? Martha would simply tell him that she wasn't there or had come and gone. Then what? Jules would have no other choice but to leave and there was no one else in Atlanta who knew her or that she was being held prisoner by this sick, incestuous mother-son duo.

Her hands were not as swollen now and the band around them had loosened. She didn't want to risk swelling them again so she made a slower, more deliberate attempt this time to free herself. Sweat beaded on her forehead. The beads connected and trickled down her face in streams and then rivers. She murmured a 'Thank You, Jesus' when the tape finally eased enough for her to slip one hand through. She pulled the sticky binding from the other hand and wiggled her stiff fingers until she felt circulation returning. Her hands were sore, making removing the tape from her mouth more difficult that it should have been. The sticky swatch finally came loose and she tossed it onto the floor.

Audrey tried to rise. A searing pain and dizziness stopped her. She held her breath and summoned her strength to try again. After several minutes she was able to sit upright. She put her hand to the huge knot on her head. It was tender but it probably felt worse that it was. Her braids were bloody and matted. Her skirt was ruined by dirt and blood. Crimson sticky wetness and sweat caused her blouse to cling to her. When she looked down at the spot where she had been laying, she understood why Paul had sounded so worried. There was a thickening scarlet pool on the floor the size of a dinner plate. Audrey shuddered thinking that this was her blood and she was likely to lose more than that if she stuck around there much longer. One of her shoes was turned on its side beneath a tiny window. She rose cautiously and wobbled in the direction of her shoe.

"Ow!" Audrey lifted her foot and looked down. A hard-shelled pink-coated almond was embedded into the ball of her foot. She dug it out and threw it against the wall before collecting the hardwood soled slide. Changing her mind, she almost cast the shoe aside. What good was one shoe going to do her? Then she realized she had no purse, nothing to use as a weapon. Who knows, maybe the shoe will come in handy. She retrieved the pitiful weapon and slid it onto her foot.

She reached for the doorknob. It was locked. Audrey felt like crying. What was she going to do? She looked at the tiny window once more. She blew away a coating of dust and tried to raise it. It was rusted shut. There was no way she was going to get her hips through that thing anyway, she thought. Think Audrey, think.

At first she thought she was in some sort of storage shed, but after closer examination she realized it was an old house. It had a rusted out basin and age crusted toilet in one corner. In the other stood a rickety iron cot. A rag pallet set up like a trundle was positioned underneath it. Dusty, moth-eaten, handmade dolls were propped beside the bed. A tiny wooden truck was parked at the foot of the bed. The scene was so eerie that Audrey found herself imagining who the owners of the battered playthings had been. She let go the reverie. She had to get out of there.

There had to be something here that she could use to jimmy the door lock. She started opening drawers and boxes that held mostly papers. Rickety furniture was piled in one corner of the room. She pushed an old chair that blocked a bookshelf. On its bottom row was a dusty red toolbox. Next to the rectangular box were the cardboard boxes that held Simone's diaries.

Audrey tried to slide the toolbox from the shelf but it was too heavy. The height of the shelf wouldn't let her open the tool chest all the way but maybe she could open it enough to extract a weapon. She pried the rusty lid, chipping two nails and drawing blood. She nearly had the toolbox open when she heard the jingle of keys. She quickly pushed the chair back in front of the bookcase and sat down just as Paul opened the door.

"So, I see you're awake…and you've managed to free yourself as well." Paul beamed, and then said disingenuously, "I like you Audrey. You're a very resourceful person."

"What's going on Paul?" Audrey tried to keep the tremor out of her voice. "Why are you holding me here like this?"

"You know damned well *what's going on*." He said the last three words with a feminine lilt, mocking her. The man was a nut, and here she was locked in this prison waiting for him to finish what his mother had started.

"You killed Simone, didn't you?"

He ignored her.

"Most of the few black athletes who are fortunate enough to make real money squander their fortunes. Many of them are just as ignorant as Bobby. The only things they care about are cars and whores. Bobby could have been like me, but he's stupid and has pissed away his opportunities."

A pain shot through Audrey's head. She wanted to lash out at him in defense of her brother. Paul's eyes twinkled evilly as he continued to vilify Bobby and other professional athletes. A shadow of hate enveloped him, curling his lips as he spoke. Icy fingers of terror did a spider's crawl up her spine as she realized that she was locked in the airless room with a madman.

"I am one of a handful of black men in America to amass an empire. We plan to go all the way to the top."

"What are you talking about?" Audrey wanted to keep him talking. She figured as long as he was talking to her he wouldn't be killing her.

"I'm going to run for U.S. Senate next year and in a few years…I'll be sitting in The White House!"

A mad glint lit in his eye. Audrey blinked in disbelief.

"The what? You're crazy."

Paul snatched her up by her blouse and brought her face to his. Her feet dangled a foot off the ground. Hot anger sizzled from every pore and heated his cologne. It was the same fragrance he wore when he lifted her the night of the banquet. It was the same cologne he was wearing when they kissed in the garden. It was the same scent that clung desperately to the handkerchief an equally desperate Simone had pressed between the pages of her journal.

"I'm not crazy!" He hissed.

When he spoke a few drops of his hot spittle sprinkled her face. His breath smelled of chocolate and almonds. Her stomach churned with nausea and then knotted with fear. He released her and she flopped onto the dusty chair, her heart pounding rapidly. Her eyes followed him as he paced, throwing his hands wildly in the air as he ranted about the things he'd done to remove himself from his impoverished roots. Audrey was afraid to blink. Taking a few steadying breaths, she asked him, "Why did you kill Simone?"

"What makes you think I killed that piece of garbage? I wouldn't waste my time."

"Well somebody did. Maybe you were afraid that she'd tell the media about Simon."

He cocked his head and his face took on a wondering gaze like he was really considering the statement.

"She threatened me." He said. "What do you think would happen if the world found out that I had a bastard son by a common street whore? The boy is a retard for God's sake. I'm not about to let anyone know that I could spawn a defective child."

"But you were trying to help me adopt him, Paul."

A high-pitched giggle escaped his lips. His eyes crinkled behind the red frames of his glasses.

"What do you think I am, a deadbeat dad?" He folded into a fit of wild laughter.

Paul was insane. After all he'd been through to overcome his speech impairment, he should have been sympathetic to others with developmental limitations. Instead, he resented them. But even his madness didn't override the powerful blood tie that he felt for his son. Paul couldn't walk away from his son. If he were with Audrey, he would know that the boy was okay.

He moved closer. His menacing face contorted until he looked like a crazed animal. "Simone kept threatening to go public." He smirked evilly. "Now she can't."

"So you *did* kill her."

"That bitch dealt with the lowest common denominator. Anyone could have killed her. All I had to do was bide my time." He gave Audrey a pitying look and smiled.

"I'm afraid you're the one who'll break my cherry." He laughed wickedly. "No, I didn't kill Simone, but I'm afraid I will have to kill you, my dear. I don't see how I have any other choice."

"I have nothing to gain by telling anyone about this. I won't say anything to anyone Paul. I swear." She backed into the musty chair. She had run out of space——and time.

"I'm going to make sure that you don't. Now where's the book?" He towered over her, casting a dark shadow; a frightening reminder of the doom that was to come.

"What book?"

Paul struck her across the face so hard that she literally saw stars. Audrey felt dizzy, like she was about to faint when he grabbed her by her blouse and smacked her again. She felt herself slipping away. Paul grabbed her shoulders and shook her until her eyes popped open.

"Where's the goddamned notebook, Audrey? If I have to ask you again, you'll be sorry."

His glare burned into her. He was going to hit her again. Audrey had never been so terrified. She couldn't take another minute of this pain.

"It's at the hotel." She whimpered. "It's not my room. It's Jules' and I don't have a key."

Paul dropped her in a messy heap on the chair. He stood quietly for a moment. Martha had taken her purse and Audrey was sure Paul had sifted through its contents and had found no hotel key. He wasn't playing around and Audrey was terrified. He snatched her up by her hair. The pain was so intense Audrey felt like her head was coming off her shoulders.

"I'll be back with a phone. You call him up and tell him to bring the damn thing or I swear to God I'll kill you."

. The door slammed behind him, the angry sound of metal meeting metal sliced into the stillness as he locked it. Audrey wiped at the spit and blood that streamed from her mouth and tried to think. She remembered the rusty red toolbox at the bottom of the bookcase. Did she have time to get a tool from the box to defend herself? If she had a weapon, would she have enough strength to use it? This would be a one shot deal for her. If she missed, she was dead.

The tinkling of keys alerted her to Paul's return. Audrey clutched the cool steel and prayed. The door opened and she swung the wrench. Its hardness met soft flesh, sounding like a muffled slap. He was much too tall for her to hit his head so she hit him in the throat instead. Paul yelped and doubled over. He clutched his throat and collapsed onto the floor in a fit of coughing. Audrey grabbed the cordless phone he'd dropped. He was lying on the wrench. With her weapon gone she grabbed her shoe in desperation and hobbled away from the shed dialing 911. She was describing her emergency to the operator when a searing pain stabbed through her leg. She listened to the vicious growl of the dog as he ripped into her. Danger tackled her onto the ground while Martha looked on. The woman's angry eyes sliced into Audrey. What Audrey saw next made her blood run cold. She feared the gleaming steel in Martha's hand would be the last thing she'd see. But first Martha delighted in the activity of her pet. The dog tore into Audrey's flesh. The pain and his horrifying growl drowned out all of her senses. With the last ounce of her will and strength she smashed the wooden shoe against his nose until his jaw loosened, then she rammed her fist, shoe and all into the dog's mouth. A gunshot rang out and Audrey neither saw nor heard anything else.

CHAPTER 35

▼

The bright hospital lighting glimmered into focus. One side of the room was filled with flowers, a color TV turned down low, and a window that opened onto sunshine and I-285. After panning the room she focused on Jules, Cordelia and Wallace St. James, Bobby, Renita and Lloyd. Their expressions were a mixture of joy and pain. Jules held her hand tight enough to break it while Renita bent over her and kissed her cheek.

"Girrrl, you scared the shit out of us!" Renita brushed her face with her fingers, smudging the red-lipped imprint left by the kiss. Everyone else kissed her too and they all cried…even Wallace.

"You're one courageous young lady." He said, patting her hand. "Glad to know that you plan to stick around with us a while longer."

"What happened?" The words rolled out as brittle as parchment. Jules handed her a Styrofoam cup with a bent straw. The water hurt and felt good at the same time as it cut through the dryness in her mouth. She moved her head and Jules pulled the cup away.

"What happened?" She repeated more clearly.

"Don't worry about that right now." Cordelia soothed. "Now that you're going to be okay, you have plenty of time for all that." She grabbed her husband's hand and they stepped away from the bed. "We just wanted to make sure you were alright."

"You get some rest. We'll see you again before you leave the city." Wallace said after giving her hand a squeeze.

They waved to everyone and brushed by a stout R.N. with dull brown hair on their way out of the room. The nurse was packed into a clean but threadbare blue and white uniform. She crossed her arms in front of her chest and issued a no nonsense look.

"The doctor's on his way to check Miss Wilson's sutures. I'm afraid I'm going to have to ask ya'll to leave." The softness of her voice belied the unyielding gaze. She stood back while they said their goodbyes. Audrey whispered to Jules when he bent to kiss her.

"Don't go too far."

He smiled and nodded, kissing her puffy mouth before making his exit.

*   *   *   *

"I'm Bradley Michaels." Dr. Michaels extended his hand and then, seeing she was too weak to respond, patted her leg.

"How long have I been here?" Audrey asked the doctor. He was tall and slender with ash blonde hair and the hard lean face of a fifteen year old. He looked up from the chart he was reading. His smile took another three years from his appearance.

"You've been here since yesterday afternoon. You got banged up quite a bit." He pointed to her head. "We stitched your head, your thigh and your leg just below your left knee. You should be okay to go home tomorrow. You need to follow up with your doctor, of course."

Now Audrey remembered Danger tearing at her leg, but why did she have the bandages on her head? She couldn't remember. Her head felt funny beneath the gauze wrapping.

"What happened to my head?"

"You sustained a nasty, though superficial cut when you were hit with a hammer. You're lucky it wasn't a lot worse."

"I always did have a hard head." She slurred.

The doctor laughed. "You're going to be fine."

"Did you have to cut my hair?"

"Afraid so." He shrugged boyishly. "We had to shave a three inch section in order to repair the wound."

"Three inches?" She tried to raise her hand to feel the area of trauma but she was much too weak.

"More or less." The doctor laughed. "If you're well enough to worry about your hair you're surely on the road to a speedy recovery."

He could joke about it. Audrey didn't think it was funny. So much for her two hundred fifty dollar braids, she thought.

The doctor finished checking her bandages, patted her hand and said good-bye. Jules was back in the room before the nurse and the doctor had time to close the door.

"So how ya' feeling?" He smiled but there was sadness in his eyes. Audrey thought she must really be jacked up for him to give her such a pitying look. He continued before she had time to respond.

"I feel awful about leaving you in the room yesterday morning. If I had only waited for you to wake up, if I had only stayed with you…"

"This isn't your fault, Jules." Audrey couldn't believe that he was accepting blame for her foolhardiness. "I made the decision to go to Paul's because I cared more about a piece of jewelry than my own life. It was a stupid thing to do."

"Yes, it was."

So much for sympathy, she thought.

"But still," he said. "I was supposed to be looking out for you. I don't know what I'd do if I'd lose you."

The words were unexpected and frightening to hear, for both Jules and Audrey. She looked into his eyes and it was like she was seeing him for the first time. He really had been concerned. So had her family to take the first flight out of Ohio to be at her bedside when she awakened. Knowing her brother and sister, they had refused to leave her room until they knew she was out of the woods. That was most likely the reason the nurse had been so firm when she'd made the request that they clear the room.

Audrey had been thoughtless. She hadn't meant to hurt anyone. The only thing that had been on her mind at the time was getting the bracelet her mother had given her. She'd nearly been killed over the keepsake. If her action had at least been rewarded by triumph, she wouldn't have felt as bad. Not only had her efforts had been in vain, she'd nearly been killed. And the bracelet was gone for-ever.

"I don't remember much of what happened." She wanted to move beyond any discussion of feelings Jules still harbored. She wasn't ready to deal with that at the moment. She told him what she could remember of her visit to the East Cobb mansion. "I never would have gone out there if I'd have suspected Paul and Martha would go off on me like that."

"That would have been the last place I would have thought you would return to. If you hadn't left the note…" Jules was holding her hand so tightly her finger-tips felt numb. His aqua eyes deepened in hue as he held her gaze. She gave up trying to retrieve her hand. Jules wasn't planning on letting Audrey go again.

"I went to the house and Martha told me she hadn't seen you since the previous night. Something told me not to trust her. I thought more and more about what you had said about Paul being the killer and I wasn't about to take any chances. I went to my car to call the police. A few minutes later I heard the dog barking and then saw it running off somewhere behind the house just as a patrol car pulled up. The cop said they had gotten an emergency call but the phone had gone dead. I was about to tell him that I suspected you were being held there when we heard the dog barking and growling and your screams…oh my God." He stopped for a moment to compose himself. Audrey was beginning to see the terror he must have felt finding her covered in blood, being ravaged by the beast.

"We both ran in the direction of the screaming and found you struggling to defend yourself against Paul's dog. I didn't even notice Martha and the gun until she aimed it at the policeman. He shot her and then the dog."

"Martha's dead?"

"No. She's in the hospital. The dog was picked up by animal control."

"I remember hearing a gunshot before I passed out." Audrey squinted, trying to dredge up memory of what happened to her. "Hell, I thought I had been shot."

"They wouldn't have done that." He assured her. "Martha and Paul were after Simone's diary and they wouldn't have harmed you too badly until they got it."

"Did you finish reading it?" Audrey struggled to find the beds remote control. She pushed the button and a whirring sound emanated from somewhere behind her as the bed folded upward.

"No. We may have to turn it over to the police. They interviewed Paul and his mother but I have no idea if they've got enough to put Simone's murder on them. They were detained and questioned about holding you but they both said you were on the property unauthorized and their guard dog was just doing his job."

"Bullshit!" Audrey was livid. "After that old lunatic beaned me with a hammer and Paul Radford beat me to a pulp in that shed, Martha stood by while that animal ripped me apart. Are you trying to tell me that they'll get off?"

"I just don't want you to be too surprised if he gets away with what he's done to you. He has quite a standing in the community and it's basically your word against his."

Audrey looked away. It angered and disgusted her that Paul and people like him had the money and position to do what ever they wanted to people and not be brought to task. Hell, she couldn't even prove to the police that she had stayed at his house as a guest just days before. To them she probably did look like some kook or groupie stalking a celebrity.

"I'm going to do everything that I can to see that he gets investigated. There's still no evidence that he killed Simone, but he had a very strong motive for wanting her dead." Jules said.

"I think he's responsible for her death, even if he didn't push her himself."

"We'll need more than a gut feeling to go up against someone as powerful as Paul Radford." Seeing her frustration, Jules stroked her swollen face comfortingly.

"What did you find out from your lawyer friend?" Audrey queried.

"I was able to access the final contract that Paul presented to Simone for her son's trust fund. It contained a codicil stating that in the event of Simone's death, all monies would revert to Paul. But according to Georgia law the boy's legal guardian could supersede the clause by simply filing a document in Circuit Court."

"So would the person Simone named as beneficiary be able to override that clause by petitioning the court?" Audrey asked him.

"Yes. And guess who she named as beneficiary?"

"Who?"

"Your brother, Bobby."

"This thing is getting weirder by the second." Audrey slid down on the bed. The family visit and all the information had exhausted her.

"Quite the contrary, my dear. This thing is getting clearer." Jules smiled like he had connected a major piece to a puzzle. "With Simone and Bobby out of the way, Paul would have the money free and clear with no one to contest it."

"So you think he killed Simone and helped to frame Bobby so that he wouldn't have to fund the trust?"

"It's plausible." Jules was excited. "He may not have had anything to do with Bobby being brought in for questioning but you'd better believe he was thankful for the added bonus his friend's incarceration would have afforded him. He took advantage of an opportunity. It wouldn't surprise me if he hired those so-called witnesses who claimed they saw Bobby and Simone fighting. Even if your brother was found innocent, Paul knew Bobby didn't want to have anything to do with raising a kid, especially after the way Simone betrayed him. He figured Bobby wouldn't contest the contract if it went that far."

"But Bobby surprised him by asking me to take stewardship of his son's affairs." Audrey asserted.

"That may have bothered Paul," Jules surmised, "but only temporarily. He knew that a simple paternity test would prove that Bobby wasn't the biological father of Simon. He probably figured Bobby would be relieved and just walk away from the boy, thus dissolving any claim he has as custodian of the fund."

"But Paul was one of the few people who was supportive of me when I initially spoke of adopting Simon."

"It was likely a front. How many people would adopt an older child who has a disability?" Jules wrinkled a questioning brow. "My guess is he assumed that once you really considered all that was involved, you would rethink the adoption and let the state place Simon."

"But he seemed so interested in helping me find Simone's folks and he helped me do the initial groundwork related to Simon's placement."

"He was just playing around with you to see what you dug up."

"And what I dug up was evidence that famous motivational speaker and author, Paul Radford had fathered an autistic son with a woman of dubious distinction." Audrey rose up on her elbows. Jules poured her a glass of water and she drank from a bent white straw. "But all of this is speculation." She said putting her hand to her chest like the move would keep the swallowing from hurting as much. Her throat was still scratchy and sore from screaming.

"True. Last I heard Paul still wasn't admitting to anything. He knows the police have no physical evidence linking him to Simone's death." Jules turned his lips downward into a bitter frown.

They were silent for a moment, looking out of the window at the billowy white clouds dancing ghostlike against the background of clear blue.

"They'll be releasing you tomorrow."

"And I can't wait to get the hell out of here." She said. "A Rosemont by any other name still smells as sweet."

"I miss the slow grind of home too." He chuckled. "Have you made up your mind about the adoption?"

"Oh, yeah. It's still on as far as I'm concerned." She tried to read Jules' face. "Cordelia hasn't said that there is a problem has she?"

"No, not at all. As a matter of fact, she's looking forward to getting everything finalized so that you guys can start your lives together."

A chill of excitement brushed Audrey's skin. She was going to be a mother. It sounded so strange and yet it was something she had wanted her whole life. When she was a young girl she had thought she would have the traditional family with a husband and three or four children. To compensate for the loss she felt after the disastrous and heartbreaking abortion, she had pushed her desire to be a mother to the furthest recesses of her mind, focusing instead on her career. But something had happened inside her of late. She didn't know what precipitated it exactly. She knew it had something to do with her mother. Esther's presence was always with her but in recent months, she could feel the spirit guiding her in all thought and action. For whatever reason, her mother had been sending a very clear message that Audrey needed to start thinking about the impact that she would make on the world while she was still in it and the legacy she'd leave once she was gone.

"The quicker you get home to get things ready, the better." Jules said.

"I can't wait." She said brightly. "I know it's going to be hard, but this is what I want to do. I'm looking forward to making Simon a part of my life."

CHAPTER 36

▼

Audrey was sleeping when Renita and Lloyd returned to the hospital that evening. Renita was glad she was alone. She looked over at Lloyd and smiled.

"She looks so peaceful." She whispered. "Maybe being a mother is what she needed. I hope she'll forgive me for taking such a hard line with her on adopting Simon."

"Of course she'll forgive you. Audrey's not one to carry a grudge." Lloyd studied her with laughing eyes.

"So you're saying that I am?"

"I'm not saying anything." He grabbed her around the waist and she made a weak attempt to resist as he pulled her to him and kissed her. "You turn me on when you try to pretend you don't want me."

Renita grimaced. She could feel the thickening lump pressing against her and was torn between moving into it and moving away. "My goodness," she thought. "The man is a machine." He was nearly sixty-five years old and he was more virile than some forty year olds that she knew. That's the reason she was in the predicament she was in now.

After she'd left Dr. Beavers' office Renita drove home in a daze. Before she knew it she was turning the key in the lock and flopping onto the couch. She looked toward the heavens, terrified.

"God, you know I am not ready to be anybody's mother."

She hadn't been with anyone but Lloyd…and Fran. What if this was his child she was carrying? She didn't want to spawn the child of Satan. That's when she seriously thought about abortion. Then she thought about Audrey and how she had wanted children all of her life and would never bear one of her own. And what if the baby was Lloyd's? Lloyd Eckstine was a good man. He had invested wisely so they wouldn't have to worry about working. He was kind and attractive and he'd never be unfaithful to her. As he said, he'd sewn his oats, harvested them, baked the bread and eaten it. He felt that there was something missing in his life. He knew what that something was and had patiently waited until Renita was ready. Renita wished she were as certain about this as Lloyd seemed to be. She was forty years old and if she didn't grow up now, when would she? Her life was about to change forever and she needed to stop wasting herself by going from man to man.

"Would you stop it?" She smacked his hand, but didn't move away from the bulge.

"Ya'll can take all that arguing somewhere else." Groggy from the medicine and the ragged sleep afforded by the uncomfortable hospital bed, Audrey gazed up at them and smiled.

"How are you feeling?" Renita bent down and kissed her face. Lloyd followed suit. He pointed at her dinner tray and gave her a parental gaze.

"You'd better eat up or they're not going to release you." He warned.

"I remember them bringing the food in but I was so tired I went to sleep before I even looked at it." Audrey yawned and stretched. "I'm starving." She pulled the tray in front of her and started removing the metal lids from the plates that sat atop a serving tray. She took tiny bites of the cold soft roll and a sip of tepid broth. She glanced up from the dish when she noticed that neither of her guests were talking.

"What?" Her brow wrinkled in concern.

"We're getting married." Lloyd was about to burst with joy.

Audrey choked on the mouthful of liquid. Renita moved quickly behind her, patting her back until the coughing subsided.

"What?" Audrey looked at them in disbelief and then started laughing. "Is this some kind of joke? Or is it the medication I'm on? I thought I heard you say you're getting married."

Lloyd appeared hurt and Renita had an even bigger question mark over her head than the one that floated over Audrey's. The thought of Renita Wilson getting married was quite a notion.

"It's not a joke." Renita said. "That's not the only news." She looked into her sisters' eyes but before she could speak, Lloyd blurted, "We're having a baby!"

Audrey opened her mouth but nothing came out. She looked from one to the other and then cracked up laughing.

"Get the hell out!" Audrey exclaimed in disbelief. She examined her sister's steady gaze and knew that she was telling the truth. As hard as it was for her to believe, it was true. Audrey's eyes clouded and her wide mouth formed a big smile. She opened her arms and Renita fell into them.

"Congratulations, Ren." She kissed her face and then moved back and looked into her eyes and whispered, "You sure?"

"Yes." Renita looked over at Lloyd. "I'm sure about everything."

Audrey opened her arms and enfolded her sister once more. Renita pushed her left hand toward Audrey so she could admire the killer diamond that adorned her finger.

"Oooh, that's nice! And we're both going to be mommies." Audrey peeked up at Lloyd and opened her right arm to include him in the embrace.

"Silver Fox——-my man!"

Lloyd flushed slightly. He bent to accept the show of support and affection.

"There might be snow on the rooftop but the fire is still blazing in the chimney." Audrey teased him. "Now you know you old enough to know better. Both of ya'll."

"I'm old enough to know *exactly* what I'm doing." A devilish glint danced in eyes that showed love and desire for Renita. Audrey had never seen Lloyd look so happy.

"Welcome to the family." She said. "Thank you for making an honest woman out of my sister."

"She's giving me everything I've ever wanted." Lloyd's eyes bathed his bride-to-be in admiration. "I'll spend the rest of my life making her happy."

Renita smiled shyly. Audrey had never seen her sister like this with any man. It was almost as if she had waited her whole life and was finally able to shed a mask she'd worn. Renita let herself relax and accept the love she had turned away from for so many years.

"I'm going to have to get out of here so we could celebrate." Audrey's eyes glistened with joyful tears.

"Celebrate what?"

Jules Dreyfus stood in the doorway with an armload of colorful flowers. His eyes danced from one of them to the other curiously.

"Renita and Lloyd are getting married." Audrey said.

Renita held up her hand and showed off a sparkling four-carat diamond that elicited an exaggerated blink from Jules.

"You won't be able to use your hand with all of that weight you'll be carrying around." Jules teased.

"We can make it without one of her hands." Lloyd winked knowingly at Jules. "You'd be amazed at what Renita can do with just one hand."

Jules laughed and patted Lloyd on the back. "Congratulations, man." Then he reached for Renita and kissed her cheek. "Be happy, my friend."

"I will." Renita replied from within the comfort of his embrace. Jules whispered loudly into her ear. "Maybe you can talk to that stubborn sister of yours into answering the call."

"I'm afraid I'm the wrong person for that job." Renita glanced at her future husband admiringly. "Lucky for me. Lloyd waited while I went all around the world to find what was staring me in the face all along."

"So there is hope for me." Jules snuck a dubious gaze in Audrey's direction. She looked away.

"My goal is to get out of this bed and get back to Rosemont so that I can get things ready for Simon."

Jules' smile faded and his expression clouded. Renita felt bad for him but if her sister wasn't ready he should just back off. She knew that Audrey wasn't going to get caught up in some marital fantasy. She'd been that route and she wasn't in any rush to go there again. Jules was certainly no Emory Kimborough. Audrey's first husband was a pompous, self-absorbed snob who wanted to control every aspect of her life. Jules was nothing like Emory. Renita liked him and she would like to see them reunite, but that was up to Audrey. She didn't want to think anymore about Jules or Audrey or a little mentally challenged boy who was once her nephew, and then wasn't, and someday may be again. Renita just wanted to bask in the glow of motherhood and the wonderful life that she knew Lloyd would provide her.

CHAPTER 37

▼

Jules stayed after Lloyd and Renita left, and Audrey could tell that their happy news had taken some of the wind out of his sails. Maybe if she got him thinking about something else he'd snap out of his funk.

"Do you still have the journal?" She asked.

"Yeah, it's in my car."

"Why didn't you bring it so we could see if it shed any more light on what happened to Simone?"

"I don't care about that, Audrey." His piercing aqua eyes bore into her deep brown ones. "You know I love you and you just keep ignoring me."

"I'm not ignoring you, Jules." She didn't want to have this conversation.

"You are!"

She had never seen him this upset. Emotion darkened his eyes. His face flushed with hurt and anger.

"I tried to forget about it but I nearly lost you for good yesterday. Life is too fucking short to be screwing around. I can't be just friends with you, Audrey." His voice quieted. He gaze pleaded. "You tell me you don't love me and I'm outta here."

Oh, hell! Why was he doing this? Why was he forcing her to do something that she wasn't ready to do? Did he think that because Lloyd had gotten lucky, shaking his hand would mean that Jules had "it" now? Renita had been in and out of love with Lloyd Eckstine for more years than Audrey could remember. Audrey was certain that if Renita agreed to marry Lloyd it was because that's what she wanted, not because the man had muscled her into it. She refused to be goaded into a relationship that didn't feel right. Things might change but it wasn't going to happen by brute force. He couldn't ram love down her throat and expect her to enjoy the meal. She saw only one way to get him to back off.

"I don't love you, Jules." She wanted the words to come out cold and blunt, using them to defuse any spark that might ignite the fire that was once their love. The heat of his anger propelled him from his place on the bed, so abruptly it startled her. Jules tore angrily out of the room, leaving behind a roaring silence that was painful to the ears and piercing to the heart.

*   *   *   *

The unsettling silence and cloying fragrance from the wall of flowers near the window gave Audrey a headache. She lay on the flat mattress wishing she could disappear into it. The tears were unexpected. They flowed from her eyes and she couldn't get them to stop. What the hell was she crying about? She knew that Jules Dreyfus wasn't the man for her. Her man had left her, gone to his hometown and hadn't so much as called to see how she was doing. She hadn't even been able to discuss her plans regarding Simon with him. She had nearly been killed and he couldn't care less. Everyone had expressed support and concern for her. Cordelia and Wallace St. James had come to visit her in the hospital and they didn't even know her. Why was she pining over Marsh who didn't even care enough to pick up the phone and rejecting Jules who would do anything for her? Was she that narrow-minded? Was she just stupid?

The door was pulled open with enough force to make it touch the wall and slam shut. Jules flung the notebook at her and was about to turn when he looked into her face. He ran to her and lifted her head, wiping away the wetness with his handkerchief.

"I-I-I love you but I'm not ready to be with you right now." She stammered like a three-year old. Her chest heaved in and out with the release of the confession. "I don't want you to go."

"I'm not going anywhere, baby." He kissed her face until his was wet with her tears. "Knowing you love me, I can wait forever." He smoothed his hand over the big gauze headdress and the few exposed braids. He rubbed her shoulders and let his hands travel down her back and inside the open-backed gown. He held her and they rocked until the tension in the room melted into an easy peace.

CHAPTER 38

▼

"You sure you want to read the rest of this?" Jules had crawled into bed with her after the nurse made the eight o'clock med rounds. Audrey felt the warmness from his skin and breath and it soothed her. But her desire to learn the rest of Simone's story gnawed at her.

She nodded and he opened the blue spiral bound notebook as she reached for the controls and brought the head of the bed upwards. They sat huddled like two campers staying up late to read *True Confessions* after everyone else had gone to sleep.

Jules read aloud from Simone's book.

> *June 4th—Got a call from that shithead attorney of P.'s asking me to come into his office to sign some additional papers. I went down there and he shoved the papers in front of me. I didn't have a lawyer, so I was taking my time to read and as best I could, understand what changes had been made and how they would affect me. I had brought my original copy along and I took my time and studied each line making sure they hadn't slipped anything in that would reverse what I had initially asked for.*
>
> *A page had been inserted. It was sandwiched in with the others, third page from the last. At the top of the page was the word CODICIL. I asked the lawyer what that meant. He said that these were amendments to the original agreement. I read the four-line paragraph very carefully. After I waded through the legal jargon the gist of the statement was that in the event of my death the money in Simon's trust would go back to P. I told the lawyer that I didn't have a problem with that as long as he made sure that our son was provided a proper home situation. I didn't want my kid holed up in some institution where they'd chain him to a bed for the*

rest of his life. The lawyer assured me that P. had only the best intentions in mind. Yeah, sure, and I'm the Governor of Georgia.

    But I signed the papers. I'm just tired. Knowing I have done everything I could to provide for my son is like having a huge burden lifted. I hope someday I'll be able to make him understand the things that I have done. I'm ashamed of the way that I lived my life. But I did the best that I could.

"Whoa!" Audrey slapped her palm onto the book. "What about this codicil? You don't think that's reason enough for Paul to have wanted Simone dead?"

"I told you about it, remember. That type of clause is not unusual. A first year law student would have advised him to do that." Jules was thoughtful for a moment. "Look, people murder for all kinds of reasons. To some a million dollars is reason enough. To others, it's the principle. It wouldn't matter if it were a penny."

They shrugged and returned to the diary.

June 9th—Simon had a seizure last night. I called an ambulance and we just got back from a night at the hospital. They gave him another EEG while I waited for his neurologist. She suggested including a medicine to control his seizures and switching him from Clonidine, which works as a mild depressant to the more potent Ritalin and seemed irritated with me when I refused. I don't want my son to be all doped up and out of it just because he doesn't want to do what they want sometimes. What if everybody was force fed pills when they had a different opinion or completed a task in a way that was different from the norm? Should we all be doped and walk around like robots? I'm so tired of fighting this fight. I cried all night. I love my baby so much. He doesn't deserve this kind of life. Neither do I.

    June 12th—I decided to take a week and go to St. Simon's Island. I tell Simon that the island was named after him and he laughs. I don't even know if he understands what he's laughing at. Maybe he can tell by the way that I say it that it's meant as a joke. Simon and I always get the nicest hotel room we can afford whenever we go to the beach. It's difficult at times handling him by myself. I'm scared to death that he might go into the water and go out too far or that he will imagine being a fish and plunge into the water when we're on one of the tour boats. I pray constantly that God will guide his steps and keep him safe. I won't let my fear keep him from having a good life.

    June 22nd—We had such a good time at the beach and the day or so following. Whenever we're around other children it's hard for me to keep from getting depressed at how far behind Simon is in his development. In light of my recent dealings with that asshole P. I've had to really look at some things that I hadn't thought about before. What would happen to him if something were to happen to me? There are so many little tricks that I use to get him to learn. If something happens to me, the person who provides his care will need all the help they can get. I've started keeping a list of all the things that Simon likes and the things that he seems to respond to in his learning. I'll start the list in the back of this book and transfer the notes to Simon's very own book soon.

Jules immediately flipped to the back of the notebook and there it was—-separated by a yellow paper index, Simone's list for Simon.

"Oh my goodness!" Audrey exclaimed. "I could never have dreamed of a blessing like this."

There was page after page of lists, notes, and what-to-do ifs. Tears sprang to Audrey's eyes as she read through the instructions. She wished she had gotten a chance to know the woman who had cared so much about her son to make sure that he had the very best of everything. Audrey would do everything in her power to make sure that she fulfilled Simone's dream of seeing Simon be the best that he could be.

Jules left Audrey alone with the notebook while he went to the bathroom and then to the cafeteria to get some dinner before they closed. When he returned with red and white Chick-Fil-A bags. He pulled out sandwiches, chips and soup for both of them. Audrey was still reading Simon's List.

"Thank you." She said pulling the cellophane from a meat salad sandwich and taking a bite. She chewed and swallowed slowly, favoring the side of her mouth that was less achy than the other. Audrey reflected in silence as they ate. The quiet was too much for Jules who filled the space with incessant chatter. In spite of his disappointment at the course of their relationship he was trying to keep her spirits up.

"It's after ten and they're going to toss my ass outta here in a minute." He said. Audrey averted her gaze to cover the cloud of disappointment in her eyes.

"There aren't very many entries remaining in the journal." She said, thumbing through the journal section of the book. "I think we can get through this in a few minutes if we hurry."

They read.

July 4th—We had fun today. Stephanie and me took our boys to Six Flags. Her son Javon is two years younger than Simon and he's so mature. He talked to us about everything. Simon was just humming to himself or uttering anything that popped into his head like he always does. It's not so bad when we're at home by ourselves but when he does this out in public people always look at him funny and it makes me sad. Javon was sweet though. He talked to Simon and treated him like he would any other kid. It didn't seem to bother him that Simon "talks funny" after I explained to him why. Stephanie was great, too. She told him that everybody is different and unique and that's what makes life interesting and special. Both of our boys are bi-racial so we are used to the looks from people trying to figure out what they are. Stephanie is able to explain to her son and have him understand how ignorant people can be. The only thing I can do is hope and pray that the world is kind to my son. I try to teach him to respect people and things. Hopefully the world will return these things to him.

July 6th—Things have been winding down at work. A lot of us older girls are being kicked to the curb by the younger ones that Portia has been bringing in. I was kind of mad at first but that's just how this business is. I know I pissed off those old heads when I came aboard. As the saying goes, what goes around comes around. All the girls that Portia brought in around the time that I started are doing their own thing on the side to keep the money coming in. It can be dangerous and a couple of the girls got sliced up and one of them got killed fucking around with the wrong element. I need to jumpstart my bank account but I have to be careful how I do it, for Simon's sake.

I found out today from one of the girls who was working the downtown hotels about a nice set-up working through a guy. His clientele are businessmen coming into Atlanta who want a little R&R. She said the only thing she didn't like was that the girls had to audition for the guy. That didn't sound so bad to me. But my girl told me that during the audition he would do everything imaginable to you to make sure you were serious and to make sure you'd do anything to please a client. She said some of the most straight-laced guys were the biggest freaks and would pay top dollar to have their fantasies fulfilled.

I figure these guys couldn't be any worse than the scum Auntie Lee set me up with. Besides, my days with Portia are numbered. My audition is tonight. If all goes well I'll be working this weekend.

July 9th—The weekend was rough. The audition was the worst thing I've ever been through in my life. The guy called himself Jelly. A woman probably gave him the name because of the long, soft, poor excuse for a penis that dangles between his legs. It was sickening. He made me suck it for what seemed a lifetime. It didn't do him or me any good. He beat me, cursed me, put all kinds of objects everywhere I have a hole and when he was finally through, he picked me up and held me and spoke to me with more love and respect than anyone ever has in my whole life. Then I went right to work. The Johns weren't so bad. It's a strain though because I still have to work at the club on weekends. I know the word is out on me. Portia knows everything so she was a real bitch to me this past weekend at the club. She had stopped letting me dance as much so my money is short, then when I try to make it up by doing something on the side she treats me bad like I'm betraying her or something. I gotta look out for myself cause I know she, Jelly, or none of them don't give a damn about me.

"With the turn in Simone's lifestyle, any one of several people could have killed her." Jules said as he pulled away from his reading and reached for the bottle of juice he'd gotten from the cafeteria. It hadn't been that cold when he got it and now it was warm and flat. He grimaced and put the bottle on the nightstand.

"I remember Paul telling me that. Between Portia, Jelly, Paul and an assortment of shady customers, anyone could have killed her." Audrey filled her cup from the plastic hospital issue pitcher and took several sips. "It could even have been one of her co-workers from the club."

They sat silently speculating on all the ways Simone Denton could have met her fate. Audrey nudged Jules.

"We'd better get finished."

They bowed their heads over the journal and continued reading.

July17th—I hate my life. I've only been hooking for a little more than a week and already I hate it. With the dancing I get to call the shots. I dance how I want to and for the most part, I choose who I give a lap to and if I want to leave the club with somebody it's up to me. Portia never made me go with somebody if I didn't feel right about it. Jelly is different. He made me go with this guy who beat the living shit outta me. All while he was kicking my ass he was telling me how Jelly always gave him the strongest girls who knew how to take a punch. When I made him stop and Jelly found out about it, he burned my inner thigh with his cigar. It hurt worse than any pain I've ever felt. He told me if I ever backed out on a client again he'd stick the thing in my face. And then he didn't pay me. I was too banged up to work my shift at the club, so I got no money this week. I'm okay right now because I got enough to go a few weeks without getting paid, but who the hell wants to get that kind of ass whipping and then if Jelly don't like the way you performed, he's not going to pay you? Fuck that! I'm not doing this shit anymore.

"My God!" Jules exclaimed. "How can anybody live like that? And she's a mother too." He shook his head, looking down at the words on the page like the vile script would give him a disease.

"It's totally foreign to me, too." Audrey felt sad and sick to think of the things people felt compelled to do just to survive. "Apparently, she didn't think she had any other way to make it."

"This is so tragic." Jules had a faraway look in his eyes. "It makes you wish you could do something to reach people who are so desperate before they get in so deep. This woman saw so little value in her life and virtually everyone she came in contact with dealt her a raw deal.

The wheels were churning in Audrey's head. When she got back to Rosemont, she would expand the sector of B.A. Wilson that dealt with young mothers. If young girls and women were able to raise their self-esteem they would be confident that they could rise above any situation. No matter how bleak things seemed.

July 19ᵗʰ—God, what am I going to do? I told Jelly that I was quitting and he told me I wasn't going anywhere until he got his investment back. What damned investment? He never gave me shit. But according to him he groomed me to be a high-class call girl and that was worth something. Hell, I'd only known this asshole a few weeks. The only thing he's given me is a hard way to go. But the worst part of the whole thing was that Karina, the girl who got me the hook-up, was one of the girls who held me while Jelly beat me silly. I took pictures of my bruises and documented all the violence. I locked it all away in my bank box. I know that I don't have enough power to bring down a man like Jelly, but you just never know. He did so many horrible things that somebody has to do something. Somebody has to stop him.

* I called Portia and quit the club. Jelly wouldn't let me go back there, plus I was missing so much time because of my black eyes and fat lips she would have fired me anyway. I asked her to help me but she just laughed.*

* "I told your ass not to mess with that pimp." She said and then told me not to come back in there no more. The other girls at the club, even Stephanie, didn't have much to say. They were the only family I knew. It really hurt me to be cast out like that. I had a little money, but it wouldn't last forever and Simon's money was held in trust until he turned eighteen. I had nowhere to go but back to Jelly.*

* July 21ˢᵗ—I met a nice man at the hotel. He's the concierge and he's been with the hotel since 1979. That's an eternity to me. His name is Wiley. He's an older black man and he's not good looking but he has a nice smile and sincere eyes. What I like about him most is that he's a gentleman. Probably the first I've ever known. He doesn't look at me the way other men do. When I'm around him I feel like a person, not a thing. He buys me a coffee or a soda and we sit and talk. Wiley was born in Buffalo, N.Y. but he has been living in Atlanta almost thirty years. He told me about how he did some time back in the late sixties and how he destroyed his life and turned his family against him. When he was released from prison he was angry and blamed everyone for what he'd gone through in there. He told me that he'd done so many horrible things he hated to even think about them. He got into trouble one time and he knew that if he stayed in Buffalo he'd end up in prison again. So he moved to Atlanta and changed his way of thinking about himself and that was when he'd begun to change his life. I told him about my life and he's the only person that I told about Auntie Lee and the men she forced on me. I told him about Simon and about P. Wiley touched my hand in a friendly way, warm and kind of comforting. He really listened to me. For the first time I felt like it was okay to have bad things happen to you. That doesn't mean it's your fault and it doesn't mean that you are a bad person. I wish I had met Wiley a long time ago. Maybe things would have been different for me. But then again, maybe I would have blown him off as some crazy old man who didn't know what he was talking about.*

* July 25ᵗʰ—Wiley asked me to marry him. I laughed and laughed—until I saw that he was serious. I told him he'd only known me three weeks and that I was*

nothing but a whore. Wiley said I had whored but I wasn't a whore. He said he was old enough to know what he wanted and he wasn't one to waste time. He had already wasted enough. He told me that he was going to love me until I started loving myself. I wouldn't give him an answer. He asked me to think about it and I told him I would.

July 26th—When I finished with my last "date" tonight Wiley was downstairs waiting for me. He looked at me different than he had before. Nobody ever looked at me the way Wiley Bates looked at me that Thursday night. He took my hand and I felt protected and good but at the same time I felt like crying. Is this what it felt like when somebody loved you? He looked into my eyes and then gave me the gentlest kiss and I knew then that I loved him too.

But this was crazy. We just met each other but at the same time I felt like I'd known him all of my life. Then I decided that this wasn't crazy. The crazy thing had been the way I had been living my entire life. Finally, the madness was about to stop. We walked together to his tiny but clean apartment on Luckie Street and for the first time in my life, a man made love to me. He left the bed and fished a small black box from the pocket of his work slacks. He opened it and gave me a delicate gold band with a small, clear diamond at its center. He put the solitaire on my finger and I said yes.

But now sitting here I feel so confused and scared. I wish I had somebody to talk to, just for some advice. I don't have a friend in the world. I look over at my son and kiss his smooth face. I want to make sure that I'm doing the right thing for him. I called Bobby Wilson because even though I hadn't told him the truth about Simon and I had been deceiving him for years, I didn't have anyone else to turn to. He hung up before I even got a word out. Then as luck would have it I found out that the hotel was hosting a banquet and the attendees were from Rosemont, Ohio. I was able to get a list of notable people who would attend and saw that Bobby Wilson would be accepting some kind of award. I called him again and begged him not to hang up. I told him that I needed to talk to him about Simon, that it was very important. I told him I had to get some things off my chest and finalize our arrangements about Simon. He immediately thought I was making a play for more money and blew his top. After listening to him hurl the usual nasty obscenities, I calmly told him that I didn't deserve to be spoken to that way. I don't know if it was the way that I said it or if he was just tired of cussing, but he stopped. The rest of the conversation was fairly civil. He told me he would be in Atlanta next weekend and he'd talk to me then. I told him to call my cell phone when he got in and we'd set it up.

The next day I told Jelly that Simon was sick and that I couldn't come to work. He was mad but I didn't care. I just couldn't see lying up with some man after the beautiful time I'd shared with Wiley. I had been thinking about everything that he'd been saying to me. I noticed that since he'd come into my life I felt good about myself for the first time ever. I kept thinking about what he said to me, that he was going to love me until I started loving myself. I knew that was what I needed. I needed to make a stable home life for Simon. I wasn't a whore and it was time I stopped living and acting like one. I didn't need anyone's assurance about the deci-sion I'd made. Accepting Wiley's proposal was the right thing to do. He would take Simon and me away from this terrible life where nobody loved us and we didn't know how to love ourselves.

"Thank God for Wiley." Jules put the book down and stretched. "Simone's life was so depressing I almost feel like flinging myself out of a window."

Audrey nudged him in the ribs. "What a terrible thing to say." She was thoughtful for a moment and then laughed. "She didn't have much to sing about, did she?"

"Maybe she'll kiss Wiley and he'll turn into a prince and swoop her away to his castle where they'll…"

"Where they'll what, wise guy? She's dead, remember?" Audrey's statement jolted him back to reality. "Nobody swooped Simone anywhere, except maybe out of a tenth floor window."

The few moments of levity abruptly ended as they remembered that they were seeing the still fresh words of someone who was no longer living. They bent their heads solemnly and read.

July 29ᵗʰ—Oh my God, no! Wiley is dead! The building manager found him in his apartment after someone complained of running water. He was getting ready to take a bath when he had the attack. He was found sprawled on his bathroom floor this morning. It was all over the hotel. They gossiped about it like he was some stranger that they'd heard about on the nightly news. I cried all night and refused to see any clients. I know that Jelly is going to beat the hell outta me next time he sees me but I don't care. The last time I was with a man, it was with Wiley Bates, a man who loved me. I'll never let another man use me and I'll never degrade myself again. Jelly can go to hell.

"Good for her!" Audrey cheered. "She finally got it. Too bad it had to take the death of the first person who ever showed her love to make her realize that she deserved better."

"Maybe that was Wiley's purpose in life." Jules surmised.

"You're telling me you think the man's sole purpose for existing was to save Simone Denton?"

"Why not? Look, the man went through hell and then he turned his life around and saved another life." Jules told her. "I believe we all have a mission in life. I think it was Wiley's life purpose to meet Simone and save her from herself."

Audrey grimaced. Wiley had saved her life only to have someone else take it. Life's a bitch and then you die. This was a case where a saying was never truer.

"I wished she had included the number to that safe deposit box somewhere." Jules said. "I would personally work with the city of Atlanta to prosecute that scum she was dealing with."

"The defender playing for the other side? That's some heavy stuff." Audrey said.

"No this," Jules tapped the manual with his finger, "is some heavy stuff."

There was only one entry left. It was dated the last day that Simone Denton spent on this earth.

> *August 2—What ever made me think that life would deal me a playable hand? I was banking on Wiley, hoping on Wiley and wishing on him. It's finally registered in my thick skull. He's gone. Nobody's going to help me and this is how I have to live the rest of my life. I had already surrendered my lifestyle, promised I wouldn't trick no more. Now what do I do? I can't go forward and I can't go back. Poor Simon. He didn't deserve any of this. I love him too much to hurt him anymore. I've given him all that I have and it just isn't enough.*
>
> *The hotel is having the banquet tonight. Bobby has agreed to meet with me. I'll tell him about my plan for Simon. I even brought Simon with me so that when I tell Bobby the truth about who his father is maybe he won't get so mad. Maybe he'll feel a soft spot for Simon and won't want him to be alone in the world. Bobby acts big and bad but he's really a nice guy at heart. Nothing like P. How could I waste so much of my time on that jerk? I'll rest easy knowing that when it was all said and done; he won't get off Scot-free.*
>
> *I haven't been answering the phone and I know Jelly has been trying to track me down. He's at the door now, banging like a crazy man. He was already here once tonight and I told him then I wasn't going to work for him anymore. He's not going to take no for an answer. Well this time no is the answer he's going to have to take. I'm not taking anymore shit off men. He knows that I've had enough and that there's nothing he can do about it. He's killed women before and I know he wants to kill me. But that's not going to happen. They wouldn't let me live the life that I wanted but I'll be damned if I'll let them dictate the way that I die. I've got something on him that would put him away for a long time. He thinks we're all so stupid that he gets careless around us sometimes. Well, I'm going to have the last laugh this time.*

Audrey turned the page. They flipped through the entire remaining pages until they reached the yellow index leading to the Simon lists. That was the end—-all she wrote.

"So she killed herself?" Audrey felt an indescribable hollowness inside. This woman who had struggled from someone who just existed to being a survivor had given up? How could she do that? What about her son?

"The police never ruled out suicide. Bobby was arrested primarily because someone had heard a fight from Simone's room and Bobby had been seen in the area around the time the fight had occurred. The police had to investigate the death from all angles." Jules said. "If he had just been honest about what he had done from the start he could have saved us all a lot of time and embarrassment."

Audrey remembered that Bobby's real reason for being away from their table that night had been because he had gone off to screw Jules' date. What a couple of sleazebags. It seemed like her brother was never going to change. But what about Paul? If he didn't kill Simone, why was he acting so crazy?

"I don't believe she killed herself." Audrey had to make sense of this nonsense. "Between the grimy people that she dealt with and that bastard Paul…" Jules cut her off.

"Read the last passage, Audrey. She was tired of being mistreated. She'd had enough."

They were suddenly interrupted by a knock on the door. An orderly entered with a roll-a-way bed. The attendant unfolded the bed and straightened the sheets around its edges.

"There are extra blankets and a pillow in the dresser drawer." He said on his way out.

Jules thanked him and looked into Audrey's surprised eyes and smiled.

"When I went to get the food I told the nurse that I was your husband and that I'd like to spend the night. She told me it would take a while but she'd try to get a bed."

Her look was a mixture of mock irritation and amusement. Jules headed for the dresser and pulled out the blanket and pillow.

"What makes you think I want you to stay here tonight?" She was actually grateful for his company but she couldn't let him know it.

"We're too old for games, Audrey." He straightened the bed, ignoring her overly dramatic attitude. "At some point you're going to relax so we can go forward with our lives. When you get tired of running, I'll be right here. I've got all the patience in the world."

Smug bastard, she thought, ignoring his prognostication. Determining that she wasn't in the mood to argue with him, she rolled her eyes and turned her attention back to the journal.

"When I had the encounter with Paul he never admitted any involvement in Simone's death." The horrifying experience in the shed flashed into her brain like a scene from a cheap slasher movie. She remembered Paul's snarling face and crazed glare. He was glad Simone was dead, but he hadn't killed her. Perhaps she had argued with the man called Jelly that night and he had either pushed her or she'd jumped. They may never know the truth.

CHAPTER 39

▼

The flight to Rosemont was uneventful. The plan was to rest up, make sure that all of the arrangements for Simon's transfer were firmly in place, and then fly back to Atlanta to get her son. She beamed every time she thought about it and sent up prayers to Simone for paving the way for an easier transition.

With all of his money and connections Paul and Martha would most likely escape any heavy fallout from the scandal of Simone's death and the allegations that she left behind in her journals. Audrey photocopied the notes on Simon's care and, for what it was worth, turned the final diary over to the police. Simone had never mentioned Paul by name and even if she had, what was the likelihood they'd choose the word of a prostitute over that of one of Atlanta's leading citizens? Audrey had been following the story by pulling up the Atlanta Journal Constitution on the Internet. Two weeks after the end of their trip it was reported that Paul had signed a new multi-year multi million-dollar contract for his talk show, which was going into new markets. The rich get richer; the poor get screwed.

Jules tried to talk her into suing Paul and his corporation. She would have to think about it. There was so much going on in her life the last thing she needed was to be tied up in court trying to recover damages from the unbalanced mother-son duo. Jules had gotten her to agree to have his office send a threatening letter naming Paul and his mother in a civil action. They would probably respond with a fat check and a letter promising that accepting the money would settle the matter. Audrey would deal with all that later. She was just glad to be home.

The first week was spent in the bed. Mrs. Mashburn continued to take care of Audrey's cat, Freedom. The orange tabby had turned up his tail to Audrey when she finally came to collect him, letting her know that he was not pleased about her absence. He swirled around Mrs. Mashburn's ankles, ignoring his mistress. But true to his feline nature, he succumbed to the keeper of the chicken gizzards, dissing Mrs. Mashburn as soon as Audrey opened the butcher's paper.

Dorothy had everything in the office running smoothly. As soon as Audrey had taken care of a series of business calls, she dialed Marsh. This was her third call to him. The other times, the phone just rang. Now a recorded message told her that his number was no longer in service. She checked the number with the phone company. Marsh had turned off his telephone service. Why would he do a thing like that? Audrey dialed his office and a girl who sounded like she was barely over the age of consent answered the phone. Audrey asked for Marsh.

"Mr. Fixx is at our Northeast Office. Mr. Pressley is in." The girly voice reported.

"Who…? Let me speak to him."

"May I tell him who's calling and what it's in reference to?"

"It's Audrey Wilson." And it's in reference to that jerk Marsh disappearing and not giving me the courtesy of a call, Audrey thought. Had he been in Boston the whole time that she had been gone? What could be so important that he would stay in Boston for two weeks?

Audrey was on hold for less than a minute before the line clicked and an unfamiliar male voice came on the line.

"Miss Wilson?"

"Yes."

"My name is Earnest Pressley. I don't know if Marsh ever mentioned me…"

"What's going on?" Audrey wasn't in the mood for pleasantries. She didn't care who this guy was; she wanted to talk to Marsh.

"Marsh has returned to Boston…"

Earnest Pressley was saying something else but Audrey couldn't hear him. Marsh was gone? Why did he wait until she was out of town to pull a chicken-shit stunt like this? He probably knew all along that he was only going to be in Ohio a short time and had never told her. Audrey's head swirled with hurt and anger. While she was in Atlanta getting the crap beat out of her, Marsh was laid up with Marlena. Of all the pain she had gone through over the past few days, nothing hurt like this. How could he leave without saying anything? It was like everything they had shared had been nothing but a lie.

"Do you want to pick it up or shall I have it mailed?" Earnest Pressley asked.

"What?" Still reeling from Pressley's disclosure, Audrey hadn't heard anything else he'd said.

"The letter."

"What letter?"

"Marsh left you a letter." Pressley said. "Do you want to pick it up or shall I mail it?" He repeated.

"I don't want anything from him." Audrey murmured softly into the phone. She felt herself weakening and tried to keep the tremble from her voice.

"But what should I do with it."

"I don't care what you do with it." She had to bite her tongue to keep from saying something out of line to him. No need in killing the messenger. She mumbled thanks and hung up the phone.

Audrey spent the rest of the day in a haze. She'd tried calling Renita at least a dozen times. She left three urgent messages but her sister didn't call until almost one a.m.

"What's up?" Renita said in a panic. "Are you feeling okay?"

"I'm feeling like shit." Audrey started crying.

Less than thirty minutes later she was turning her key in Audrey's door.

"What happened?" Renita ran to the bedroom and sat on the bed that was covered with snotty tissues. She ignored the mess and pulled her sister to her.

"Marsh is gone." Audrey whimpered.

Renita stopped the rocking motion that was meant to soothe and swallowed the lump that had formed in her throat. Guilt slapped her hard across the face. She'd forgotten to tell her about Marsh and felt terrible. She had let her down in a big way. Audrey was going to be mad at her for not telling her sooner but she would be even more upset if she found out later that Renita knew and didn't say anything.

"Audrey, I knew about Marsh and I forgot to tell you." Renita held her tight as she made the confession but was unable to contain her sister as her fury tore her out of Renita's grasp.

"You knew and you didn't tell me?"

"There's been so much going on…as soon as I was ready to tell you something else was happening and the next thing I know, I'm sitting on your bed and it just occurs to me that I never got around to telling you." She rubbed Audrey's arm. "Honey, please, please forgive me. I feel awful."

Audrey shook her head and then waved her hand dismissively.

"Don't worry about it, Ren. It's not your fault he turned out to be such a bastard. When did you find out?" Audrey sniffed.

"The day I got back to town. I tried calling you but I couldn't reach you, then everything started happening..."

"It's okay, Ren. Really." Audrey had a faraway look in her eyes. Her lips curled into a sad smile and she looked at Renita with glassy eyes. "It wasn't going so hot anyway with us lately. I could feel him pulling away for a long time. I always knew he still had feelings for his ex. I tried to put on the breaks, but I couldn't. I love him so much, Ren."

The tears fell. Renita rubbed her shoulder soothingly.

"Don't worry, sweetie." Renita assured her. "I'm sure he'll call you at some point and explain everything. Or we can hop a flight East and whup his ass."

"For what, Ren?"

"Aren't you pissed?" Renita's brow furrowed into a deep angry rut. "Don't you at least want to give him a few quick jabs to the ribs?"

Audrey smiled in spite of everything. Renita was a trip.

"To tell you the truth, I'm too tired to be mad. Maybe it hasn't sunk in yet."

"Well the least he could do is call you and tell you what happened in his own words."

"That guy told me he left a letter but I told him I didn't want it." Audrey grabbed another tissue and honked into it.

"I probably would have said the same thing. But you know later on you gon' wish you had read that letter." Renita massaged her shoulders. "Why don't you get some rest?" She kicked off her shoes and climbed onto the bed with her sister. She sang soft comforting melodies until Audrey fell asleep.

*   *   *   *

Renita answered the door at nine fifteen a.m. A white FEDEX truck could be seen from the window. She opened the door and signed for the package.

"What is it?" Audrey asked her. She had done her best to clean herself without wetting her bandages and was feeling a little better than yesterday. She looked curiously at the large square envelope in Renita's hands. She handed the mail over and watched as Audrey pulled the tab and looked inside.

"It's a letter." Audrey said pulling the white rectangle from the mailer. She ran her nail along the top and pulled out a single sheet of paper. "It's from Marsh."

"I guess that little pop-eyed dude from his office went ahead and mailed it to you." Renita said.

Audrey spread the sheet out and read it aloud.

Audrey,

I can only imagine what you must think of me. I couldn't face you and I'll be the first to admit this is the coward's way out. I feel like a total jerk and I'm sure I'd get no argument from you on that.

The time I spent with you has been incredible. You are one of the best people I've ever known. But my heart is with my family. My son is growing and needs me in his life and try as I might I never got Marlena out of my system.

Please know that I will always love you and appreciate the times we shared. I've just got to make this last attempt at seeing if this will work with us. If I don't at least try, I would spend the rest of my life wondering. I couldn't dishonor you in that way.

Please try to forgive me and try to understand.

Love,

Marsh.

The paper quivered in Audrey's hand. She skimmed the lines once more. This was her last physical connection with a man that she had felt a unique bond with. Unfortunately, his feeling for her hadn't been as deep.

"Damn." Renita finally said.

"Yeah," Audrey said, "Damn." She looked up from the letter and wiped her wet lashes with her hand. "I'm not mad at him though, Ren. What can I say? The man is in love with his wife."

"Yeah, but he never should have gotten involved with you if he was carrying a torch for her." Renita was less forgiving. She hated seeing her sister hurt.

"I'm sure if he had any indication that she would take him back he wouldn't have gotten involved with me. I can't be mad at him for going with his heart, Ren. There's nothing I can do but pick myself up and go on with my life."

Renita wrapped her sister in a comforting embrace. She knew Audrey's bravado was just an act so when she felt Audrey's trembling shoulders against hers, it confirmed that the charade was over. Renita patted her back while she cried. The tears washed over her pain and diluted the ache in her heart.

Minutes passed as the water washed away the bitterness and hurt, the sadness and the feelings of loss. He had returned to his family. His home. How could she hate him for that? Family is an important thing and despite the pain she felt at the breakup, a part of her felt glad for him. In spite the tacky way he'd ended their relationship, she would always cherish the good times they had shared.

CHAPTER 40

▼

One thing Audrey realized more and more was that she was getting tired of her profession. She had worked in finance for nearly twenty years and while she valued and appreciated her knowledge and everything she'd achieved, she felt that professionally she was being moved in a new direction.

Audrey decided to let go of her financial consulting business. It hadn't been profitable and the work was no longer challenging. B.A. Wilson, on the other hand, was thriving. She would still be able to use her extensive finance background there. Since most of their B.A.W. clients required little time and had more money than they could ever spend, Audrey could carve out more time teaching the working poor about saving and investing. She would also develop a plan for working with single mothers. Audrey was sick and tired of stories of mothers not having adequate childcare while they struggled to work or educate themselves. Her concept was to create a network where the working poor could go for quality daycare services. The thought of a new career path and her new life with Simon made her smile. She couldn't wait to get started. But first, she had to get well.

It was warm outside and late summer sunny. Audrey's favorite way to relax was reclining on her chaise lounge on her back porch. Mrs. Mashburn would come by and fix her a light lunch and a pitcher of sweet-tart lemonade and they'd sit and talk and shoo away flies. It reminded Audrey of the time she'd spent with her mother. Ruth Etta Mashburn couldn't imagine the gift her company was. She eased into a peaceful recovery listening to her neighbor's stories and relishing her hearty laughter.

Audrey spent another week resting and reading the novels she'd bought in Atlanta. She was in constant communication with Cordelia St. James getting updates on Simon and making sure that she could be as prepared as possible for his arrival. Audrey was still searching for the best school setting for him. She had about a month to get everything established so that the only worry she'd have would be helping Simon make the transition.

Mrs. Mashburn would be her first line of defense and then Renita, Syd, and Carmen would act in a sort of surrogate capacity. Audrey's excitement had ignited the ever-cold heart of Renita. The others were a piece of cake. They were all excited about Simon coming to live in Rosemont and being a part of their lives. Since her family and friends loved children, Simon would get so much affection he might start talking just to tell them to shut up and give him some peace.

She would return to Atlanta in a few weeks and she and Simon would stay with Cordelia, Wallace and Jonah so that Audrey could get acquainted with her new son.

Audrey leaned back on the chaise and smiled. She was feeling pretty good about her life and looking forward to the future with more enthusiasm than she'd felt in a long time.

*   *   *   *

It took nearly two weeks for Audrey to get strong enough to walk without a cane. There were still a few sore spots and her hair was jacked-up. She looked at herself in the mirror and couldn't help getting depressed. The scissors glinted in the morning sunlight, daring her to do what she wanted but wasn't sure she had the nerve to do. The first cut hurt her feelings more than anything else. After that, the others were easy. A few minutes later, her reflection showed a head full of sharp black wisps flecked with sporadic strands of silver. Now she was *really* depressed.

Audrey had a ten o'clock appointment with her stylist. It was just after nine now. Renita offered to take her but Audrey declined. She needed to start getting around on her own. Besides, she didn't want Renita to see her until her hair was fixed. Audrey grabbed a loosely woven straw hat from her closet and pulled it over the short soft tufts of hair and headed out the door.

*   *   *   *

Audrey's friend, the former Detective Rob Hollingsworth, was fulfilling his lifelong dream. He was in negotiations with Jackson Waller to buy The Spice Rack and turn it into an upscale restaurant. With ten thousand dollars and a handshake, Rob plunged into the renovations with the zeal of a child with a deluxe Lego set——and a secured bank loan. Waller hadn't given Rob an official departure date, but that didn't stop Rob from going forward with his plans. They all had been invited to a pre-opening party that night where they would sample some of the culinary delights Rob had learned in his recent studies at a famed New York cooking school.

As far as Audrey was concerned he couldn't have made the career change at a more opportune time. She was starving. Thanks to her recent adventures in Atlanta, Audrey had lost a considerable amount of weight and was able to ease into things from her closet that she hadn't worn in nearly a decade. She chose a shimmering platinum Yves St. Lauren slip dress that accentuated every curve. Make-up would hide the souvenir bruising that remained from her rumble with Paul, Martha and Danger the dog. She hated that she limped without the cane, but she was just too vain to use it.

She checked herself in the mirror a final time. It was going to take some getting used to wearing her hair this short. But she liked it. The real test would be the reaction she'd get once she reached the restaurant. Audrey grabbed her bag and keys and took measured steps to the car.

*   *   *   *

The rundown street where the Spice Rack was located was nearly deserted. Audrey parked the car and took diffident steps to the door. She put her hand on the handle and pulled.

The walls had been stripped bare of the artsy posters and the garish Caribbean paint that were the old club's trademark. She passed the empty tables, and stepped toward the front where the bandstand was. There was only one table dressed for dinner. At it were seated her sister and brother, Jules, Lloyd, Syd and Carmen. Rob had been courteous enough to warn Audrey that he was inviting his brother, Jerry. Her old flame sat at the table with his new wife. Audrey was glad she hadn't married him. Looking at Jerry now she felt none of the old feelings of desire for him. He was just another guy at the club. She took in a breath and released it. It felt so good to be home. Audrey cast a dazzling smile at the people seated before her. They all turned their attention in her direction.

"Oh my God!" Renita was up and running in her direction. She put her hand to Audrey's tiny golden curls that hugged her head like a chic cap. Everybody raved about her hair and how good she looked—except Jules. He just stared at her. A slight smile turned the ends of his mouth upwards. He glanced at her throughout the evening but didn't say anything about her new look. Audrey guessed he was one of those guys who didn't like women with short hair.

The food was excellent. Rob was excited and his enthusiasm filled the air as he spoke of his plans for the club. He had light jazz spinning in the CD player and it was a good time with good friends. Audrey even liked Jerry's wife.

When the party was over, Jules moved behind her to help her with her seat.

"Can I see you to your car?"

"That would be nice." She replied. He had been so quiet all night she hoped he was okay.

Jules hung back for support as Audrey took tentative steps to the front of the restaurant and out to the parking area. Audrey had worn comfortable shoes but she wished she hadn't been too cute to bring her walking stick. Her leg didn't feel good at all.

"Why don't you let me drive you home." Jules offered. She accepted without hesitation.

"Okay."

They stopped in front of a sleek black Cadillac. Audrey heard a beep and the passenger door swung open.

"This is nice." She slid onto the butter-soft black seat as he held the door.

"I spend too much time in my car to be uncomfortable." He shut the door and jogged around to the driver's side.

"So you don't miss the Beetle, huh?"

"Are you kidding? I couldn't wait to get rid of that piece of shit."

They laughed. He put the key in the ignition, and then let go of the steering wheel.

"Oh...I almost forgot." Jules said turning around he started rummaging around in the back seat. Whatever he was trying to do was obviously giving him some difficulty. He mumbled a curse and turned all the way around so that his waist bent over his seat. Audrey looked at his tight little rump pooched up over the seat and smiled. You can take the boy out of the bug but you can't take the bug out of the boy, she thought, giggling to herself.

"Here it is." He said before letting out a relieved sigh. Jules brushed the wisps of hair away from his face with one hand and presented Audrey with a plush black jewelry box with the other. She looked down at it with a mix of delight and weariness. It was too big to be a ring so she knew he wasn't about to propose to her or nothing crazy like that. But she could tell by the box that its contents were not some dime store trinket. She hesitated.

"Well, aren't you going to open it?" Jules asked, smoothing his hair once more for good measure. He smiled mischievously and Audrey's curiosity got the best of her. She reached for the box and opened it. Jules clamped his hands over his ears as her scream flooded the interior of the vehicle.

"My bracelet! Where did you find it?" A lump burned in her throat like hot coal as she blinked back the tears that flooded the rims of her eyes.

"I'm afraid I'm a bit of a slob and had I not left so many wet towels laying around, you would have seen your bracelet underneath a sloppy pile of them on the hotel room floor." Jules gave her his handkerchief. His eyes danced in the glow of the parking lot lighting as he watched her dab the wetness from her face.

"But I looked on the floor." She sniffed, giving him a glassy-eyed gaze.

"I guess you're about as good at looking as I am at cleaning." He said. Then he moved closer.

"Thank you." She smiled at him as she slipped the bracelet around her wrist. Jules fastened the clasp.

"Speaking of good-looker, I love your hair, Audrey." He ran his fingers over the golden curls and smiled in wonder. "You're so pretty. I miss you so much."

She tilted her head toward him. His lips hesitated near hers. Audrey closed her eyes and accepted his slow, gentle kiss. The heat of her passion drew her closer. The kiss she returned burned with all the desire she had denied herself for so long.

"I don't ever want to lose you." Jules whispered between kisses.

"You never will." She promised, falling into his arms, losing herself in his love.

When they finally parted, they began to giggle and neither of them knew why. Jules looked into her eyes and then put his hand on hers.

"If I take you home tonight I'm not going to want to leave." His words were heavy with wanting. His eyes held hers beseechingly.

"I'm feeling so weak I may not be able to make it to bed without help." She smiled at him seductively. "So I guess you'll have to stay."

ATLANTA

---▼---

"Don't cry, Remmi."

"I can't help it. I'm so sick of this shit. We sang our guts out and we only made two dollars forty-one cents."

"Baby, it's like that sometimes. Come on. Be strong for me." Lonnie pulled her into his arms. "Here, you eat my Krystal."

"What *you* gonna eat?" Remmi eyed the sandwich hungrily.

"Don't worry about me, I'll find something." Lonnie clutched his stomach so Remmi wouldn't hear it growl. He felt like shit too. They had been performing on the streets for a while but after Remmi lost her job at Lockheed and they had to let the apartment go, things had gone from bad to worse. He felt less than a man for not being able to support them, but the money from the settlement he'd gotten was long gone and his back was too messed up to work.

When they were both working he would get his sax and they would sit in at Café 290. He would blow and Remmi would sing. They'd drink and smoke and hang out with the other musicians every Sunday night. It was cool.

It was amazing how quickly they'd gone from having so much to being out on the street. The truth of the matter was Lonnie had nixed any chance of being called back to work because he couldn't stop smoking crack. But he thought it was all a bunch of bullshit. Half the people at the job were drunks or meth heads. Why they have to fuck with him? It seemed every time he turned around somebody was asking him to take a piss test. He thought about it now and his handsome face darkened at the memory.

"Mutha fuckas set me up." He mumbled.

"What?" Remmi was trying to act like she was thinking about more than the little square burger that she had started unwrapping.

"Nothing." Lonnie grumbled. He wanted to push away the bad memory and the evil thoughts he had about how he could avenge his former employer. He felt he had an airtight case against them. He'd even filed a grievance with EEOC. They said he didn't have a case. Fucking government puppet bullshit organization. That's what they were. He knew entrapment when he saw it, even if they pretended not to see it. The shit never would have happened if he hadn't been black. But there was no point in dwelling on the past. He wanted desperately to change his life for the better. He just didn't know how.

Lonnie had his faults but he really loved Remmi and he loved God. He prayed for strength to put down the pipe and that he would be able to give Remmi everything that she deserved. It was working too. He hadn't spent any of the money they made this week on drugs. It was only Monday, but it was a start. It was hard as hell but he was determined to find a way to kick it. He unwrapped the knapsack and tried to find a descent spot for them to squat before all the riff raff came out. He might be a bum but that didn't mean he couldn't make their space as clean and comfortable as possible.

"Fuckin' litterbugs." He muttered, picking up garbage and putting it in a nearby trashcan. A bright yellow square of paper stuck in the chain link fence near the spot he planned to bed down caught his eye. Lonnie pulled at it until it came free. It was hotel stationery. Beneath the bold black heading *RENAIS-SANCE HOTEL*, the writing was neat—a woman's writing, Lonnie thought. He read the first line and frowned.

> *To the finder of this note:*
> *My name is Simone Denton. Jelly Anderson is trying to kill me. But I won't let him. I'll kill myself before I let him decide the end of my story.*
> *Take this note to Mr. Andrew Schyler at the Roswell Wachovia Bank.*

Dear Mr. Schyler,

This letter gives authority to bearer full access to the contents of safe deposit box # A273.See that the tapes inside go to the district attorney's office. The money is the sole property of the bearer of this note.

Yours truly,

Simone Denton

4751 Tuxedo Canyon Drive, Atlanta
Account # 7133487

Lonnie read the note again. Simone Denton. That's the chick that took a leap out a window at the Renaissance, he remembered. Word on the street was she had been some high-class hooker who worked for the same syndicate that owned The Platinum Club. She was rumored to have connections to John "Jelly" Anderson, too. If this note is authentic, the rumors were true.

The yellow paper glowed like a hot poker in his hand. He read the note at least another half dozen times while his mind cleared and absorbed the treasure he'd just found. He looked over at Remmi who had eaten Lonnie's hamburger and was still complaining about the day's take.

"Baby, get up." Lonnie pulled at her arm trying to get her off the ground.

"What? You just told me to get over here and sit down, now you telling me…"

"Baby, we ain't got time for that now. Get up."

"Where we going?"

"To the bank."

"The bank? Ain't no banks open now. Are you crazy?"

"No baby. I'm not crazy." Lonnie held her at arms length. The gleam in his eyes was contagious and Remmi lifted the corners of her mouth into a cautious grin.

"We'll wait outside until that sucker opens up." He said.

"Baby, what is it?" Remmi was suddenly feeling his excitement. Lonnie wrapped his hands around hers.

"First we going to the bank, then the office of the *National Tattler* and then we going to church."

Thank you for taking your valuable
time to read my work. I hope it was
as enjoyable to read as it was to
write. Please take a moment to
review the book at www. Amazon. Com

0-595-27821-3